THE ADVOCATE'S LABYRINTH

TERESA BURRELL

SILENT THUNDER PUBLISHING

COPYRIGHT

This book is a work of fiction. References to real people, events, establishments, organizations, or locales are intended only to provide a sense of authenticity and are used fictitiously. All other characters and all incidents and dialogue are drawn from the author's imagination and are not to be construed as real.

DEDICATION

To Robin Thomas—Your help has been invaluable to my business, and your sweet disposition makes you a delight to work with. Your concern for others is a shining light in these stressful times. I wish the rest of the world had just a tenth of your loving character, for you are the very essence of kindness. This world is a far better place because you are a part of it. Thank you for being you.

ACKNOWLEDGMENTS

A special thanks to those who made this book possible.

Attorney Ralph Hekman
Attorney Robert A. Pullman
Dr. William Clark, PhD, LPC
JP

Thanks, **Dana Conrad,** for choosing the title for my book.

And My Loyal Beta Readers:

Beth Agejew
Melissa Ammons
Linda Athridge-Langille
Vickie Barrier
Melanie Cardullo
Teresa Harden
Gena Fortner Jeselnik
Crystal Kamada
Sheila Krueger
Janie Livingston
Rodger Peabody
MaryAnn Schaefer
Colleen Scott
Nikki Tomlin
Uma Van Roosenbeek
Brad Williams
Denise Zendel

THE ADVOCATE SERIES

THE ADVOCATE (Book 1)
THE ADVOCATE'S BETRAYAL (Book 2)
THE ADVOCATE'S CONVICTION (Book 3)
THE ADVOCATE'S DILEMMA (Book 4)
THE ADVOCATE'S EX PARTE (Book 5)
THE ADVOCATE'S FELONY (Book 6)
THE ADVOCATE'S GEOCACHE (Book 7)
THE ADVOCATE'S HOMICIDES (Book 8)
THE ADVOCATE'S ILLUSION (Book 9)
THE ADVOCATE'S JUSTICE (Book 10)
THE ADVOCATE'S KILLER (Book 11)
THE ADVOCATE'S LABYRINTH (Book 12)

THE TUPER MYSTERY SERIES

THE ADVOCATE'S FELONY
(Book 6 of The Advocate Series)
MASON'S MISSING (Book 1)
FINDING FRANKIE (Book 2)

CHAPTER 1

Sunday Morning

"The ambulance"—Goldie struggled to speak—"on its way."

"Don't try to talk." Sabre Brown put her aunt on speaker phone, so her boyfriend, JP, could hear. "I'll meet you at the hospital."

"No," Goldie said sounding riled. "I need you ... to do something ... for me."

Sabre was already on her feet, keys in hand. JP Torn, who was also her private investigator, followed.

"I'll drive," JP said softly as they walked to his truck.

Sabre spoke into the phone. "Auntie, what happened?"

"Chest pain ... stomach." She breathed heavily. "Listen to me."

"First tell me, will they take you to Sharp Grossmont? That's the closest hospital, right?"

"Yes." Goldie took a deep breath. "Come ... my house ... change code on garage door. Code is ... 4746."

"What should I change it to?"

"Anything ... just change it. People know ... or could figure it out."

"I'll meet you at the hospital, then I'll go do it."

"No," Goldie insisted. "Do it now. When I'm gone, it won't be safe."

"Auntie—"

Goldie cut her off. "Please, now"—she breathed heavily—"before it's too late."

Sabre heard sirens in the background as the first responders pulled up to her aunt's home.

"They're here." Goldie sighed. "Promise me ... take care of it and take care ... *duly*."

Sabre climbed in the truck. "I'm on my way. And I promise I'll do it right after." Still not sure what her aunt meant, Sabre asked, "Is that what you meant by duly?"

The line was silent.

Sabre and JP parked near the emergency room entrance at Sharp Grossmont Hospital. An ambulance pulled in behind them.

"Maybe that's her," JP said.

"I'll find out." Sabre jumped out of the truck. "Go change the code. It's 4746."

"Do you really think we should do that?"

"Yes." Sabre was adamant. "I promised her."

"Okay."

Sabre ran over to the ambulance as they pulled out the gurney with her Aunt Goldie, who was lying very still.

"You need to step back," an EMT said in a strong voice.

"Is she alive?" Sabre asked.

"Yes. Now move."

She complied as another EMT asked, "You wouldn't be Sabre Brown, would you?"

"I am," Sabre said, a little surprised. "She's my aunt."

"She wanted to make sure someone reached you." He pushed the gurney toward the entrance. "I'm glad they did. She kept saying your name over and over. Now please go wait inside."

Sabre retreated, but followed them into the hospital. She was soon left behind when the guard stopped her from entering the swinging doors that led to the emergency room. "You need to check in." The large, African American guard spoke in a soft, understanding voice. "If they can, they'll call you back there."

Sabre walked to the counter, provided her aunt's details, then took a seat and waited. She called her brother, Ron, to let him know about their aunt. She and her brother were very close, and she knew he'd be concerned. Of the two, Ron was more sensitive, but if their aunt didn't make it, they'd be there to comfort each other. Sabre wanted to call her mother, but she was out of the country, so she would wait until she knew more.

Forty-five minutes later, JP walked in. "Heard anything yet?"

"Nothing," Sabre said. "I've checked in a couple of times, but I couldn't really get any information."

JP sat down and took her hand. "I'm sorry, baby."

"She doesn't deserve this. She's still young."

"I know."

3

They sat quietly for two hours, watching as people came in. Only a few left. A doctor finally came out and spoke to the guard, who pointed toward Sabre. The solemn-looking doctor approached, carrying a manila envelope.

"I don't like the look on his face," Sabre said.

"They're never smiling when they come out," JP said. "Don't jump to conclusions."

The doctor stopped in front of them. "Who are you here for?"

"Goldie Forney," Sabre said.

"Are you Sabre Brown?"

"Yes."

"Do you have any identification?"

Sabre reached in her pocket for her driver's license, then showed it to him. "Why do you need to see my ID? I've never been asked for it before at a hospital. Is there something wrong?"

He glanced at her ID photo, then at her. "You're an attorney?"

"Yes."

"I have strict instructions from your aunt to only talk to you. I don't know why, but that's my patient's right, so I will honor it." He paused for a second. "I'm so sorry, but she didn't make it."

No! Sabre tried to be strong, but her eyes filled with tears. The doctor was still talking, but she heard little of what he said. When he held out the manila envelope, JP tried to take it, but the doctor wouldn't give it to him. Sabre looked at the inscription. Written in big, black letters across the front was: *GIVE TO SABRE BROWN ONLY!* She took a deep breath, cleared her throat, and held back the tears.

"Your aunt said to give you this if she passed."

"Thank you, doctor."

He handed her a plastic baggie with a necklace in it. "She was wearing this when she came in."

"Thank you." Sabre shoved it into her jeans pocket. She was not ready for any of this.

"Do you know if she made arrangements for a funeral home?" the doctor asked.

"I don't know."

Sabre tried to compose herself. She wasn't sure what the doctor had already said, so she asked, "Was it a heart attack?"

"Yes, but we think she might have had some food poisoning as well. We're running lab tests. Do you know what she had to eat today?"

Sabre shook her head. "I didn't see her until she was brought in."

"Do you have any other questions?" the doctor asked.

"Can I see her?"

"Yes. I'll take you to her."

CHAPTER 2

Sunday Afternoon

Sabre held her aunt's beautifully manicured hand. Her skin was already starting to feel cold. Sabre stared at Goldie's face and thought how beautiful she still was. She remembered the thin woman she'd met as a child, and how she was enamored by her beauty and her flaxen, stylish hair. Aunt Goldie had gained a lot of weight since then, but Sabre could see her inner beauty, which never changed. Her hair was still blonde but weaved with silver strands. A lock hung over her aunt's eyebrow. Sabre brushed it back where it belonged, knowing Aunt Goldie would want that. She was no longer crying, but she felt an ache in her chest. Sabre sat in silence for a few minutes, then stood and kissed Goldie's cheek.

"I'm so sorry, Auntie. I love you, and I'll miss you."

She stepped out and joined JP, who waited for her in the hall. They walked in silence to the truck, his arm wrapped lightly around her shoulder. The only sound was the clicking of JP's western boots on the concrete.

Once inside the vehicle, Sabre said, "She called me yesterday, but I didn't answer, and then I forgot to call her back. I can't help but think it might have made a difference."

"You have to let that go. More than likely, it had nothing to do with her heart attack today."

"I'll never know," Sabre said. "You got the code changed for her, didn't you?"

"Yes, of course." JP paused. "When were you last at her house?"

"I can't remember if I've ever been there, not at the house where she last lived. We usually just met for lunch. Why?"

"Something struck me as odd. The yard looks great. The lawn was manicured, and the plants around the grass were beautiful. She has a little flower garden on one side of the yard and more flowers under the windows in front. The fence is freshly painted, and I think the house is too." He paused and scowled. "But when I opened the garage door to reset the code, it was packed full of boxes and junk. There's only a narrow path between the overhead door and the one that goes into the house."

"That's probably where she stored everything."

"I guess, but the house is so cute when you drive up. I just found it a little strange. Did Goldie like gardening?"

"She loved it and talked about her flowers all the time. She'd even bring our family a bouquet now and then. She was very meticulous about things. When she would bring Christmas presents, each package was beautifully wrapped and adorned with a huge, gorgeous bow. She made them herself."

JP started the truck. "Where to?"

"Let's go by her house just to double check the code." She

7

glanced at the envelope in her lap. "Wait. Let's stay here while I see what's in this" she said, holding it up.

JP shut off the engine as Sabre opened the package. She pulled out a key with a red and white plastic tag. It read *HOME* in her aunt's perfect script.

"It must be the key to her house." Sabre felt a little foolish for stating the obvious, but her thoughts were jumbled.

"Is there anything else in there?" JP asked.

She reached inside and pulled out a three-page handwritten note on bright pink paper. Sabre took a deep breath, then read it aloud.

My Dear Sabre,

If you're reading this, I must have passed on, hopefully to a better place than this earthly one afforded me.

I'm sorry to put this on you, but you are the only one I trust to take care of things, and the only one who won't judge me. You are the only one who ever saw me for who I am. You never expected or demanded anything of me. You have always been like that, even as a small child. You made me feel so special and welcome in your family. I realized as you grew, and I got to know you, that you were like that to everyone. That it came directly from your heart, not from anything I did or was, but I felt your love just the same. And for that, I will always be eternally grateful.

So, where do I begin? With my children, I suppose. You must notify them. I would like to tell you not to and just wait to see how long it takes them to discover I'm gone. That would be fun for me, but it would only make it harder on you, and since I won't be there to see it, you may as well tell them. But before you do—and I can't stress the importance of this enough—I need you to go to my house and take photos of everything, the walls, the floors, the furniture, everything in every room. You need to have a record for when the vultures come—and they will come. Also, please change all the locks on my house and the storage units. I don't think any of my children have keys, but I can't be certain. Hopefully, you can get that done in a day or two and then call them. They'll be mad that you didn't call them immediately, but they'd be mad even if you did, so it doesn't matter. Oh, and give them a chance to see my body before it's cremated, in case they want to make sure I'm really dead.

"Are her kids that bad?" JP cut in.

"I haven't seen them in years, so I don't really know any of them as adults." Sabre went back to reading the note.

Then get that envelope I gave you when we met for lunch a few months ago. It will lead you to what you need in order to handle the legal matters.

"What envelope?" JP asked.

The memory was still vivid. "In June, Aunt Goldie asked me to join her for lunch at a restaurant in La Jolla."

"Did you go?"

"Yes, and it was nice." Sabre paused. "For the most part."

"What wasn't nice?"

"I don't know exactly." Sabre struggled to put her feelings into words. "Aunt Goldie kept saying how proud she was of me and how she wished she had a daughter like me. I felt so sorry for her. She said her kids were all a mess, and she couldn't trust any of them. It's been years since I've seen any of my cousins, but I'd heard there were some problems."

"That probably explains some things. I suspect she chose you to take care of business that she didn't trust her kids to handle."

"Like what? Funeral arrangements maybe? I doubt if she has much of an estate. As far as I know, she didn't work much. She certainly didn't get a windfall from my Uncle Bill, and from what I understand, her last husband didn't have anything to speak of."

"It's probably more personal than that." JP squeezed Sabre's hand. "She liked you and wanted you to make sure she had a good ending."

"Maybe." Sabre sighed. "Aunt Goldie gave me a small envelope at lunch that day and asked me not to open it unless something happened to her. I was afraid she had cancer or some other terminal illness, or maybe was contemplating suicide. But she assured me everything was fine and that it was no big deal."

"So, where is it?"

"In my briefcase at my office. It's just a business-sized envelope. I left it there because I thought it was as good a place as any."

"You usually bring your briefcase home." JP gave her a puzzled look.

"I didn't bring any files either," Sabre said. "Remember? We were planning a completely non-work weekend with the kids." JP's niece and nephew were living with him while their parents were in prison.

"So much for our plans." JP nodded at the letter Sabre was still holding. "Sorry for interrupting."

She went back to reading.

I hope you don't mind doing this for me. I know that even if you do mind, you wouldn't say so, because that's who you are. I don't mean to take advantage of your good nature, but I'm convinced you are the only one in the family who will carry out my wishes. I could have another attorney handle it, but they wouldn't have your heart. And this task needs someone with a big heart and your skill set.

I've made all my funeral arrangements so that won't be an issue for you. If the kids don't like it, too bad. They'll be happy to know that everything is already paid for, and they don't have to dish out a dime. They also won't get to fight about any of it because I've taken care of it all. Every detail.

"So, she doesn't need you to make the arrangements," JP said, "but possibly to see that they get carried out as she wished. She clearly doesn't have any confidence in her children.

"Sabre continued reading.

I still expect some squabbling. Those five have never been able to agree on anything. Don't let them get to you. They'll try, but you have the power. They have none.

This will be a long, arduous journey for you. I know you are up to the task, but I hope, in the end, that it doesn't destroy your love for me. It will change what you think about me. I know that. Because I am far less and far more than what you knew. When you're done, you will know my intimate thoughts like no one else ever has. I trust you with them. I trust no other. I can only hope and pray that you won't judge me.

11

Your favorite aunt, Goldie

P.S. Don't forget to take pictures of the house, and please don't be too shocked at what you see. I lived the only way I knew how.

Sabre folded the letter and choked back tears. Then she removed the last item from the envelope.

"What's that?"

Sabre glanced over the page. "It's a notarized legal document giving me power of attorney over her health, burial, finances, and every other decision that might need to be made in her stead."

JP started the truck again. "Where to?" he asked.

"Let's go take some photos."

CHAPTER 3

Sunday Evening

The house in La Mesa sat on a hill in an older neighborhood, where most homes were owner-occupied and well kept. The street was narrow, and tall palm trees lined both sides. Goldie's small front yard bloomed with geraniums, and a crepe myrtle tree hung over one corner of the narrow, yellow house. Eight wooden steps led up to the porch, which stretched the width of the front. The home looked small from the street, but when Sabre walked up the long driveway, past a gray, Toyota van, she saw that the house extended deep into the lot.

The garage sat at the end of the driveway with an old Corvette parked in front. The car's protective cover was weather worn, torn in a couple places, and hung halfway off the vehicle. The garage door looked new.

"It's a cute place," Sabre commented. "It looks so… neat. But then Auntie always did too. Her hair was always styled, and her nails were perfectly polished. She wouldn't leave the house without lipstick, and when it would start to wear off, she would re-apply it."

JP walked up to the security pad and punched in the new code. "I chose my birthday, by the way. Yours would be too obvious to family members." When the door started to rise, he pressed the button and stopped it. "It's a mess in there. I'm afraid things may start to fall, but we know the new code works. Let's try the key to the front door."

They walked to the front and up the steps to the porch. Two white, wicker rockers with floral seat cushions sat on green indoor-outdoor carpet. Sabre sat for a moment and looked across the street at the houses below. "What a view," she said. "You can see for miles."

The only other thing on the porch was a stainless-steel container about eighteen inches tall with a big paw decal on the side.

JP opened it. "Did your aunt have a dog?"

"I don't know. Maybe."

"This is full of Milk Bones. We better go inside and see if there's an animal in there. Didn't she tell you to take care of 'dually?' Maybe that's her dog's name."

"Who names a dog that?"

"Someone who had a dually truck. I think it's a pretty cool name."

Sabre stood, removed the key from her pocket, and opened the locked door. She gasped, shocked by the sight and the smell. "Oh, my! This can't be!"

JP put his hand on her shoulder. "Let me go first, something could fall."

"Or we'll find a dead dog," Sabre added. She glanced around at the junk. The stacks were so tall, they left only a foot of space between them and the ceiling. Sabre's mouth was agape as she flattened herself against the door, giving JP room to step past. The open space was only the width of the door, which allowed it to swing out to a ninety-degree angle. They stood face-to-face with a wall of junk, most of it higher than JP's six-foot frame.

To the left was a path through the stacks. The rest of the room was too densely packed to navigate. Beyond the doorway, the pathway narrowed. The most disconcerting thing about the junk pile was the banner taped to it: *CALL SABRE BROWN.* Underneath was Sabre's phone number. The note had been written with a purple marker on old, dot-matrix printer paper that had been torn off a long sheet. It looked like it was straight out of the 1980s.

"Well, butter my butt and call me a biscuit," JP said, shaking his head.

Sabre stared in disbelief. "Aunt Goldie was odd, but I never imagined this." *No wonder her aunt had never invited her over.*

"Dually," JP called out. "Come here, Dually."

"I don't think there's a dog in here. Maybe she said something else, maybe *duty* or something."

"Be careful," JP said, leading her through the narrow pathway.

"There's a sticky note with the same message," Sabre said, spotting a yellow square on a pile of newspapers.

After a few more steps, JP said, "And another one."

They continued to call for the dog but got no response. Along the way, before they reached the next room, they passed seven brightly colored sticky notes, all with the same message and all written in purple ink.

"I think she made her point."

"She sure did," Sabre said, examining a note more carefully.

JP turned sideways to avoid a basket sticking out from the rest of the stuff. "I don't think there's a dog here, at least not a living one."

"This opening is barely big enough for my aunt to get through." Sabre stopped. "Wait. I need to get photos. That's why we're here, right?"

"Go ahead. I'll make a quick check everywhere for the dog, then meet you back at the front door."

Sabre walked back to the entrance and started taking pictures, but it was hard to get a good angle. She stepped out onto the porch and took a few from there.

JP returned a few minutes later. "I didn't find a dog, just lots of black hair. She must have had a pet at one time."

"I've noticed a lot of hair too," Sabre said. "Stand there against the junk so I can get a photo showing how tall it is."

JP did as she asked. Sabre took photos of everything she could, then handed her phone to JP. "You're taller. See if you can get some shots of the top."

They continued taking pictures as they walked carefully to the next room, which appeared to be a den or small dining room. To the right was a door. It was lodged open, and behind it sat a toilet. The tub-shower enclosure was barely visible because of the stuff piled inside. They couldn't see a sink at all. The path hugged the window, which had closed shutters that allowed little light. But there was enough to see the notes of different sizes, taped or stuck to the junk, all beckoning someone to call Sabre Brown. JP found a light switch and flipped it on, but nothing happened. He took out his phone and turned on the flashlight.

"Do you think the electricity is off?" Sabre asked.

"I don't know. Maybe she just couldn't get to the light fixture to change the bulb."

"I hope that's the case. I'd hate to think she was living without power."

"I hope there's another bathroom, because this one hasn't been used since Moses was a teenager."

They headed for the open door at the other end, which led into a bedroom. It looked like more of what they'd seen so far. Piled full, except for a path next to the large windows. They had closed shutters too, but a little more light came through. Sabre shook her head in confused wonderment as she took photos, occasionally handing her phone to JP to get a shot of something she couldn't quite reach. The sporadic sticky notes of different sizes and colors, all with her name, and all in purple ink, surprised and confused her too.

That room led to another which appeared to be the master bedroom, although no bed was visible.

"This is a strange floorplan," Sabre commented. "There's no hallway, which means you have to go through one bedroom to get to the next one."

"I think at one time the house ended with that last room, and at some point they added these back rooms. I noticed the window construction is a lot older in the front rooms. The glass in the two windows in the front is blown glass, probably around a hundred years old."

"I wouldn't want to live here," Sabre said and continued down the narrow path which led to an aging recliner in the far corner. Near it was a dresser with a sixty-inch television on top.

A closet ran the length of the room, and its open sliding door exposed half the contents. The rest of the room was stacked full. The walls around the recliner and everything within reach were wallpapered with the same note: *CALL SABRE BROWN.*

Sabre and JP continued in awe through another open door. This one led to a hallway with a bathroom on the left. The toilet was accessible, but nothing else was. The sink, tub, and counterspace—all filled. Clothes hung from a rod around the bathtub. The shower curtain had been torn down from the weight of the junk, and the adjacent wall had numerous sticky notes.

"At least she had a toilet," JP said. "But how did she shower or wash her hands?"

Sabre shook her head.

JP flipped the switch on the bathroom wall, and the light came on. "She has power."

They continued on, snapping photos, but it was difficult to see anything but piles of boxes, clothes, and junk. The third and fourth bedrooms were packed so full, they had no pathway. The doors were propped open with junk, but they couldn't step more than a foot inside. The hallway led to another open door, but the room was stacked so full they couldn't walk in.

But JP could see over the stacks. "It's the kitchen," he said. "There's an opening on the other side that appears to lead back to the living room." JP held up the phone and took photos, getting as many angles as he could so Sabre could see everything. "Goldie apparently hadn't cooked here in a long time. She must've eaten in restaurants or gotten take-out."

They turned around and walked back the way they came. No words were spoken. The only sound was Sabre's occasional sigh, as she looked around in disbelief. When they reached the front room, JP asked, "Are you ready?"

"Yes." Sabre stepped outside, taking a deep breath of fresh air. She heard JP lock the door and turned to him. "My aunt was a hoarder." She sighed again. "How did I not know she was living like this?"

CHAPTER 4

Monday Morning

"My Aunt Goldie is dead," Sabre said, still feeling solemn as she approached Bob, her best friend and colleague. They sat down on a bench in front of Department One at the San Diego Superior Court, Juvenile Division, where they both worked.

"I'm so sorry," Bob said. "What happened?"

Sabre explained the events of the weekend, including the crazy house.

"So, you have to handle everything?" Bob looked concerned for her.

"That was Goldie's wish."

"Are you her only living relative?"

"No. She has five children." Sabre looked up. "She was pretty adamant that she didn't want them handling anything."

"Were you and your aunt close?"

Sabre heard the sympathy in his voice. He was quite caring, and seemed to understand her better than anyone. She loved him for that. But mostly she loved his sense of humor. Even in the worst of times, he could make her laugh. But not now. He was consoling her.

"She was my favorite aunt, even when I was growing up. She was married to my Uncle Bill, my mom's brother, so we're not even blood related."

"She probably wanted you because you're an attorney." Bob widened his eyes and spoke in a sinister voice. "Or maybe someone murdered her, and she wants you to find the killer."

His humor was back. Sabre gave him a sideways look, but she enjoyed the relief from her glum state.

"Maybe she was rich, and she gave you all her money."

Sabre rolled her eyes. "She wasn't rich, and even if she were, she has five heirs."

"All of whom she doesn't trust."

"Believe me, she doesn't have any money."

"Okay, maybe she has legal matters she wanted you to handle."

"Maybe." Sabre took a deep breath.

"You said she *was* married to your uncle. I take it that's no longer the case."

"He's dead," she said coldly.

Bob hesitated, then asked, "Was he the uncle who mol...?"

Sabre closed her eyes, so Bob didn't finish the sentence.

"Yes. He's the one I found hanging from the rafters in our guest house when I was four." She paused to regain her composure. "Goldie and Uncle Bill had only been married a few months when they moved to Bakersfield where her family lived. They stopped in San Diego on their way to visit my mom, as kind of a honeymoon. That's when he committed suicide."

"Lucky you."

"Auntie had a lot of tragedy in her life, at least when she was younger."

"Like what?"

"Her first husband was a biker guy who couldn't seem to stay out of trouble. Four months after the wedding, she gave birth to Michael. She had identical twin girls two years later and within another two years was divorced. She moved to Florida, and that's where she met Bill. He was clean cut, worked in sales, and very different from her first husband."

A woman walked up to Bob and asked, "When are we doing my case?"

"We're waiting on the social worker," Bob said. "It shouldn't be much longer."

She walked away, not looking happy.

"Sorry, go on," he said to Sabre.

"Aunt Goldie was pregnant when she and Bill came to visit us. A few months after his death, she had another set of twins, boys this time. She was living in Bakersfield, so her older children could have a relationship with their dad."

"Did she go back to him?"

"No, they didn't get along at all. But the kids liked him, and from what I've heard, he was good to them. Then she met Norm Perkins and married him. At that point, she was only a few years older than I am now—and on her third husband."

"Geez, she was a slow learner."

"For sure, but Aunt Goldie was a sweet lady. She didn't have much of a family of her own. Her mother died when she was very young. She only had one sibling, a sister, who never married or had children, and she died over twenty years ago.

Her father wasn't around much either; he passed away a long time ago too. I think that's why Goldie tried so hard to be a part of our family. She even drove to San Diego from Bakersfield for my sixth birthday party. We hadn't seen her since Bill killed himself, and we'd never met the youngest twins, the only ones I'm actually related to. She brought both sets of twins, and she was pregnant again. The youngest twins were still toddlers, and the girls, Michelle and Rochelle—or Micki and Rocki, as we called them—were two years older than me."

Sabre paused, remembering the tragic events. "Unfortunately, Michael stayed home with his father who took him along to rob a convenience store. He left Michael outside on the motorcycle, and when he tried to make his getaway, the cops chased him. He tried to beat a train as he raced across the tracks, but his timing was off. The train hit them, and both Michael and his father were killed."

"Oh, that's horrible."

"It was pretty sad. I didn't fully understand it because I was so young. But I'd find my mother crying sometimes. And she didn't want to let us out of her sight for quite a while after that. I remember Ron saying it was because she was afraid one of us might get killed like Michael."

"That makes sense." Bob stared at the floor. "I can't even imagine what it would be like to lose a child."

"After the accident, Aunt Goldie and the two sets of twins moved to San Diego with her new husband, Norm."

"What about the new baby?"

"Aunt Goldie lost the child when she *fell* down the back steps." Sabre used air quotes when she said *fell*. "We didn't see her much during that time, even though she was in the same town. We actually saw her more when she lived in Bakersfield.

We thought she was caught up in her new husband's family. According to my mom, Norm was abusive. When Aunt Goldie got pregnant again, she left him and filed for divorce. I guess she didn't want to lose another child to that monster."

"Let me get this straight." Bob had an expression of disbelief. "Before your aunt reached forty, she had been married three times—to a criminal, a child molester, and an abuser—and widowed twice, for all practical purposes. She'd given birth to six children, miscarried once, and lost a child. On top of all that, she lived in *Bakersfield.*"

"That about sums it up."

"That's tragic," Bob said seriously.

They both stopped talking when two men standing about ten feet from them started yelling at each other. People backed away as the confrontation escalated. A bailiff burst out of Department Four, but before he could reach them, one of the men punched the other. The other caught his balance and charged the first man, slamming him against the wall. Another bailiff flew out of Department Three, and two others dashed down the hallway. Within seconds, the two men were handcuffed and led away.

"That was cool," Bob said.

"Do you know what it was about?" Sabre asked.

"The guy who threw the first punch was Collicott's client. The other guy molested his kid. I saw them earlier this morning. They almost got into it then."

"That got my heart pounding."

"Where were we?" Bob asked. "Oh yeah, your aunt moved to San Diego. Did you see her more often then?"

"She came to see us and told my mom about the divorce. After that, we saw her occasionally. I was a pre-teen and too busy with my friends to make much effort toward my aunt. I'd see her sometimes when she came over, and I always enjoyed her company, but I mostly wanted to be with my friends. Then Goldie stopped coming around for years. My mother tried reaching out several times though."

"How'd that work?"

"Mom offered to go see her, but Aunt Goldie always refused. I see now why she didn't want visitors. That's probably why she started coming over again, so Mom wouldn't go to her house. They'd have lunch about once a year. A few years ago, Auntie started coming to our house for Christmas."

"Instead of spending it with her kids?"

"She said they were all busy with their work or friends. She seemed lonely, so Mom tried to make her feel welcome. Goldie was a little odd, but very caring and sweet. She'd bring huge bags of presents for us, always with the most unusual and interesting gifts. It was her way of thanking us for including her. She was a sad woman."

Sabre looked away, grieving again. When it passed, she reached for her briefcase and opened it. "I just remembered; I haven't looked at the envelope yet."

"What envelope?"

"When Aunt Goldie and I had lunch recently, she gave me an envelope and told me to open it if anything ever happened to her."

She removed the pink envelope from her leather case. It had her name, *Sabre O. Brown*, in purple ink with perfect lettering. Sabre sat for a moment, holding it, not understanding her apprehension at opening it.

"Don't keep me hanging. Open it."

Sabre squared her shoulders and opened the seal. She pulled out a key and held it up for Bob to see.

"That's it? Just a key?"

Sabre slid out a note, handwritten on purple paper, and read it to herself.

"Come on. What does it say?" Bob prodded.

Sabre read the note out loud, choking up as she read.

If you're reading this, I must have passed. I know you are one of the few who will grieve for me, and the only one I can truly trust. This key is to Angie's Storage on Ashford St. Unit #12. Inside, you will find a gold Suze Orman container with your name on it. I trust you will follow my instructions and do what I've asked.

Always, Aunt Goldie.

CHAPTER 5

Monday Morning

S abre's stomach turned as she read the allegations on the new detention she'd just received. She slumped into the only chair in the court's tiny attorney lounge. These cases were the worst.

> *The parents neglected to protect the children in that five-year-old, Perry McCluskey, was found dead in his bed with multiple bruises on his scrotum...*

Sabre stopped, shuffled the petition to the back of the file, and read the report instead. There were five children in the family: Dale (11), Fayth (9), Harmony (6), Perry (5), and Ivory (3). At the time of the incident, the children were all in the home of their mother, Ellie McCluskey, who had custody, with open and regular visitation with their father. The mother's boyfriend, Kenny Yarborough, had also been in the house at the time of the death. Perry had slept, as he usually did, in the same room as his brother Dale, who had woken about eight. Thinking his brother was asleep, he hadn't tried to wake him. About an hour later, his mother sent Dale to wake Perry, and the older boy found him dead.

The estimated time of death was approximately 1:00 a.m. According to the mother, the children had all been asleep, as were she and her boyfriend, who lived with her.

Sabre left the lounge and walked down the hall toward Department Four, where Bob waited for her.

"I called JP and told him about the storage unit," Sabre said. "He's going with me when I'm done here this morning."

"Can I go?" Bob pleaded. "I want to see the house too. I've never been in an actual hoarder's home before. I've seen them on TV, of course, but I bet it's pretty cool."

"That's not exactly the word I'd use to describe it. Certainly unusual, but I just keep thinking how sad and lonely she must've been."

"You're right. But it's still fascinating. I'm really good with finding treasures, so if you need any help assessing anything, I'm your man."

"Thanks. I wouldn't recognize an antique if it bit me, but you have some gorgeous pieces in your house."

"My mom is into antiques, so I've learned a lot from her. And if you find any old jewelry, I'm pretty good at recognizing stones and jewelry construction. I know the real stuff from the fake."

"You might come in handy at that."

"What do you have on calendar this morning?" Bob asked.

"*We* have the McCluskey detention. Did you see the

reports?" Before he could answer, she added, "They haven't declared the boy's death a homicide, at least not yet."

"I think the mother and/or her boyfriend did it," Bob announced. "I'm glad I represent the father on this one. The abuser had to have been someone in that house, and the only adults were the mother and the boyfriend."

"But the mother claims the bruises on the little boy's scrotum were there when he returned from a visit with the father."

"Yeah, she's also saying someone must have snuck into the house while everyone was asleep, killed her son, and snuck out again. Besides, if she saw the bruises before, why didn't she report it? Or at least confront the father?"

"That does seem odd." Sabre had come to expect the worst from parents. "Maybe she was afraid of what CPS might do. The mother has been reported several times, and nothing was ever filed on her before. It's such a shame little Perry had to die before something was done."

A tall, lanky man in jeans walked toward the bench where Bob and Sabre sat. He kept tugging at the collar on his short-sleeved, button-down shirt. "There's the father now," Bob said.

"That shirt seems to be making him uncomfortable," Sabre noted.

"I think he's a t-shirt kind of guy. He's very nice. I bet you'll discover that the kids really like him."

Bob stood when Mr. McCluskey got closer. "Hi, Adam." Bob turned toward Sabre. "This is Sabre Brown. She's the attorney for your children."

"Nice to meet you, ma'am." He nodded. "Can I talk to you for a minute, Mr. Clark?"

"Sure," Bob said, leading him away.

Sabre called JP while she waited. "I have a new investigation for you," she said. "A young child suffocated in the night, wedged between the mattress and the wall."

"Was he murdered?"

"The police are still investigating. The ME did an autopsy, but I don't have the report yet. I know they found bruises on his scrotum. The mother claims the bruises were there prior to his death. Hopefully, the examination will give us the timing."

"What do you want me to do?"

"I need you to talk to the neighbors of both the father and the mother. See what you can find out about Ellie McCluskey and her boyfriend. I'll bring you the file when we meet up today. You're still going to the storage place with me, right?"

"Yep."

"This is my last hearing. Do you want to meet me at home or at the office?"

"Home would be good. That'll give me time to pick up Conner from school."

"If I'm done in time, I'll pick him up on my way home. I'll call you before I leave here to confirm."

JP's nephew, Conner, and his niece, Morgan, were in JP's custody while his brother, Gene, served out the last of his prison sentence. The children had been living with him for a couple of months, and Sabre had been there most of the time as well to help out. The kids liked having her around too. Unlike JP, Sabre wasn't certain she ever wanted children of her own. They'd had a couple of discussions about the matter, but she hoped his time with these kids would be enough for him. Still, she'd discovered she was enjoying their little family unit more than she expected to.

"The court is ready for us," Bob said, interrupting her thoughts.

"Good." Sabre picked up her files and followed him inside the courtroom.

Judge Hekman, a gray-haired, sixty-something woman, called the case to order. Bob stood from his seat at the counsel table. Adam McCluskey sat next to him. Bob introduced himself and his client for the record.

Sabre stood. "Sabre Brown for the children, who are not present in court, Your Honor."

The tall, dark-haired man sitting next to Ellie McCluskey stood next. "Your Honor, I'm Attorney Casey Oakes. I've been retained by the mother, Ellie McCluskey, who is present in court."

Sabre wondered why he felt it was necessary to say he'd "been retained." It sounded a little arrogant. Most of the attorneys at juvenile court were on a panel and were appointed by the court. Since they were there every day, they knew the innerworkings of the court far better than most of the retained attorneys. Perhaps he thought it would impress his client.

The claim, however, did not seem to impress the judge. "Have you done any prior juvenile work, counselor?" she asked.

"I have, Your Honor; albeit the majority has been in delinquency. However, I have done a couple of dependency cases as well." He barely took a breath before continuing. "If your concern is whether my client will be duly represented, I can assure you, she will. I'm a graduate of Harvard Law. I have been litigating for ten years, and I have a very capable staff and research team at my fingertips. I'm very familiar with both the civil and criminal rules of procedure and the evidence code, which, when I last checked, was the same in every California Superior Court."

"Don't get on your high horse, counselor," Hekman said

with a smile. "I'm well aware of your reputation as a criminal attorney. I was merely curious. I guess I should've waited until after the hearing to ask, but hey, I gave you a chance to put your credentials on the record."

"Thank you, Your Honor," Oakes said. He smiled back and sat down.

The judge made the appointments on the record, and the parents entered denials to the petitions.

Oakes stood. "My client would like the children detained with her, Your Honor."

"I'm sure she would, Mr. Oakes," the judge responded, "but that's not going to happen until we know what happened to Perry."

"The death of this child is a horrible tragedy," Oakes argued. "But it is through no fault of my client. She's suffering and feels a strong need to protect her other children."

"I understand that, but until we have more information, I believe it's in the best interest of these children to be elsewhere."

Bob spoke up. "The father would welcome the children in his home, Your Honor. He has been a stable, involved parent, and it would keep all the children together."

Judge Hekman turned to County Counsel. "Has the father's home been evaluated?"

"Yes, Your Honor," Linda Farris said. "I just spoke with the social worker, and we are recommending detention of all the children with the father."

"No," the mother said.

All eyes turned to Ellie McCluskey, and her attorney leaned down and whispered something. She shook her head and argued, some of which was audible. Oakes kept telling her to lower her voice. Finally, her lawyer said, "My client is not objecting to detention with their father at this time, but she requests unsupervised visits for herself."

"The children will be detained with the father," the judge ordered. "Supervised visits with the mother. The social worker has discretion to lift the supervision, with approval of minors' counsel. No," Judge Hekman said, apparently changing her mind. She looked directly at Attorney Oakes and then County Counsel. "If you want to lift the supervision, set a special hearing."

CHAPTER 6

Monday Afternoon

Sabre and JP drove to Angie's Storage, found unit #12, and parked in front. JP unlocked the roll-up door and carefully opened it. The space was full of boxes stacked almost to the eight-foot ceiling. In front, on top of the center stack, was a gold, ribbed-metal Suze Orman case. Still shiny, it looked unused, except for a few minor scratches. At the top, in raised two-inch letters, were the words: *SUZE ORMAN'S PROTEC-TION PORTFOLIO*. Underneath was a large sticky-note, taped down on all four sides. It read: *FOR SABRE BROWN*. JP moved a couple of boxes to form a makeshift table about four feet high and set the case on the top.

Sabre hesitated before opening it. She'd had so many surprises already; she didn't know what to expect. When she finally popped the latches, she found a well-organized accordion-style file folder held in with a Velcro strap. Each folder was permanently labeled according to the documents inside. The folders also had tabs with corresponding labels. The first file, *Personal Documents,* contained a stack of papers. Other thick folders were labeled *Real Estate, Investments,* and *Taxes.* The *Estate Planning* file was surprisingly empty.

Then Sabre discovered a notebook in the bottom of the gold case. She picked it up and opened it.

"What's that?" JP asked.

"I hoped it was her trust documents," Sabre said, "but there's nothing except an old will, dated over fifteen years ago." Sabre saw a bit of lavender paper sticking out of the front pocket and reached for it. "Another handwritten note." She began to read aloud.

My Dear Sabre,

I must start with an apology for what I did to you as a child. Whether you blamed me or not, I'll never know, but I never forgave myself. Regardless...

"What did she do?" JP asked.

Sabre was dumbfounded. "I have no idea what she's talking about. Goldie never did anything to me that I'm aware of." Sabre searched her memory for anything that might be related, but nothing came to her. She turned back to the note and read more.

... it appears you have decided to help me through this. I knew you would, because you are a kind and loving person. I wish we could've spent more time together. If you're thinking the same thing, please don't blame yourself. This was all on me. I wouldn't have been able to stand the look on your beautiful face if you had

discovered the way I lived. So, I hid it from you. I went to great lengths to keep it from the world, as you can tell by the outward appearance of my house. Many days I had to force myself to go outside and keep up the front yard and my flower beds. The odd thing is that I actually enjoyed it once I started. I could have hired a gardener, but for some reason that didn't feel right. It was my punishment and my joy all rolled into one.

My second apology is that I didn't get a chance to put all the necessary information and documents into this case. Some will require hunting through my house to find, but I assure you, they're all there. I couldn't even find the deed to my home, but I do have it. As you know by now, I had a hard time throwing things away, but that is especially true with paperwork and receipts. They somehow connected me to real life. If it had a paper trail, it had to be real. At least, that's what one shrink told me. Not that it was true, but that my mind thought that way. Needless to say, it'll take some time to go through all the paperwork. This will and testament is very old, but I have since written a pour-over will and had a trust drafted, naming you as the trustee. I know it's a monumental task, but I'm counting on you.

Apology number 3: My children are a handful—all of them. They'll fight you all the way, even if they don't know what they're fighting for. I'm sorry I didn't do a better job of raising them. I guess my own problems were harder to handle than I thought at the time. The more I realized I was messing up as a parent, the more guilt I felt, and the worse job I did. Don't trust them. They're very manipulative. Don't let them suck you in. Micki and Rocki will play good cop/bad cop. Travis will try to charm you,

Langston will bully you, and Chase can be very sneaky. The constant conflict will be enough to run you off, but I'm begging you, please do not let it.

Apology number 4: I'm sorry for what I'm about to ask. Before I do, you need to know that every year in the first few days of January, I re-write this note. I take the old one out and replace it with the new one. I do that to make sure this letter is up to date and to add anything new. Sometimes, I just do an addendum to the old letter, but this time I started fresh. As with everything else, I saved the previous notes. You will find them in the "Personal" folder in this case.

There are four other storage units besides this one. They're all at this location and all require the same key: units 14, 16, 23, and 25.

Now, for my last request. I need you to continue the work I've started. It's very important to me. No one else knows about it, and I need you to keep it that way.

Your loving Aunt Goldie

"She didn't say what the work was?"

"Nope, but maybe it's in her files somewhere." Sabre reached for the gold case and found a solid plastic sheet that clipped into place.

On the backside in raised print were the words: *PEOPLE FIRST, THEN MONEY, THEN THINGS.* Sabre read the motto aloud. Under the plastic were small compartments lined with dark blue felt. Each was filled with different items and tagged. She picked up a cameo pin and read the tag: *For Micki.* Next to it was a diamond ring tagged with Rocki's name. Sabre glanced at the other items, thinking they were probably everything of value her Aunt Goldie owned. She closed the lid and latched it into place.

Sabre picked up her phone and searched for the lawyer whose name was listed on the will, but she couldn't find him online. She took a photo of the name and texted it to JP. "Could you try to find this guy? He may have done the trust for her too."

"I'll get on it as soon as I get home."

Sabre put the letter back in the pocket of the notebook and placed the notebook back into the case.

"I'll look at the rest later. I have to go see some kids at Polinsky before they're moved. Their father is picking them up around six-thirty and taking them to his home in Lakeside. I'll visit them there in a few days, but I'd like to meet them before they go home to Dad. You can come along if you want. It's the McCluskey case I called you about earlier. It might help for you to hear what happened."

"I'll meet you there."

On the way to Polinsky, Sabre called Ron. "Are you busy tomorrow?" she asked. Ron was a few years older than her and presently unemployed. Both JP and Sabre tried to give him work whenever they could. JP often enlisted her brother's help with his investigations, but it wasn't really what Ron wanted to do with the rest of his life. He loved the outdoors, and Sabre was confident he would soon be back doing something he loved. In the meantime, she would help him any way she could.

"What do you need?" Ron asked.

"I need you to go to Aunt Goldie's house and change all

the locks on her doors. She also has five storage units that need new padlocks. Key them all the same so we only need one master key for them. Pick up what you need from Lowe's. But come by the house first, and I'll give you my credit card."

"I've got it."

"I'll pay you back."

"No need. Aunt Goldie was quite a character. I really liked her, and if that's what she wanted, I'm glad to help out."

"I'll take the money out of her estate to repay you, if she has any. If not, I'll be glad to pay for the supplies if you provide the labor."

"Deal."

"Please let me know when it's done. I don't want to wait too long before I contact our cousins and let them know she passed." Another call came in on Sabre's phone. "JP's on another line. I'll talk to you later."

Sabre switched over. "Hey, Kid," JP said. "The lawyer who wrote Goldie's will has been dead for fifteen years. He was a sole practitioner and, without a lot more digging, I don't know if I can find his files. But I'll keep looking if you want me to."

"Let it go for now. I expect we'll find something in that house." Sabre's phone beeped. "I have a call coming from the hospital. I'll talk to you later." She switched connections again and said, "Sabre Brown."

"This is Dr. Yadav at Sharp Grossmont. I treated your aunt, Goldie Forney, yesterday. I have lab results for the serum we had tested. Where would you like me to send them?"

"Can you email them to me?"

"Sure."

Sabre gave him her email address, then asked, "Did you find anything unusual?"

"There was a trace of botulinum toxin in her blood."

39

"Food poisoning?"

"That's most likely. The toxin can come from open wounds as well, but she didn't have any."

"Where else could she have gotten it?" Sabre asked. "I thought it all came from food poisoning."

"She could've ingested the toxin itself."

"You mean intentionally taken poison? As in suicide?"

"It's possible. Or someone could've given it to her. But those are unlikely scenarios, and we have no reason to believe the toxin came from anything other than bad food. The amount was minor and not likely the cause of her death. As per protocol, I reported it to the County Health Department, so you may receive a call from them."

CHAPTER 7

Monday Afternoon

S abre and JP sat in the interview room at Polinsky
Receiving Home, waiting for Dale McCluskey.

JP was reading the report from the social worker to famil-
iarize himself with the case. He looked up at Sabre. "The
mother's boyfriend is Kenny Yarborough."

"Do you know him?"

"No, but I knew a Zack Yarborough. He was my trainee
when he first joined the force. The report says Kenny has a
brother named Zack. I wonder if he's the same one."

"Could be. Yarborough's not that common of a name."

They were interrupted when a young man walked in,
escorting a short, skinny kid with bushy blond hair and brown
eyes. "This is Dale McCluskey," the attendant said.

Sabre introduced herself and JP, then explained their roles
in the legal proceedings.

After the attendant left, Sabre said to Dale, "We work for you and your siblings. I'll represent you in court, and JP will be investigating for us. But right now, I just want to get to know you a little bit. I also want to give you my information in case you need to reach me, as well as answer any questions you have."

Dale stood silently, looking overwhelmed.

"Have a seat." Sabre gestured to a chair and handed the boy her business card. She and JP sat on the sofa across from him. "I know this is a lot to handle, and you're grieving the loss of your brother, but right now we need to make sure you have an appropriate place to live. Do you understand?"

Dale nodded.

"I understand you've spent quite a bit of time at your father's house since the divorce. Is that right?"

"Yes, we go there a lot."

"What's it like? Is it much different from your mom's?"

"Way different," he said, with little change of expression. "I like living there. It's where we used to live. It's kind of in the country, and we have a lot of land where we can ride our bikes and explore and stuff."

"Tell me one special thing about your father," Sabre said.

"That's easy. He does things with us. He takes us fishing and to the park, and sometimes we camp out in the backyard." His voice sounded more upbeat now, but there was still no smile. "We have movie night every Saturday when we're there. Even when he's tired, he'll make us popcorn and sit with us. He falls asleep sometimes, so we throw popcorn at him until he wakes up. He just laughs and says he wasn't really sleeping, just testing us."

"It sounds like you get along with your father."

"He's the best. He never yells or spanks us or anything like that. But he does make us do our chores and our homework. But he helps us when we need it. Usually, my sister, Fayth, helps Harmony, but sometimes she helps me. Fayth is real smart in school, a lot better than me."

"Does your mom help you with homework when you're at her house?"

He hesitated. "Not so much. She never liked school. She lets Fayth do it."

"What about Kenny? Did he ever help you?"

"No." Dale scoffed. "Kenny just sits around playing his guitar and drinking beer."

"Tell me one thing you really like about your mother," Sabre said.

When he didn't answer right away, Sabre wondered if the boy was trying to make sure he got the answer correct, or if he was having trouble thinking of something good to say. Finally, he said, "My mom's a good cook." He paused. "At least she used to be. She doesn't cook as much as she used to."

"Why is that?"

Dale shrugged. "I dunno." He thought for a moment, then added, "But she taught Fayth, and now Fayth cooks sometimes."

"Is your dad a good cook?"

"Not really, but we barbeque a lot, and he's good at that."

After that, Sabre tried to keep the conversation light, hoping to get a smile from Dale, but she never did. She wondered if he was always this solemn, or if he was just grieving for his little brother. She decided not to bring him up. Things were still pretty raw. "Do you have any questions?"

"Do we get to go home?"

"You won't be able to stay with your mother for a while."

Before she could continue, Dale interrupted. "Not my mom's house. Home with my dad."

"Yes, your dad will pick you up about six-thirty this evening, probably after dinner." She looked in the little boy's eyes, trying to get a read on what he was thinking, but he remained locked.

"Are my sisters coming home too?"

"Yes. Is that what you want?"

"Yeah," he said, showing the most enthusiasm he'd mustered so far.

"Be sure you eat your dinner here, so no one has to cook when you all get home." Sabre smiled, teasing a little. But the boy didn't smile back.

After he left, JP said, "That's one sad little boy."

"I know. I just hope it's because he's grieving Perry, and not something else that's going on."

"Do you think he might have seen what happened?"

"I thought about that. Or maybe he witnessed other things that have gone on in that home."

They were still chatting when Fayth came into the room. Her mousy, straight, brown hair hung just below her ears in a cute messy look. She was tall and thin and carried herself with confidence. Sabre explained who they were and reassured Fayth that anything she said was confidential. She seemed to grasp the idea quicker than Dale had. Fayth had a serious, almost business-like attitude. Although she didn't smile much either, she didn't look as sad as Dale.

"I hear you're a good cook," Sabre said.

The girl shrugged. "Someone has to do it, and I don't mind. Mom doesn't really like it anymore."

"Do you cook every day at your mom's?"

"Not every day. She brings fast food home sometimes."

"What about at your dad's?"

"I help Dad when he cooks." Without skipping a beat, she blurted, "Since you're my attorney, you're here to help me, right?"

"That's right. It's my job to let the court know what you want, but also to recommend what's best for you. Those things aren't always the same, however."

"What I want is to go home to live with my dad, and I want my brother and sisters to go with me. I can take care of them all. Harmony and Ivory listen to me, and I can help Dad with cooking and cleaning. And even though Dale can be a pain sometimes, he'll be happier at home." She talked fast, as though afraid her time would run out. "I'll be real good, and I'll make sure Harmony and Dale go to school. If Dad has to go to work early, I can make breakfast and pack sack lunches." Before Sabre could respond, the girl's pitch turned into begging. "Please, please, let us go home. Tell the judge to send us home. Tell him ...."

Sabre raised her hand, palm up, to stop her. "Fayth, your father is picking you up this evening and taking you home."

Her eyes brightened, and she jumped up and hugged Sabre. "Thank you! Thank you!"

"It's what the judge thinks is best for now."

"This isn't for good?" The jubilance faded from her voice.

"That hasn't been decided yet. There'll be a lot of investigation and court hearings before we know that."

"I'll go to court and tell the judge that we should be with my dad."

"That time may come. But for now, I'll be able to appear in court for you. At some point, you may need to testify too. If so, I'll make sure you are well prepared for it. In the meantime, you'll all be living with your father and going to school in Lakeside."

"That'll do for now." She stood up almost dismissively.

Sabre liked this girl's attitude, but she was concerned she was taking on too much of a parental role.

"Can I tell Harmony and Ivory?"

"Why not?" Sabre stood. "Just wait here. I want to meet them anyway, so I'll send for them." Sabre picked up the wall phone and asked to have the girls brought in.

A few minutes later, six-year-old Harmony came in holding the hand of her three-year-old sister, Ivory. Harmony had a full head of red curls that fell softly about her face and neck, much like her father's, only longer. She also shared his deep-green eyes, but hers were filled with a distant, empty stare. Ivory looked more like Fayth, the same coloring and similar features, only not so serious. Unlike Harmony, she smiled the whole time she was in the room.

Fayth took charge as soon as they walked in. "This is our attorney, Ms. Sabre Brown. She's helping us in court. And this is Mr. Torn. He's helping us too."

Sabre chatted with them for a bit and gave her card to Fayth. "If you ever need to reach me, call me at this number."

Harmony held out her hand, palm up.

"Would you like one too?"

She nodded, her red curls bobbing up and down. Sabre handed her a card, then said, "I'll come to see you again real soon, but right now, Fayth has something to tell you."

Fayth got down on her knees so her eyes met theirs. "We're going home to Daddy today."

For the first time, Harmony's face showed some emotion. Her eyes seemed to brighten, and her mouth turned up ever so slightly. Sabre had been told that Harmony had turned inward since Perry's death. They were the closest in age, and she probably least understood how to deal with her loss. In a soft voice, she said, "Yay."

Fayth turned to Ivory and waved her arms. "Yay! We're going home to Daddy."

Ivory smiled and did the same thing. Sabre wasn't sure if the little one was happy about what she'd heard or just mimicking her big sister.

CHAPTER 8

Tuesday Morning

S abre woke to the aroma of brewing coffee. She loved the smell but had never gotten hooked on the taste. That, coupled with her intolerance for caffeine, made hot herbal tea her drink of choice. But she occasionally indulged in a decaf mocha, which tasted more like dessert than coffee. She looked at the time on her phone: *5:49 a.m.* She rolled out of bed and strolled to the kitchen. JP sat at the table reading the newspaper.

"Good morning, darlin'," he said as she walked in. "I turned the teapot on, so your water should be hot."

"Thanks," Sabre muttered, trying to get her morning mouth to function. She picked up a cup, dropped in a teabag of summer peach, and poured in hot water. Then she walked to the table and sat down next to JP. "Anything exciting in the news?"

"There's an article on the Incognito Angel," JP said. "It's kind of interesting. Want to read it?"

Sabre tipped her head to the side and looked at him sweetly. "Would you mind reading it to me? My eyes aren't focused yet, and I love the sound of your sweet voice."

"No need to pile it on. I don't mind." JP shuffled the paper and began to read.

Just over a year ago, I discovered a student who had received a gift to attend a local college of her choice, which she chose to use at the University of San Diego. It included tuition for four years, housing, books, and incidentals, as long as the student went full time, maintained a B average, and worked toward a four-year degree. There were no other strings attached. There was no indication of where the money had come from, other than the initials, IA, and this investigative reporter has not yet determined the source.

When I posted the story last year, I asked for others to come forward if they had a similar experience. I received hundreds of responses and discovered anonymous gift-giving that ranged from a free lunch at Jack in the Box to a Silverado truck. Thanksgiving and Christmas dinners had been provided to impoverished families, and Santa had delivered gifts. School tuitions were paid, team uniforms donated, and housing provided for the homeless.

It has been difficult to determine how many of these gifts came from the same source. However, similarities lead me to believe that quite a few were likely from the Incognito Angel. The size of the gift is not one of the consistencies. The Angel seems to give in all values. However, one thing I discovered is that he/she favors children and young adults. I discovered a few other subtleties, but I choose not to make those public yet. I'm still investigating and think I'm getting close. The obvious ones have instructions or notes signed IA. I haven't been able to determine what the initials stand for and have assigned my own label—Incognito Angel.

The most recent report was a week ago when a young woman was given a pre-paid package to Victoria's Wedding World, where she'll be able to have the wedding of her dreams. Upon investigation, I'm convinced this is the work of the Incognito Angel.

If you received an anonymous gift in the last five years, please contact me through this newspaper. I would also appreciate any information pertaining to who the Incognito Angel is.

"That Angel is really something," Sabre said. "What a kind heart."

"And a large bank account," JP added.

"It would be a fun thing to do if you had lots of money." Sabre wrapped her hands around her cup. "What's on your schedule today?"

"I thought I'd get started on the McCluskey case. I'll see if I can find out who's handling the police investigation. Bob said he'd go with me to see his client, Adam McCluskey, and I'd like to get his take on the mother and her boyfriend. If I get a chance, I'll talk to some of the neighbors too." JP laid down the newspaper. "How about you?"

"I'm going to take a quick run then shower and head to court. I only have a couple of cases on calendar this morning, so it shouldn't take long. Then I'll go back to my office and reach out to all of Aunt Goldie's kids."

"I take it Ron got the locks changed."

"Yes, and he'll bring the keys to my office when I'm done at court."

"Good."

"I've been debating whether I should set up a meeting with Goldie's kids and explain things all at once, or if I should meet with them one at a time. Or maybe I should talk to them over the phone and not meet with them at all. That would be the easiest way."

"Do you want my opinion, or is that debate with yourself?" JP asked.

Sabre grinned. "I'd like to know what you think."

"What would be the point in meeting with them together?"

"I would only have to explain things once."

"True, but they're far more likely to gang up on you. I don't want you diggin' up more snakes than you can kill."

"I don't scare easily," Sabre said.

"I know you can hold your own, but do me a favor. If you have such a meeting, please let me be there with you. Just to be safe. From what Aunt Goldie has said about her own children, they may be pretty mean."

Sabre knew there was little point in arguing with him, so she acquiesced. Besides, she felt a little better about the whole thing. She remembered the twins, Rocki and Micki, ganging up on her when she was little. She'd always had Ron around to back her up, and they were a little afraid of him. It probably had something to do with the pocketknife he carried and the stories he told about skinning a coyote who'd come after him, which were all fabricated, but they'd believed him.

Sabre's thoughts were interrupted by a phone call from the

County Health Department. She put the call on speaker for JP. After the woman introduced herself, she asked, "Do you know what Goldie Forney ate the last few days before she passed away?"

"I have no idea, but…" Sabre hesitated.

"But what?"

"My aunt was a hoarder. If she ate anything in that house, it could've been tainted."

"If you find food wrappers near where she sat or any suspicious canned goods that appear to have been recently opened, please bag them and let me know. And if you're handling anything that might be contaminated, use disposable gloves."

CHAPTER 9

Tuesday Morning

I t didn't take JP long to find out which homicide detective was handling the Perry McCluskey case, and fortunately, it was someone he knew. He picked up his phone, searched his contacts, and placed the call. He leaned back in his desk chair, enjoying the peace and quiet of his home now that everyone had left for the day. Louie, JP's beagle, walked up, plopped himself down, and put his head on JP's knee.

"Detective DuBois," the man answered.

"Hey, Vinny. This is JP Torn."

"Nice to hear from you, McCloud."

JP smiled. His old friend would never stop calling him that. Vinny had always teased JP about his boots and cowboy hat. Vinny said he reminded him of Dennis Weaver on an old TV show, who'd played a cop named McCloud from New Mexico who'd been transplanted to New York City.

"I see you're on the Perry McCluskey case," JP said. "Sabre is representing the siblings in juvenile court, and I'm investigating for her. I was surprised to learn you were handling it. I thought you were retiring."

"I changed my mind. Another year gives me a bigger retirement check."

"You'd probably be bored to death anyway."

"Not to mention my wife would get tired of seeing my mug every day. But you're not just calling to say hello. What can I do for you?"

"Have they ruled the boy's death a homicide?"

"Just did. I talked to the medical examiner, and it's her professional opinion that the child was intentionally smothered. Whoever did it, left bruises on his scrotum. We're still sorting that part out. We're not sure if there was molestation of some sort, or just targeted violence. It's always hard to determine with boys. The ME checked for anal penetration, but there was none."

"The mother claims the bruises were there when Perry came home from a visit to his father, three or four days earlier, but neither DSS nor the court believe her."

"According to the ME's report, the bruises were not more than a day old. I guess it's easy to tell by the coloration."

"Do you have any suspects?"

"Unless someone snuck into the house and killed the boy, it has to be the mother, the boyfriend, or one of the other kids. At this point, we're not making any arrests."

"Thanks, Vinny."

"Be careful, McCloud, when you're nosing around that you don't interfere in my investigation."

"I won't be tipping over any outhouses," JP said.

"Good to know."

"Any chance you can email me the coroner's report, or do I need to go through other channels?"

"I'll get it right over to you." Vinny paused. "Those kids aren't going home to the mom, are they?"

"No, not right now anyway. They're living with their father in Lakeside."

"Good. Keep me posted if you come across anything that might help."

"You know I will."

JP hung up and called Bob, who was still at court, but said he would be available in an hour.

JP headed outside, got in his truck, and drove to the address listed for Ellie McCluskey. She had remained in the home where her son had died. JP wouldn't be able to speak to her without her attorney's permission, which he was pretty sure he wouldn't get. He could, however, question her boyfriend, Kenny Yarborough. But that wasn't his plan for today. He wanted to see the area and question the neighbors who might prove to be helpful.

JP double-checked the address when he arrived, making certain he was at the right house. He climbed out and started taking photos, trying to be subtle. Several windows were boarded up, and black curtains hung over the others. The yard was overgrown with weeds, and the grass needed cutting. Dry, overgrown bushes lined one side of the property forming a wall between them and the neighbor.

JP walked to the house on the other side and knocked.

A woman in her fifties opened the door, leaving the security screen closed. "Can I help you?"

"My name is JP Torn. I have some questions about your neighbor, Ellie McCluskey."

"Are you a cop?"

"No, I'm a private investigator on behalf of the children." JP sometimes found it difficult getting people to talk without giving out confidential information. It had been different when he'd had a badge backing him, but as a PI, he had to make people trust him. Before she could turn him away, he asked, "Do you know the McCluskeys?"

"As well as anyone in the neighborhood, I guess. Which is to say, not really. They're loners. I've seen them come and go but never really talked to any of them."

"How long have they lived here?"

"Less than a year."

"Do you know any of the children?"

"No. I see them leaving for school in the morning and returning in the afternoon. They go straight into the house and don't come out."

"They don't play outside?"

"No. I don't think they're ever allowed to go out."

That seemed odd. "What makes you say that?"

"My daughter sees the kids at school. She's in the same class as Fayth, and they're friends at school. But she never sees her after because Fayth isn't allowed to come over here."

"You don't allow her?"

"Oh, she's more than welcome to come here. But she says she can't because she has chores and has to watch her younger siblings. My daughter has never been invited over there either, but I wouldn't let her go anyway." The woman shook her head. "Not without meeting the parents first, which they're not interested in doing. The longer they've been there, the more adamant I've become about it. And now that poor little boy died, and I'm really glad I stuck to my guns."

"What do you know about his death?" JP asked.

"Not much. I heard all the sirens, and then the fire truck

and cop cars arrived. I saw them bring the body out. But most of what I know, I read in the newspaper. A detective came here and asked a bunch of questions, but as I told you, I didn't really know any of them."

"Did you hear any commotion or anything unusual during the night it happened?"

"Not really. There's just a fence and a short distance between the mother's bedroom and mine, and sometimes they get loud at night." She rolled her eyes. "But that night wasn't any different—just the usual yelling at each other."

JP gave her his card and thanked her for the information. He went to several other houses and got similar information. No one in the neighborhood seemed to know the family. Standing in front of Ellie's house, JP could see the tops of the two houses behind hers. They sat on a hill, facing the next street over. One house had a long back deck. If someone was on that deck or looking out an upstairs window, they could see everything that went on in the McCluskeys' backyard. JP decided to check them out.

He drove around the block and parked in front of the two-story house that sat directly behind Ellie's. He got out and rang the bell, but no one answered. He tried knocking. Still nothing. JP hurried to the nearby house with the deck, and this time a young, shirtless man came to the door.

"Yes?" he asked.

"I'm JP Torn. I'm investigating an incident that happened last Friday in the house behind you."

"Where the little kid died?"

"Yes. Do you know the people who live there?"

"Never met them."

"How did you know about the child?"

"I heard all the sirens that morning, but I didn't go outside.

57

One of my roommates told me what happened, at least what he had heard."

"Were you home the night before?"

"No. I stayed at my girlfriend's house. I had just gotten home when I heard the sirens. I live here with four other students, and I think Norint was the only one home that night." He turned and yelled, "Norint. Come here." Then he pivoted back to JP. "Come on in."

JP walked inside, surprised by how clean the house was. With five students living together, he'd expected a mess. From the living room, JP saw a young Asian-American man come inside through the sliding glass door that led to the deck.

"This is Norint," the shirtless guy said. "I've got to run."

JP reached out to shake Norint's hand and introduced himself. "Do you mind showing me your deck?"

"Not at all." Norint stepped toward the slider.

JP followed him outside. "Do you know the people who live there?" He pointed down to Ellie's house.

"I've never met any of them. I know there's an older guy, about your age."

How old did this kid think he was?

"He comes out back to tend his marijuana plants." Norint pointed at a small crop of weed growing in a corner of Ellie's yard, then frowned. "A bunch of kids live there, but they don't come out much. I've only seen them a few times. Except the older boy who comes out more often."

"What does he do in the backyard?"

"Not much. He mostly just walks around like he's bored to death."

"I understand you were here the night the five-year-old boy passed away. Is that correct?"

"Yeah. I had a paper due, so I didn't go out with my

friends. I was out on the deck working on it until about two-thirty in the morning." He walked over to a high table with a tall chair. "I was sitting here. It's where I study and write papers. It's quiet and peaceful."

"You have a good view of the house from here. Did you see anything unusual that night?"

"Sort of."

"What do you mean?"

"I was working on my laptop, and something got my attention, so I looked up. I thought I saw something move in their backyard."

"What exactly did you see?" JP asked.

Norint pointed toward the yard below again. "I saw someone walking across the backyard and toward the side gate." He pointed to the side of the house. "I didn't see where he came from. When I first spotted him, he was near that big rose bush. I watched as he went to the gate, opened it, and left."

"You said *he*, are you sure it was a male?"

"Not absolutely. I only got a glimpse because it was dark, but he or she was wearing pants. I know that much."

"How tall would you guess?"

"No idea."

"Could it have been a child?"

"Not a little kid for sure. I really didn't see him for long, maybe a couple of steps, and then he was out the gate."

"Is there anything else you remember about him?"

Norint shook his head, paused, then added, "I think he was carrying a bag of some kind."

"Any idea what time?"

Norint shrugged. "Sometime between midnight and two is my best guess."

JP thanked him and headed back out to his truck. He called Vinny DuBois, told him what he'd learned, and gave him Norint's contact information.

"That's the first I've heard of anyone outside." Vinny grunted. "I went to that house twice yesterday but didn't catch anyone home."

"I guess I got lucky."

A pause. Then Vinny lowered his voice. "I've been interrogating Ellie McCluskey and Kenny Yarborough. They're pointing the finger at Dale, the oldest kid."

"They both are?"

"Kenny was more insistent, but the mother is dropping hints. I got the feeling they rehearsed what they planned to say. Neither mentioned it the first time we talked."

"That makes them look more suspicious."

"Maybe. But I'll question the boy. Please tell Sabre I'll call and set it up soon. I know she won't let me talk to him alone."

"But Dale's not a suspect at this point?" JP asked.

"Just a person of interest."

CHAPTER 10

Tuesday Morning

Sabre finished her morning calendar and drove back to her office, dreading the phone calls she had to make to Aunt Goldie's children. *Maybe it won't be so bad,* she thought. *Although, it was never easy telling someone their loved one had died. But this was their mother, and they deserved to know. They would never have her to lean on again.*

Sabre thought about her own mom. They'd had their differences, but nothing like these kids. She wished she could call her mom and talk to her right now, but she was on a cruise and there was no reason to bother her on her trip. She'd be home at the end of the week, and Sabre would tell her everything then. They wouldn't hold a service before then anyway. Aunt Goldie had been very specific about how that should take place. She had planned every detail.

At her desk, Sabre decided to read through the instructions

again before she made the calls. She opened the gold case and pulled out the folder marked *End of Life Instructions*. The details were also incorporated into Aunt Goldie's will.

The executor of my estate, Attorney Sabre Orin Brown, is to follow these instructions to the letter.

1. My family and friends do not need to know of my death until my trustee has had all locks changed on my house and storage sheds.

2. Call each of my children and let them know that I have passed.

3. My remains are to be cremated. I have the documents attached for Soft Slumber Mortuary and have paid for all their services.

4. My celebration of life is to take place at the German American Societies Clubhouse in El Cajon. I have made all the arrangements. The date will be determined after my passing, at the facility's earliest convenience, as coordinated by Sabre Brown.

5. Distribution of my cremated remains to be done by Sabre and/or Ron Brown. I requested the mortuary to provide small tubes of ashes for each of my children, should they want them. The funeral home will provide four urns, and my ashes are to be distributed in the following places, each of which have special meaning to me:

- *Glacier National Park*
- *The ocean off the coast of San Diego, California*
- *Payne Park in Sarasota, Florida*
- *The grave of my son, Michael Nogard, in Bakersfield, California*

All of this will take some time and does not need to be rushed. I've provided the funding and made arrangements where I could.

Really, Aunt Goldie? Sabre took a deep breath. Distributing the ashes would take some effort, but she didn't have to think about that yet. She picked up her desk phone, and dialed Micki Nogard. She'd pulled the heirs' information from Goldie's phone. The strategy was to tell Micki first, hoping she would pass the word on and leave Sabre less explaining to do with her siblings.

"Hello." Her voice was noncommittal and a little cold.

"Is this Micki?" Sabre asked.

"Yes. Who's this?"

"Sabre Brown. Remember me?"

"Of course. I'm just shocked to hear from you." Micki sounded a little friendlier. "I didn't recognize the number and thought it was a sales call for insurance, or car warranties, or something. What's up?"

"I'm afraid I have some bad news." Sabre paused, bracing herself. "I'm so sorry, Micki, but your mother has passed away."

"What?" A quick breath. "What happened? When?"

"She had a heart attack. She passed away on Sunday afternoon at Sharp Grossmont Hospital. Her body is at Soft Slumber Mortuary in La Mesa. You can go see her there if you choose. She'll be there until Friday when she's scheduled for cremation."

There was an uncomfortable silence for a few seconds. Then Micki said, "Wait. How do you know all this?"

"Your mother called me on Sunday and asked me to meet her at the hospital."

"Why didn't you call me then?" Micki raised her voice, angry now.

Sabre had anticipated the question and was prepared. "Micki, I'm sorry, but I didn't have your number, and then Aunt Goldie gave me very specific instructions."

"She told you not to call me?"

"I'm sure she didn't want any of you to worry," Sabre lied. "She probably thought she'd get better in a few days."

"I guess one of us has to start doing some paperwork," Micki said. "I suppose that'll be me since I'm the oldest. I'll go to her house and see if she left anything."

"There's no need for that." Sabre cut her short. "I have her will and last instructions."

Silence.

"Why?" Micki asked.

"Why what?"

"Why do *you* have her will and last instructions?"

"Because she gave them to me. Let's have a meeting, and I can catch you all up at once."

"Okay." Micki sounded hesitant. "Let's meet at her house."

"No," Sabre said softly, but with conviction. "We'll meet at my office this afternoon at three o'clock. Can you be there?"

Silence for several seconds. "Yes."

Sabre gave her the address, said goodbye, and hung up before Micki could say any more. She waited a few minutes before she called Rocki. Micki had already contacted her as Sabre expected. When Rocki started to ask questions, Sabre invited her to the meeting. Rocki agreed to be there and hung up.

The calls to her cousins, Travis and Langston, weren't much different, except Travis was sweet, and neither seemed surprised to hear from her. Sabre was certain they had both already been contacted by Micki or Rocki. It was evident they knew their mother had passed. Travis maintained his sweet tone throughout the conversation. Langston, on the other hand, had been crying when she called, and he sobbed occasionally as she gave him the time and address for the meeting.

Chase Perkins, Goldie's youngest, didn't answer his phone. Sabre left him a message, along with her phone number, and asked him to confirm. Her next call was to JP, who was on his way to see Adam McCluskey.

"Please check on the kids while you're there," Sabre said. "I'll visit them soon, but just try to get a feel for how they're settling in."

"Will do. And Sabre?"

"Yes?"

"I don't think you should have that meeting alone with Goldie's kids. I'll reschedule McCluskey."

"You don't need to do that. I'm sure they're all harmless."

"A dead bee can still sting, you know."

"It's all right. I'll call Ron. He'll want to see his cousins anyway."

"I'll try to get back before it's over," JP said. "By the way, I checked on Kenny Yarborough's brother. He's a cop, around the right age and description. I bet he's the same guy I trained fifteen years ago."

"He might give us some insight."

"I'll contact him and set up a meeting first chance I get."

Sabre hung up and immediately called Ron. "What are you doing this afternoon?"

"Nothing important. Why?"

"Can you come to my office a little before three? I'm meeting with Goldie's kids, and I think it would be good to have a witness."

CHAPTER 11

Tuesday Afternoon

JP picked up Bob at the courthouse, then headed east out of town to Adam McCluskey's place. On the way, they passed several horse ranches on the otherwise sparsely populated road.

When they arrived at the ranch-style home, Adam was in the front yard, pushing Ivory on a swing hanging from a large magnolia tree. Fayth and Dale rode their bikes on a dirt path that ran the depth of the property which seemed to cover several acres. The kids disappeared from sight for a while, then returned bent over in race mode. Dale was in the lead, but Fayth wasn't far behind.

JP got out, stretched his legs, and looked around. The property was filled with eucalyptus trees and bare dirt except for patches of grass near the house.

Adam stopped the swing, hugged Ivory, and sent her

inside. Then he invited JP and Bob to sit at a picnic table a few feet from an old-fashioned tire swing in the shade of the magnolia tree.

They exchanged pleasantries, then JP asked, "What do you know about what happened the night Perry died?"

"Not much. Just what Ellie is saying, and what the kids told me. Everyone claims they were asleep, and the next morning, Dale found him dead." The father choked back tears.

"I'm so sorry, Adam, but I have to ask you these questions."

"I know. The cops said the same thing. I've told them everything I know." He swallowed hard. "Ellie tried to blame me for Perry's bruises, but I'm sure they didn't happen here. He went swimming with the other kids on Sunday, and he was fine when he got dressed after."

"Did they swim here?"

"Yeah. I have an above-ground pool in the backyard. Come take a look."

They followed Adam around to the back of his house. The pool was just big enough for young kids to swim around and stay cool. The temporary fence around it had a locked gate.

"Dale and Fayth can go in without me if they're together, but the younger kids are only allowed in the pool with adult supervision. It's a good pastime for all of them."

"Why do you suppose Ellie blamed the bruising on you?"

"To divert attention from herself. I don't know what went on in that house that night, but only two adults were there."

"Do you know that for a fact?"

Adam looked pensive. "Not really. The kids went to sleep, so I suppose Ellie could've had someone else over. But why wouldn't she just admit that?"

"I don't know," JP said. "Have there been other problems in that home before? Either from their mother or Kenny?"

Adam hesitated.

"What is it?" Bob cut in. "You need to tell us everything you know."

Just then Dale rode up on his bike. "Dad, can Fayth and I go swimming?"

"Sure," Adam said. "Ask Aunt Olivia if she'll take the girls in for a while. I'll be with you in a little bit. I may take a swim myself."

Dale rode off.

"I don't really know anything," Adam said. "It's just a hunch." He paused again. "I know there's been some drug use, but I'm hoping it has just been marijuana."

"What is it you know, exactly?" JP asked.

"Fayth said they have skunks around their house because she's smelled them several times. We all know what that means."

"Have any of the kids seen them do drugs?"

"I think Dale has, and he told me Kenny is growing pot plants in the backyard. The kids don't say much about their mom, and I haven't really pushed them. I wanted them to be comfortable when they were here on weekends, and I didn't want them to feel like I was grilling them. In retrospect, I realize that wasn't the right thing to do. Maybe I could've prevented..." Adam couldn't finish the thought.

Bob put his hand on the big man's shoulder. "It's not your fault, and JP will do everything he can to find out what happened."

Adam cleared his throat. "I'm sorry. I'm like this all day long. I try to hold it together when the kids are around, but if I talk about it, I fall apart."

"I know," JP said. Although he couldn't imagine what it must be like to lose a child. He knew how devastated he would be if anything happened to Conner or Morgan, and they weren't even his. *It must be about the greatest pain in the world,* he thought. He decided to take a different tack. "What can you tell me about Kenny Yarborough?"

Dale and Fayth dashed past them, running toward the pool ten feet away. Dale opened the gate, and Fayth pushed past him in an obvious attempt to get in first. Dale let go of the gate and grabbed her.

"Close the gate," Adam yelled.

"Aunt Olivia is right behind us with the girls," Dale said, struggling to hold onto Fayth. When he let go, Fayth scrambled up the ladder, and Dale went over the side and hit the water seconds before Fayth did.

"Sorry. They're excited." Adam kept his eye on the gate. "What did you ask me?"

"About Kenny Yarborough."

"Oh yeah. He seems kind of worthless. He doesn't work much, and he and Ellie have been partying a lot since he's been around. But I don't really know him that well. The kids could probably tell you more." Adam glanced at the house, then walked to the gate and closed it. He pointed at the pool. "As you can see, there isn't really anything in the pool that Perry could have hurt himself on, and they didn't do much after. The kids were all tired, so we watched a movie and ate popcorn." Adam's eyes watered up again. "Perry loved popcorn."

"You don't need to concern yourself about the bruising, at least not as far as the timing," JP said. "According to the medical examiner, the bruises happened about the same time"—JP quickly rephrased—"sometime that night."

Adam nodded, but didn't speak.

"I went to your ex-wife's house to see where they were living and found several of the windows boarded up. The others had black curtains over them. Do you know why?"

"The kids say Kenny is a little paranoid. He's always afraid someone is watching them."

"Have you confronted Ellie about it?"

"No. Again, I probably should have."

JP changed course again, asking, "Have you been inside the house?"

"Not lately."

A woman came out with the two younger girls, both wearing floaters. *Aunt Olivia,* JP presumed. She wore shorts and a halter top and flashed their group a quick smile. Adam opened the gate to let them inside. They all watched as Harmony went up the steps and jumped in. Olivia handed Ivory to Dale, who put her on a floating swan, then the aunt got in too and stayed with the girl as she floated along.

"How are things since the kids came home?" JP asked.

"They're excited to be here, and I'm thrilled that they are. My sister, Olivia, came from Riverside to stay with me for a while. She's a big help."

"Good. I'd like to say hi to the kids if you don't mind."

JP, Bob, and Adam passed through the gate and stood near the pool. Olivia had taken Ivory off the swan and was teaching her the breaststroke. The little girl seemed to love the water as much as the others.

When Adam introduced everyone, Olivia smiled, waved, and said in a friendly voice, "Nice to meet you both." She was a petite woman with short, red hair that made her look like a pixie.

"Ivory can swim underwater and dog paddle." Adam beamed with pride. "All the kids are good swimmers."

JP watched the interaction between the children and their father and felt comfortable with the court's decision to place them here. It was obvious how much Adam loved them, and they him in return.

After he dropped off Bob and headed home, JP used the hands-free system he'd finally mastered to call the next person on his list.

"Zack Yarborough," the man said when he answered.

"This is JP Torn."

"Officer JP?"

"The one and only."

"Nice to hear from you. It's been a long time."

"Since Hector was a pup," JP said.

They made small talk for a bit, then Zack asked, "What made you decide to call me?"

"I'm working as a private detective now. My main client is an attorney who advocates for abused kids in juvenile court."

"And?"

"Do you have a brother named Kenny?"

"Oh no, what has he done now?"

"I'm not sure, but—"

Zack cut him off. "I'm sorry but I have to go. I'll call you later."

CHAPTER 12

Tuesday Afternoon

Ron arrived at two-thirty, and Sabre watched him through her office window as he walked across the parking lot. He was a handsome, blond man, and for the first time, she realized how much he looked like their deceased father. She loved her brother dearly and wished he had someone in his life who made him as happy as JP made her. Ron did have Addie, and they seemed to be getting closer, but Sabre wasn't convinced she was right for him. Ron had been in love twice before, but both relationships had ended in heartbreak.

"Hi, Bro," Sabre said when he walked in. "I'm so glad you're here."

"I couldn't let you face that bunch alone. If Micki and Rocki are anything like they were when they were kids, they'll try to chew you up and spit you out."

"I'm a lot tougher now," Sabre said.

"And they have no idea. I know you'll hold your own." Ron took a seat. "The truth is, I didn't want to miss the fun."

"I'm glad you think it'll be fun. I'm dreading it."

"Just remember, you have all the power."

"I know. It's just sad that we're dealing with Aunt Goldie's death. I don't know what to expect. Grief? Anger? Guilt?"

"Probably all of the above. But you'll manage. You always do."

"Thanks." Sabre shifted in her chair. "By the way, you're on the payroll for this."

"You don't have to pay me to be here. I want to support you."

"This is a technical strategy. You have to be on the clock, so there's no confidentiality issue. It's simpler this way."

Sabre and Ron talked about old times, remembering the tricks Micki and Rocki had played on them as kids. They were identical, and their mother had always dressed them alike. They loved changing places or showing up—to unsuspecting victims—in two places at once. Ron always seemed to know which was which, but he had refused to tell Sabre how he knew. Sabre finally decided he was just good at guessing.

"Remember the time Micki had a race with our neighbor, Vincent? He didn't know there were two of them."

Sabre laughed. "Yeah, when he got to the end, Rocki was waiting for him."

"He was so confused. I don't think we ever told him the truth."

"He probably wonders to this day how that girl was so fast. Remember? Vincent was even convinced that he heard her rush past him just before he got to the finish line."

Ron was laughing so hard he had trouble speaking. "That's

because I was hiding in the bushes and made a *whooshing* sound as he passed me."

"You stinker."

In the front office, the door squeaked open.

"Shh. I think someone's here."

Ron stifled his laughter.

"I asked Elaine to keep them in the waiting area until three, so they can't come in one at a time." Sabre glanced at her phone: *2:48*.

She made sure she had all the files she needed at her fingertips, and Ron brought in three extra chairs from another office. Sabre lined up the five chairs across the room, just a few feet back from her desk. Ron would stand near her or sit on the credenza behind her desk.

"It's cozy," Ron said, "but it'll work."

Sabre sat back down and fidgeted with her files.

"Are you nervous? You don't usually get stage fright."

"A little. I wish Aunt Goldie hadn't told me what to expect. I hope she exaggerated."

"More likely, she sugar-coated it."

"You're not helping."

The door opened and Elaine stepped in. "They're here," she said in a sing-song tone.

"Uh oh. What's wrong?"

"The lady twins are dressed exactly alike." Elaine smirked.

"How many are here?"

"Just four, but it's past three o'clock."

"Okay, send them in." Sabre turned to Ron. "So, Micki and Rocki don't want me to know which is which. I can't imagine that they still dress the same when they go other places together. They're playing games already."

"No problem," Ron said, "I'll let—"

The two women stepped in, interrupting Ron. Their blue tank tops and black yoga pants were both stretched a little thin on their slightly overweight bodies. Sabre wondered how they maintained the same weight. *Did their twin thing make them have the same eating and exercise habits?* Their shoulder length mousy brown hair sported the same hairstyle as well. They appeared to have taken extra steps to look alike today.

Langston and Travis followed. These twins were in complete contrast to one another. Travis stood about six feet tall, had a good build, jet-black hair, and blue eyes. Langston, on the other hand, was a few inches shorter, had brown hair and eyes, and weighed least three hundred pounds.

"Please have a seat. I'm your cousin, Sabre."

The woman on the right mumbled, "You're not *my* cousin."

Sabre ignored her. "I'm sure you remember my brother, Ron. He works with me."

They all exchanged greetings, and Travis shook hands with both Sabre and Ron. The others made no effort. The women sat on one end of the row next to each another. Travis and Langston left a seat open between them.

"First of all," Sabre started, "I'm so sorry about your mother. She was very special to me, so I can't even imagine the loss you're feeling. She was a kind, loving woman." Sabre watched their faces as she spoke. The woman who mumbled earlier rolled her eyes. The other looked blank. Langston looked angry, and Travis had watery eyes. Sabre stopped and looked directly at the women. "Micki and Rocki, I'm sorry I don't know who is who. Would you mind telling me?"

The grumpy one muttered, "It doesn't matter, just go on. We want information."

The door opened, and Elaine came in, followed by a skinny, young man with long blond hair and in need of a shave. He looked around, nodded at the group, and sat in the empty chair. Travis smiled at him, but the others just looked away.

"Thanks, Elaine." Sabre nodded at him. "You must be Chase."

"Yeah," he said.

Sabre kept her composure while she told them about the phone call from Aunt Goldie, the trip to the ER, and the envelope she received from the doctor. She left out a description of the house and didn't mention changing the locks. She assumed they must know their mother was a hoarder. That mess didn't happen overnight.

"Why are *you* taking this on?" the grumpy woman asked. "It should be one of us. It's not your business."

"That's right." The other woman spoke for the first time.

Sabre stayed focused on the woman who had challenged her. "Because, Micki or Rocki, whoever you are—"

"I told you, it doesn't matter."

The secrecy was starting to make her mad. "Your mother made it clear that she wanted me to handle this." Sabre kept her voice professional, despite her feelings. "Goldie wanted me to be the trustee and executor of her estate. I'm just following her wishes." Sabre knew she was on thin ice since she had no legal document. She hoped she could put them off long enough to locate the paperwork. Otherwise she wouldn't be able to do what her aunt obviously wanted. At least not without a court battle.

"Her estate?" Grumpy Twin asked. "You say that like she has a lot of stuff."

"She does have a lot of *stuff*," Langston muttered.

Ron unexpectedly walked past the women, then reached over to the window and closed the blinds. When he came back, he put a sticky note on Sabre's desk that read: *Micki is the one on the end doing all the talking.*

"But nothing *we* can't handle," Micki said. "We can go to the house and take what we want. Then I'll sell the house and split the money. How hard can that be?"

"There's more to it than that," Sabre started to explain.

Micki cut her off before she could finish. "And I suppose you're the only one in the room smart enough to do it," she snarled.

"No," Sabre said. "I'm the only one who has the legal right to do it. I expect Aunt Goldie didn't want to burden any of you with this task."

"Don't call her that. She wasn't your aunt."

"I'm sorry you feel that way, *Micki*, but she was married to my uncle and very much an aunt to me."

Micki looked surprised and a little perturbed when Sabre said her name, but she didn't correct her.

"Regardless," Sabre continued. "It was important to Goldie that things be done a certain way, and I'm going to see to it that they are."

Langston leaned over and glared at Micki. "Why should you sell the house and split the money? You're not in charge here."

"Because I'm the oldest. Anyway, I want my Barbie collection."

"Your Barbie collection?" Rocki challenged. "They're half mine. But they should be all mine. You didn't even like playing with them."

Within seconds, they were all bickering. They argued about baseball cards, comic books, and jewelry. After several minutes of talking over each other in loud voices, Travis shouted, "Enough!"

They went quiet for a few seconds, then Micki said, "I have some things in that house, and I'm going to get them." She looked at Sabre. "You have no right to stop me from getting my personal possessions."

"Micki," Sabre warned. "Do not break into that house, or I'll be forced to turn you in."

"Don't be dramatic. I have a key."

"The key won't work," Langston grumbled. "I tried mine on the way over. The locks are all new."

Micki stood and took a step toward Sabre. She stopped when Ron moved to block her. "You changed the locks?" she yelled.

"Your key hasn't worked for years," Travis said. "Mom changed the locks a half dozen times since any of us have been there. You know she hasn't wanted us inside for ages." He looked around at his siblings. "Have any of you been inside the house in the last ten years?"

They all shook their heads.

"I *did* change the locks," Sabre clarified. "But at your mother's request. She didn't want you fighting with each other, and frankly, I don't think she wanted you to see just how bad things had gotten in her home."

They started yelling again, all of them on their feet now. Except Chase, who sat quietly, tears rolling down his cheeks.

CHAPTER 13

Tuesday Afternoon

Sabre sat back and observed as the siblings tore into each other. Rocki glanced at Chase, who refused to engage, and rolled her eyes. Any moment Sabre thought Langston and Micki might come to blows. Langston had sat back down, and Micki stood over him, calling him names, the nicest of which was "idiot." Finally, Travis stood, directed a reluctant Micki back to her seat, and told them all to shut up.

"What happens now?" Travis asked Sabre.

"I'll make sure your mother's instructions for her burial are followed." Sabre was disappointed, but not surprised, that no one had asked about a memorial service. "Goldie asked to be cremated and gave specific requests for her ashes."

"I'll decide what we do with her ashes," Micki said.

"You're not in charge here," Langston snapped. "Let it go."

"Yeah, didn't you hear Sabre?" Travis said. "Mom has already decided where she wants to be."

"And I doubt she wants to be on your fireplace mantle, listening to you bitch all day," Langston added.

Before anyone could argue, Sabre took charge again. "Her service will be scheduled, and I'll notify each of you."

"And then?" Micki asked.

"I'll get the death certificate and begin to determine the extent of her estate. I'll distribute any personal items she bequeathed, as well as other assets she has specified. At some point, everything else will be liquidated and distributed according to her will. However, I won't be able to distribute the assets until I determine what they are, their value, and what debts and taxes need to be paid."

"How long's that going to take?" Their heads all turned toward Micki. "Oh, please," she whined. "It's what you all want to know. I'm just the only one who isn't afraid to ask."

"It could be done in weeks, or possibly months. But it depends on what she had, besides the house, and how easy it is to access the paperwork."

"She doesn't have much, so it shouldn't take long," Rocki said.

"She has more than you know," Langston mumbled.

"You don't know what you're talking about," Micki snapped back. "Just because Mom had a lot of stuff, doesn't mean it's worth anything."

"That's true," Sabre said. "And I'm sure you know more about her assets than I do, but I need to make sure everything is accounted for."

"What if there are other wills that you don't have?" Micki asked.

"Do you know of other wills she wrote?"

"Maybe."

The others looked at Micki suspiciously.

"If they predate what I have," Sabre explained, "or are not properly executed, they are void. If you have something that's more recent, you should bring it to me."

"Why?" Micki barked. "So you can destroy it?"

"No, so your mother's last requests can be granted."

Shortly after everyone left, JP arrived.

"You missed all the fun," Sabre said with a sigh.

"How bad was it?"

"I guess it could've been worse. They clearly don't get along, and most seem more interested in what Goldie left them, than in the woman herself. Micki wanted to control everything, and I'm pretty sure Chase was stoned. By the way." Sabre turned to Ron. "Are you sure that was Micki?"

"I'm sure," Ron said.

"You always knew the difference when we were kids, but how?"

"Micki still has a habit of tucking her hair behind her ear."

"That's what you based it on?" Sabre was skeptical. "Rocki could have picked up the habit as well. Or she could be aware of it and wanted to mess with us."

"That's true, but Micki has a small birthmark at the top of her ear. That's why I shut the blinds. I wanted to get close enough to be sure."

"You devil."

"I told you I'd be helpful."

"This seems like a lot of work, Sabre." JP looked at her with concern. "Are you sure you want to do this?"

"I have to … for Aunt Goldie … who's not really my aunt, as Micki had to point out."

"What?" JP asked.

"It's not important. But yes, it'll be a lot of work. Going through that house and those storage sheds will take weeks." Sabre turned to her brother. He could be even more helpful. She certainly didn't have time to do it by herself. "Hey, Bro, want some work?"

"Sure. Doing what?"

"Aunt Goldie's house needs a lot of attention. We need to go through every box, bag, and piece of paper. I'll pay you out of the estate. She owns the house, even if there's nothing else of value." Sabre paused. "Unless she didn't have any equity, but I'll try to determine that early on. Either way, you'll get paid."

"You know I would help either way," Ron said. "She was my aunt too, or *not* my aunt too, according to Micki. The job won't be as exciting as some of the stuff JP has me do, but it might be kind of interesting."

"But not as dangerous," Sabre added. "I hope it doesn't interfere too much with your time with Addie. I know you two already have some trouble getting together because of her work schedule."

"That won't be a problem," Ron said, his face reddening.

"Why? Is there something wrong?"

"Are you ready to go?" JP asked, interrupting the conversation.

"Just let me grab my things." Sabre picked up the files from her desk, and they started out. "Are Ron and Addie having problems?"

"How would I know?"

"Because you intentionally interrupted us when I was asking him about her."

"He was obviously agitated, and if he wanted to tell us he would. Give him some space."

"Dang. I was hoping it would work between them, even though I didn't really think it would."

"We don't know that yet, do we?" JP said as they reached their vehicles. "By the way, I called Zack. He confirmed that he has a brother named Kenny, but then he had to get off the phone. He said he'd call me back."

Sabre gave him a questioning look.

"You think he's blowing me off."

"It's possible. Some siblings look out for each other even when they don't deserve it."

CHAPTER 14

Wednesday Morning

After breakfast, Ron drove to his aunt's house to have a look around and determine what equipment he needed. Even though Sabre had described the house, Ron was shocked at the condition. The thought of Aunt Goldie living in this squalor made him nauseous. He suddenly had a pang of guilt for not reaching out to her more often. The sharp contrast between the outward appearance and the interior made him even more bewildered.

Ron stepped out onto the porch for fresh air and spotted a white SUV slowly passing the house. He didn't see the driver, so he waited a few minutes to see if the SUV returned. It didn't.

He walked around the side of the house and opened the wooden gate.

"Oh my God." He stared, open-mouthed, for a moment.

Finally, he took out his cell phone and started snapping photos as Sabre had instructed. Mountains of junk were piled as high as the fence with only a narrow path leading to the backyard. A large vinyl shed sat back about fifteen feet, but the door wasn't accessible. Ron walked to the side. A stack of sun-faded plastic containers leaned against the wall, along with three ladders. One still had a store tag on it.

He followed the path through mounds of more junk than he'd ever seen in one place in his life. The yard was about forty feet deep and about as wide, and every square foot was piled as high as the fence. Most of the content was contained in battered boxes, and he couldn't tell what was in them. But two shopping carts were partially visible, and behind the shed, he found a stack of weather-beaten, orange emergency cones. *What the hell?*

Ron followed the path until it reached a wall of solid junk. He went back to the plastic containers and pulled them away from the shed wall. A huge rat ran across his feet and scurried off. The sudden movement startled him, and he pushed away from the containers, knocking them over. Several pieces of plastic broke off the brittle boxes.

Ron sighed, left the backyard, and called Sabre, who picked up right away.

"Hey, Sis. I need to run to Lowe's and buy gloves and containers," Ron said. "I also need trashcans and a huge dumpster. Or two. Most of the stuff in the backyard is worthless. It's been out there a long time, and the weather has taken a toll."

"Get whatever you need. I'll order a dumpster and have it delivered as soon as possible."

"Oh, and I need rat traps."

"You have my credit card and don't need permission to use it. Just save the receipts. And, Ron, be careful."

Ron drove to the nearest Lowe's, purchased what he needed, and drove back to the house in La Mesa. When he pulled up, he saw a white Mazda SUV pull away from the curb. He wondered if it was the same one he'd seen earlier. He shrugged it off. There were thousands of white SUVs on the streets.

He sat in his car, gathering his thoughts. The project was so overwhelming, he didn't know where to start. Since the back-yard piles needed a dumpster, he headed inside. He parked a large, black container in the entrance to prop the screen door open. Next to it, he set a trashcan, leaving enough room to pass through to the porch. He took a smaller container inside, which he placed on the floor. He began to take apart the mountain, dog hair flying as he moved boxes.

He grabbed a box from the top, and several things fell out. One was a plastic skull with red-jeweled eyes that he assumed lit up with batteries. *Not exactly a collector's item, but someone might want it.* Ron placed it in the large black container. Receipts and documents he put in the smaller container on the floor. Obvious trash, he threw away. It wasn't long before his containers were full, and the trashcan nearly so, but he could see little progress.

Ron worked his way along, widening the path. By three o'clock, he'd made enough space to put the black tubs inside and still shut the door. He had to continuously clean up the floor when items fell, but he did that as he moved along. All four trashcans were full and so were five of the large contain-ers. He put the two smaller tubs with paperwork in his car for Sabre to sort through at home.

He was about to lock the house and leave when he saw the white Mazda parked across the street with a woman in the driver's seat. He couldn't see her well enough to know if she was one of the twins. He locked the door and crossed the street, being careful in case she decided to pull away and possibly run over him. But instead, she lowered her window.

"Can I help you?" Ron asked.

"Is Goldie okay? I haven't heard from her, and I was getting concerned."

"Who are you?" Ron asked.

"Oh, I'm so sorry. My name is Judy Reed. I'm Goldie's best friend."

"I'm Ron Brown."

"You're Sabre's brother, right?" She climbed out of the SUV, reaching for Ron's arm, her plump body making her awkward. "I'm afraid my knees don't work as well as they used to."

"No problem." Ron helped her as she stepped down. "Yes, Sabre is my sister. Do you know her?"

"Not really. I met you both before—when you were teenagers. I'm sure you wouldn't have any reason to remember me. But Goldie talked about the two of you all the time, so I feel like I know you both. And I do know your mother, Beverly. We've been to lunch together with Goldie a few times."

Ron smiled. "Well, it's nice to see you again, Judy."

"I'm sure you're wondering why I keep driving by the house. I'm just worried, that's all. Is Goldie okay?"

"I'm afraid she's not." Ron took a breath. "Aunt Goldie has passed away."

"Oh no!" Judy gasped, her hand over her mouth.

She leaned back against the car, and Ron again offered her his arm. "Are you okay?"

"I didn't expect to hear that. I knew something was wrong, but I figured she was in the hospital or something. I talked to

Goldie Sunday morning, and she seemed fine. She said she had a little stomachache, but I didn't think anything of it."

"Her heart attack happened later that day," Ron said.

"You're here cleaning her house?" Judy asked, seeming skeptic.

"I am."

"It's pretty bad in there," she said.

"Have you been inside?"

"A few times. When Goldie wasn't feeling well, she'd let me bring her food, and I would stay with her in her bedroom and chat, but she never let anyone else in. I tried to get her to let me help clean, but she wouldn't hear of it."

"I think she was pretty embarrassed by the whole situation."

"I'd be glad to help with the cleanup. I've got a lot of spare time."

"Thank you, but we have it covered," Ron said.

"Do her children know?"

"Yes, we've told them. Do you know the kids?"

"Goldie and I have been friends for twenty years, so I knew them when they were young. They don't come around anymore. Chase graduated from high school and seldom comes back. The other boys tried to visit, but she wouldn't let them inside. The girls have always had a beef with her." Judy took a breath, as though a little winded. "I'm not sure what it was, but Goldie blamed herself for it. She always said she was a terrible parent, but I didn't see her that way. She tried so hard, always reading self-help books and getting the kids the services they needed. If you ask me, they didn't do right by her after all the sacrifices she made for them."

Ron didn't respond.

"You probably know all that anyway." Tears pooled in

Judy's eyes. "I feel so bad for Goldie. She was one of the kindest people I've ever met. She was so generous and helped so many people. All she wanted was to be loved, especially by her children." Judy took a small step toward the house. "I'd be more than happy to give you a hand. That's quite a job you have ahead of you."

"Thanks again, but we're good. Nice meeting you." Ron waved and walked to his car. It had been a long day, and he needed a shower.

CHAPTER 15

Wednesday Evening

I t was nearly nine o'clock before Sabre could sit down on the sofa and sort through the plastic containers Ron had dropped off. The first thing she picked up was a twelve-year-old receipt from McDonald's for two hamburgers and a soft drink. Sabre got up, retrieved a plastic trash bin, and set it on the floor. She tossed the receipt and picked up an unopened statement from Bank of America. The postmark was also twelve years old. She opened it, surprised to see a balance of $24,328. Sabre wondered if that was Goldie's life savings. The next item was a journal. Sabre began to read.

> *Chase turned twelve today. He is such a sweet, kind little boy. I wish Langston wouldn't pick on him so much. Chase worships Travis, who completely ignores him. At least Langston gives him some attention. I hope he*

doesn't follow in Langston's footsteps. It's such a battle with that kid.

Rocki called this morning. I tried to get her to come over, but she was too busy. I still haven't heard from Micki.

I did a good deed today. I went to the grocery store, and when I got out, I found a small change purse, the kind my mother used to carry with a clasp at the top. I opened it and found a twenty-dollar bill and a bank withdrawal receipt. I looked around, but no one was in sight. I figured whoever lost it could be in any of the stores, so I waited to see if someone came to claim it. Twenty minutes later, an elderly gentleman walked up to a nearby car and opened the passenger door. He looked around inside, then started searching on the ground. I asked if he lost something, and he said his wife dropped her change purse. He smiled and thanked me when I gave it to him.

This act of kindness was dropped in my lap, but I've decided to do something kind every day. Perhaps that will make up for my failures.

Sabre glanced at a few more pages in the journal, then set it down. She was getting to know her aunt in a new way. Goldie was an unusual, but remarkable, woman. Sabre sighed and got back to work.

She threw away hundreds of old receipts and set aside more bank statements on the coffee table. The account balances only fluctuated a few thousand dollars. She found several old birthday cards addressed to Goldie, checked inside, then tossed them. A second stack on the table held photographs.

As she started a third stack of handmade cards from

Goldie's kids, JP came into the room. "Anything interesting?" he asked.

"Ten or twelve years ago, Aunt Goldie was keeping a journal. She wrote in it every day. Nothing earthshattering, based on what I've read so far, but it's obvious she was trying to be a better person. I just found articles on teenage drug addiction and a handout titled *Teenage Alcohol and Drug Usage Spectrum*. It has a phone number in Orange County. I'm not sure who these documents pertain to since there aren't any names attached."

"It could have been any of them—or all of them. You said Chase looked stoned at the meeting."

"Ron thought so too."

Sabre pulled an envelope from the tub and opened it. "Here's another bank statement," she said. "The ones I saw earlier showed she had over twenty grand." She looked at the balance. "This one has $35,723. It's from around the same time."

"So, she added a little to it."

Sabre shook her head. "No, this is from Wells Fargo. The last one was Bank of America."

"Maybe she changed banks," JP offered.

Sabre shuffled through the other statements. "No. This statement is dated in between two of the others from Bank of America. At one point, Goldie had over fifty-thousand dollars in these two checking accounts."

"That's not so much. I mean, it's a lot more than most people have, but if she was frugal and wanted to make sure she had ready cash, it's not that unusual."

"True. Or she could've received an insurance settlement or something."

JP sat down and started reading. Sabre continued to sort

Goldie's papers, tossing birthday cards, thank-you notes, and printed articles on the kids' do-it-yourself projects, along with a stack of unusual recipes. She checked each receipt carefully after finding a return slip with $23 folded up inside. When she pulled out a Ziploc baggie, she held it up to show JP.

"What's in there?" JP asked.

"They look like gift cards to me."

Sabre pulled out the cards, some of which were still in little envelopes. "Eight from Starbucks and four from McDonald's."

"Do the cards have a value on them?"

Sabre shuffled the stack. "The Starbucks envelopes each say $25." She turned the others over and looked at both sides. "These don't say, and the cards could've been used. Goldie saved everything, so it wouldn't surprise me to know she saved depleted gift cards."

The next item was an unsealed Hallmark card with just the name *Dené* on the front. Sabre opened it, wrinkling her brow.

"What is it?" JP asked.

"It's a birthday card for a one-year-old, and it appears to have not been sent. It's signed, *All my love.*" Sabre held up a fifty-dollar bill. "And this."

"That's a lot of cash for a toddler."

"I guess it doesn't matter if she never sent it."

"Still very generous," JP said. "Your aunt must've meant to give it to her at some point."

"It's not signed, so we don't know if it was even from her. Although, it's addressed in her beautiful handwriting."

Sabre continued through the box. After a while, JP commented, "I'm glad we took photos before doing anything in the house, in case we forget how bad it was."

Sabre took out her cell phone and opened her photo app.

She hadn't looked at the pictures since they were taken. She flipped through, then stopped. "Oh no."

"What?"

"Look at this photo." Sabre handed her phone to JP. "Look on the stand next to Aunt Goldie's chair."

"What am I looking for?"

"Zoom in. You'll see it."

JP did, but shook his head.

"See the large manila envelope?"

He shifted the photo and zeroed in. "It says, *My Trust*."

Sabre took the phone and scrolled to a photo Ron had sent her. She held it out to JP. "Look, the envelope is not in Ron's photos."

Sabre riffled through the bins again, looking for the trust, but to no avail. "It's not here."

"Well hell. Someone got inside the house between the time we took the photos and Ron changed the locks."

CHAPTER 16

Thursday Morning

After Sabre finished at juvenile court, she drove to Lakeside to see the McCluskey children. The older ones were in school, but she decided to pull Dale and Fayth from class, then visit the younger girls at their father's home in the next few days.

Sabre checked in at the school's office and provided her court documents. The receptionist led her to a small, empty office, then sent a student helper for Dale. While Sabre waited, she checked her phone and found a shrill voicemail: "This is Micki Nogard. Call me and update me about what's going on. I have a right to know."

When Dale came in a minute later, he was cordial, but still no smile.

"I just have a few questions, Dale, then I'll send you back to class."

"It's okay. I don't mind missing language arts. We're writing compositions, and I don't like it."

"I still won't keep you long because you'll probably have to make up what you missed."

"That's okay. Fayth will help me."

"Dale, I need to know a few things about the night Perry passed away."

The boy stiffened and looked down at his shoes.

Sabre felt bad about bringing it up, but she needed to find out if Dale knew anything more. Detective DuBois hadn't called to set up an interview with Dale yet, but it wouldn't be long. In the meantime, she wanted to make sure there wasn't a reason to keep the boy from speaking to him.

"A detective is investigating your brother's death, and he'll call me soon to set up an appointment to talk to you."

Dale looked up with wide eyes.

"You don't need to be afraid. I'll be there with you. But before he comes, I need to know everything you know, so I can protect you."

"I don't know anything," Dale blurted.

"We have recently learned there was someone in the back-yard that night. Did you see anyone out there?"

"No," he mumbled.

"Do you know anything about someone being in the backyard?"

Tears welled in Dale's eyes. "It's my fault, isn't it?"

"What's your fault?"

"That Perry died."

"Dale," Sabre said softly, "did you hurt Perry?"

"No," he said loudly. "I'd never hurt him, but I should've been protecting him. Instead, I left the door unlocked. And someone must've come in."

"When did you leave the door unlocked?"

"I saw Fayth sneak out the door, and I didn't want to lock her out." He sobbed. "I meant to go back later and lock it, but I forgot and fell asleep. Someone must've come in and killed Perry."

"Dale." Sabre put her hand on his shoulder. "Calm down. We don't know if anyone came in through that door. It's not likely that someone just happened to find the only unlocked door in the neighborhood and came in to kill someone. If they found an open door, they would be more likely to burglarize the house, and no one did that."

Dale's sobs lessened.

"Why was Fayth sneaking out?" Sabre asked.

"I shouldn't tell you."

"Yes, you should. I need to protect her too."

"I can't." He sniffled. "You'll have to ask her."

Sabre asked Dale about life at his dad's and about school, making sure he was calm before she sent him back to class. Then she called for Fayth.

After some small talk, Sabre asked, "Did you go into the backyard the night Perry died?"

"W… what?" Fayth stammered, gasping a little.

"Before you answer, I already know you were outside. What I want to know is whether you were in the backyard at any time."

"No."

"Why did you sneak out?"

Fayth was silent, her eyes darting around to avoid contact with Sabre's.

Sabre waited.

Finally, Fayth said, "I don't want to get in trouble."

Sabre again explained about the confidentiality between

them and encouraged her to speak. "I can't help you unless I know what you were doing."

The girl looked down at the floor. "I was stealing vegetables."

Sabre almost laughed. "Where were you stealing vegetables from?"

"A woman up the street has a big vegetable garden in her backyard. I only take what we need, and she has plenty. I'm careful so she won't miss 'em."

"Why?" Sabre pursed her lips to keep from smiling. "Why do you steal them?"

"Because I like fresh vegetables, and Mom never remembers to buy them. I tell her what I want, but she always comes home with a bunch of frozen food. The vegetables in that garden are so good, and I use them for soups. Sometimes I just cook them with meat, if we have any."

Sabre wasn't sure what to say. She was angry at Ellie and concerned for Fayth, who was taking on such a parental role. It wasn't unusual in homes where children were neglected. The older kids often became responsible for their siblings, but this was extreme. Sabre wondered if this girl would ever get to enjoy just being young.

"Do you know what time you went out?" Sabre asked.

"It was after midnight. I usually wait for Mom and Kenny to go to sleep."

"Were they asleep that night?"

"I could still hear them, but I figured it was late enough that they wouldn't check on us."

"How long were you gone?"

"I don't know. It takes a while because I have to be real quiet, so I move slow through the garden."

"How many times have you done this?"

"Five or six."

"And no one has ever noticed you?"

"No, but once, Mrs. McGregor—that's not her real name, just what I call her—turned on a light, and I laid down in the garden until the light went out. Then I waited for a while after to make sure she wasn't coming out. That was only the second time. I had plastic bags, and they made a lot of noise when I put the vegetables in. After that, I started taking pillowcases with me. I carry one in each hand, but I don't fill them up. I just take what we need."

"When you came back into your house, was anyone awake?"

"Yes." The girl hesitated. "Someone was in the bathroom."

"Did you see who?"

"No. I hurried into my room and checked on the girls. They were both asleep. I was going to check on Perry, but I was afraid to."

"Why?"

"Because I didn't know who was in the bathroom. I wanted to get Perry up to pee, because he got in trouble the night before when he wet the bed. I didn't want that to happen again."

"Who did he get in trouble from?" Sabre asked.

"Mom and Kenny were both mad, but Mom did most of the yelling. I think Perry got a spanking. He wouldn't stop crying, and that made them both madder. Then Mom made him go to his room, and none of us were allowed to go in until his punishment was over."

"When was that?"

She shrugged. "A couple of hours maybe. Then he was allowed to come out. I snuck in once to take him food, but he'd fallen asleep, so I let him be."

Fayth's eyes filled with tears, but she fought them back and swallowed hard. "Do you think that's why he died?"

"What do you mean?" Sabre asked. Her heart ached for this girl.

"Did they hurt him when they punished him, and that made him die that night?"

Sabre looked deep into Fayth's eyes, then got up and wrapped an arm around her. The girl willingly relaxed into Sabre's hug. "I don't know what may have happened. Hopefully, the medical examiner will figure it out."

They sat together for a few seconds, then Fayth pulled back, and Sabre let go. "Did you ever go into Perry's room that night?"

"No. I was waiting for Mom and Kenny to go to sleep, but they started yelling at each other. Mom was especially loud. I covered my head with my pillow so I couldn't hear them. I must've fallen asleep because I don't remember anything else until morning."

CHAPTER 17

Thursday Morning

Ron opened the door to Aunt Goldie's house and sighed. He followed the path back to her bedroom, where Sabre had suggested he start. She wanted him to look for documents that might be more current and to double check for the envelope marked *My Trust*. He gathered all the paperwork around Goldie's recliner, including a fast food receipt from last Sunday, and put it all in a tub for Sabre, adding documents as he came across them. He tossed in several newspapers, some still in plastic sleeves, and threw away empty fast food containers and water bottles. He put unopened Amazon packages in another bin. Three heart-shaped rocks sat on the nightstand, and he saved those as well.

A couple of hours later, Ron had cleared a spot approximately two feet around her recliner. He left the lamp and the remote control on the stand. Aunt Goldie's television sat in a direct line across the room on top of her dresser. A path led almost to the flat screen, but stopped short, making the dresser drawers inaccessible. Her sliding closet door was open on one side, allowing access to some clothes. The other half of the closet door was blocked by more boxes and junk.

Ron wanted to remove the recliner and create some space, but there was no way to get it out without taking it apart, and he wasn't sure he had enough space to even accomplish that. It would have to wait. He went back to the living room and started sorting. At least he could make room to stack bins, and he wanted to create a path to the kitchen. He found some old throw rugs, covered in dog hair, and tossed them in the trash. Another box contained old pots and pans that might be of use to someone and more heart-shaped rocks of different sizes and colors. One was amber with a beautiful grain. He wondered what kind of stones they were and started a bin just for those. Later, he would look them up online.

Ron took a break to drink some water, eat a banana, and create tags for the bins. The labels included *Paperwork, Garage Sale, St. Vincent de Paul, Heirlooms*, *Heart Stones,* and *Re-sort*. He started to make one for *Trash*, then realized he didn't need it. But he did need to empty the trashcans. The bins for the paperwork and heart stones were clear plastic, fifteen-quart containers. The others were heavy-duty, black ones with yellow lids. He had cleared enough space that he could start stacking them by category. None of his organization was set in stone. Sabre would eventually go through everything, but this would at least make it easier.

At the end of the day, Ron loaded the five paperwork bins, along with four gallon-sized cans, and took them to JP's house. Sabre wasn't there when he arrived.

"I brought these for Sabre to go through," Ron said, as he stacked the tubs near the sofa.

"You've been busy as a hound in flea season." JP stared at the stack. "That's a lot of paperwork."

"I think Goldie saved every receipt, every document, and every check she ever wrote."

"Oh boy." JP gave a little shudder. "What else have you found?"

"Come help me," Ron said. "I'll show you." He led JP to his car, and they retrieved the metal cans, taking two each.

"These are heavy. What's in them?"

"You'll see," Ron said smiling. "I also found lots of dishes, pots and pans, books, and tons of silverware." Ron set the cans next to the stack of paperwork tubs. JP did the same.

Sabre walked in, and Ron turned to her. "Hi, Sis. I was just telling JP about the treasures I found today."

"Such as?"

"Aunt Goldie seemed to like heart-shaped stones. I found fifteen or more so far." He reached in his pocket and pulled out the polished amber stone. It covered most of his palm. "Here's one." He handed it to Sabre. "I think it's a paperweight."

Sabre took the stone, flipped it over, and rubbed it. "It's so smooth and pretty."

"I think so too. I'm putting them all in one box. I'm curious to see how many she has. Oh, and she has tons of coasters. I don't think Goldie was concerned about getting rings on the furniture because—well, you know—but I came across at least forty coasters so far. Many are still in their packages."

"Why would she have so many coasters?" JP asked.

"Who knows?" Ron shrugged. "She doesn't have just one or two of anything. I must've thrown away fifty batteries today. And I kept as many that hadn't leaked. I think she kept every coat hanger she ever owned, and I can't tell you how many empty egg cartons. She just couldn't get rid of anything."

"It's a form of mental illness," JP said, sounding solemn.

Sabre nodded silently. Then she spotted the stack of tubs. "That's all from *today*?"

"Yes, and there's a lot more where that came from." Ron suddenly felt tired. "She even kept the kids' elementary schoolwork. And there's old papers belonging to someone named Joseph Albrecht. Is he a relative?"

"Maybe," Sabre said. "But I think Goldie picked up a lot of stuff from thrift stores and garage sales."

"She has old wills, military papers, a bunch of German documents I couldn't read, and a couple more journals like the one I found yesterday. Oh, and a lot of dog hair. Do you know when she had the dog?"

"No idea, but getting to know Aunt Goldie has been interesting." Sabre smiled sadly. "I just wish I had done it when she was alive. By the way, did you find the envelope that said *My Trust*?"

"It wasn't there. I looked at the photo you sent and checked the exact spot. It was gone."

"Someone has to have gone in and taken it. I wonder what else is missing." Sabre spotted the cans. "What's in those?"

"Open them and see," Ron said.

JP picked up one and set it on the table for Sabre to open.

"Oh, my," she exclaimed, as she discovered the coins. "There must be over a thousand dollars in here. All quarters, dimes, and nickels." She dug down into the can. "I don't see any pennies."

JP lifted the other four cans onto the table, and Sabre

opened them. Ron stood back, knowing the contents. One was filled with pennies, two more were like the first one, with quarters, dimes, and nickels. The fourth contained silver dollars, fifty-cent pieces, Susan B. Anthony coins, and Sacagawea dollar coins. "Someone needs to go through all these to make sure there aren't any valuable coins." His sister cast him a hopeful look. "You may be busy for a while."

Sabre reached for the last can. "What's in here?"

"Just look," Ron said, smiling.

"It's not going to jump out at me, is it?"

Ron laughed. "Nothing like that."

Sabre peeled off the lid. "Are you kidding me?" She walked over to the dining room table and dumped the contents.

"Are those twenty-dollar bills?" JP asked.

"Not just twenties. There are hundreds and fifties in here too." Sabre stood there with her mouth open. "What was Goldie doing with all this cash? This is a lot of money to have lying around."

"Especially when you don't have any to spare," Ron said. "How much do you think is here?"

"Thousands," JP said.

"Count it," Sabre said to Ron.

Ron picked up a handful of bills, then spotted something. He pulled out a note written on green paper and folded over. It had Sabre's name on it, so he handed it to his sister. "Maybe Aunt Goldie will answer your question."

Sabre read the note out loud.

My Dear Sabre,

I hope you're the one who found this can. It's seed money for you. I know it will cost a great deal to get my mess cleaned up, and it may be a while before you can get access to my bank accounts. So, please use this to get rolling. Hire someone to help, but make sure you trust them. (That would not include any of my children. They would take whatever they could get their hands on.) Perhaps your sweet brother can help you. He was always such a lovable, honest young man.

Sabre looked up, rolled her eyes at him, then went back to reading.

Once again, I apologize for the time this project will take, but you will be rewarded for your work.

Your loving Aunt Goldie

CHAPTER 18

Thursday Evening

Sabre had only been working on Aunt Goldie's papers for about an hour and had already uncovered another $247 in cash—some in birthday and Christmas cards that hadn't been sent and some wrapped in receipts. As she unrolled another receipt, JP walked in and sat beside her.

"More money?" JP asked.

"Another twenty-one dollars. That makes $268 from this tub alone."

"She was awfully careless with her money."

"I know. And she never seemed to have much, although she would give us tons of Christmas presents."

"Did she always do that?"

"No, just the past few years when she came to Mom's for the holidays. She was very generous."

"Are you sure? Or was it more about her compulsion to shop?"

"I assume that was part of it, but she was a very kind person, and she loved to give."

"I'm sure she was," JP said.

"Want to know something strange?" Sabre asked.

JP raised an eyebrow. "*Everything* about this is strange."

"So true." Sabre smiled. "I found two birthday cards and a Christmas card for Dené, each with a fifty-dollar bill, all signed *with love* in Aunt Goldie's handwriting. But she obviously never gave them to Dené, whoever she is. Do you think you could find out?"

"We'll need a lot more information than what you have."

Sabre picked up the pamphlets about drug dependency and a generic letter from Zion Teen Center. "At least one of Goldie's kids must've had a drug problem. I keep finding information about treating drug and alcohol dependency. This is a letter to parents, inviting them to participate in the Parents' Program."

"It doesn't say which kid?"

"No." Sabre pulled out another letter. "But this one does. It's from Zion Teen Center as well and dated ten years ago." She read the letter to JP.

This correspondence is to confirm that Chase Perkins is complying with a chemical dependency treatment program through Zion Teen Center. He is working on N.A. and A.A. steps, as suggested by the chemical dependency counselors.

Chase is looking for a sponsor and attending both community and hospital-based chemical dependency meetings. He demonstrates a strong commitment to his sobriety and is complying with all the rules and expectations of the programs.

"So, Chase had a drug problem," JP said. "That isn't a big surprise."

"No, and apparently he still has one."

The next bunch of papers contained fast-food receipts, pamphlets on cooking, and more drug rehab information. Sabre tossed them in the trash and picked up another journal. It was from the same time period as the letters from Zion Teen Center. Sabre glanced at a few entries, which were mostly about Chase and his drug problem. Goldie wrote about her sweet little baby who had changed almost overnight.

Sabre placed the journal with the other one she'd found. "Maybe I'll use those for my bedtime reading once I collect them all. I can't take the time right now, and I'd like to read them in order."

"That's smart." JP picked up the newspaper.

Sabre continued through the bin until she came across legal papers with Hans Joseph Albrecht as the plaintiff. She removed a large manila envelope and emptied it. The more she read, the more interesting it became. "I don't know who this guy is, but he must've been important to Aunt Goldie."

"Why's that?" JP looked up from his reading.

"Why else would she have all this paperwork? And it's not the first thing I found with Hans' name." She shuffled through the papers. "Hans was born in 1920 in Iowa. In 1939, he married Alice, who soon gave birth to a child, Virginia Albrecht. A few years later, Alice died. Then in 1945, Hans filed this lawsuit."

"Over her death?"

"No. Apparently, Hans claimed to be an illegitimate son of

some man in Germany. His two half-brothers had turned their father's estate into an empire and became one of the wealthiest families in Germany. I can't tell exactly who they are because parts are redacted. The bottom line is they settled the case, and Hans received a million-dollar payout."

"Wow. That was a lot of money in 1945. But what does it have to do with Goldie?"

"I don't know. Maybe nothing. Aunt Goldie spent a lot of time at garage sales, so it's possible she found the papers in a desk or something, thought the case was interesting, and brought it home with her."

"Leave the document with me. I'll see if I can find more information online tomorrow."

"Thanks."

JP shuffled his newspaper. "Looks like the Incognito Angel has struck again."

"Who was the lucky recipient this time?" Sabre asked.

"The article doesn't give their names, but apparently fifteen years ago a man had a sinus infection that went to his brain. He spent four and a half months in the hospital, had twenty-one surgeries, and came home with the mental capacity of a child. Most of his frontal lobe was removed, so he's not capable of reasoning." JP glanced at the article, then continued. "His wife had been taking care of him all that time, but she's now seventy-five and dealing with her own health issues. He seems to be quite a handful. A few years ago, he snuck out, walked a few blocks, and was hit by a train."

"No kidding? And survived?"

"Yeah, who does that?" JP said. "Gets hit by a train and lives?"

"So, what did the Angel do for them?"

"He provided in-home care, so the wife could get a break

now and then. She can't leave the poor guy alone, so she's either stuck at home, or he has to go along. The Angel also gave them a new car and is renovating their home."

"If I had lots of money, that's exactly the kind of thing I would do," Sabre said. "I wonder how the Angel decides who the lucky ones are."

"Maybe they're people he knows. But he's smart to donate anonymously. Can you imagine if people knew about the gifts? Everyone would bug him for money."

"Yep." Sabre went back to her task and eventually found an old wedding photo in a cardboard frame. She removed the picture and turned it over. It was dated August 1, 1957. "Look at this." Sabre handed it to JP. "I wonder if there is a connection after all. I think these might be Goldie's parents."

JP read the back of the photo. "Virginia Albrecht and William Forney."

CHAPTER 19

Friday Morning

J P sat down at his desk with a cup of coffee and a sheet of information about Goldie Forney. He hadn't finished investigating the McCluskeys yet, but this family history was more interesting. He started with a Google search for William Forney and found an Alabama legislator who had been a brigadier general in the Confederate States Army during the Civil War. He died in 1894, so he was definitely not Goldie's father, but he could have been related.

JP opened another link and found a William Forney born in 1947, which made him too young to be Goldie's father. The third William Forney had also been a brigadier general, but this one served in Vietnam and spent thirty years in the Marine Corps. He passed away on Christmas 2018. JP didn't have the date of Goldie's father's death, but he knew it happened when she was much younger. He kept looking.

He extended his search to genealogy records and finally found a William Forney who had married Virginia Albrecht. They had two daughters, Gladys Jeanne and Vivian Marie. Figuring one must be Goldie's aunt or cousin, he jotted down the information for Sabre. He searched for Virginia Albrecht Forney and discovered she died in 1968 at the age of twenty-eight from an intracranial aneurysm. He couldn't find her obituary though.

Sabre finished her last hearing, left the courtroom, and headed to the restroom to change her clothes. As she slipped into her jeans, something fell from the pocket. She picked up the small plastic bag with Goldie's necklace the doctor had given her in the ER. Sabre removed it from the bag for a closer look. The vintage, heart-shaped locket was gold and beautiful. She shoved it back into her pocket, left court, and drove to Aunt Goldie's house.

Sabre stepped inside, pleased to find Ron working on the front room.

"I see you've made progress," Sabre said, noticing the path to the kitchen was now about two feet wide and three feet long.

"It sure goes slow, but I have three more containers of paperwork for you. I also started putting photographs in a separate tub."

"Good idea. Have you found anything else interesting?"

"Some baseball cards, but I didn't look through them. I'll look them up online later and see if they're worth anything."

"Thanks, I'd appreciate that."

They heard the door open and turned to see Bob step inside.

"Whoa!" Bob scanned the room. "This is amazing. I bet there are tons of treasures in here."

"Hi Bob," Ron said. "I started a box for you to sort through with things that might be antiques. I hear you're the resident expert."

"I know a thing or two, especially about jewelry and furniture," Bob said. "And I know a guy who'll give you an honest appraisal if you need it."

"I haven't found much furniture yet except that china cabinet over there." Ron pointed across the room. "You can't see much of it, but the corner that's showing looks interesting. And I just discovered one leg of what seems to be a large dining table. For now, it's still piled under, over, and around with stuff."

"What a mess," Bob said. He turned to Sabre. "What do you want me to do?"

"I have a box of jewelry you might want him to look through," Ron said. "From what I've seen, it's likely cheap, costume jewelry, but I'm no expert. I've been throwing old coins in as well."

"Before you do that, have a look at this." Sabre handed Bob the vintage locket. "Aunt Goldie was wearing this when she died."

Bob pulled his thick glasses down and peeked over them examining it carefully. "I can't be sure, but this seems like a very old German piece."

"You can tell just by looking at it?" Ron asked.

"It helps that there's German writing on the back." Bob laughed. "Even some old costume jewelry is valuable if it's old enough, but I think this is authentic." He glanced at Sabre. "Did you open it?"

"I tried but couldn't get it."

Bob turned the locket and, with a little effort, pried it open. "Aw, it has a picture of a cute, little baby." He handed the necklace to Sabre. "Do you know who the baby is?"

She looked closely at the color photo. "No idea. One of Goldie's kids, maybe?"

"She has five. How do you decide which one to wear next to your heart?"

"Maybe it's Michael," Ron suggested. "The child she lost."

Sabre put the necklace in her pocket, Ron went back to work, and Bob picked up the jewelry container and sat down next to Sabre. He started through the box, looking at each piece carefully and putting it into one of two piles. Sabre trusted that he knew what he was doing.

Ron opened a taped cardboard box with three items, all carefully bundled in bubble wrap and tissue paper. He extracted one and held it up. "What is this?"

"Wow," Bob said. "That's a kachina doll."

Sabre tilted her head and raised an eyebrow. "A what?"

"A kachina doll," Bob repeated. "The first ones were made by the Hopi Indians, hundreds of years ago. Then the Navajo started to make them in the 1900s. Each originally depicted one of the four-hundred mythical beings in the Hopi religion. They were used in ceremonies, and the Hopi Indians traditionally carved them from the roots of cottonwood trees. Little girls received two each year, but they were not toys. They generally hung on a wall and were used to teach young girls about spiritual beings."

"You know the strangest stuff," Sabre said.

"I read a lot." Bob grinned and turned to Ron. "Can I see it? I think it's a buffalo kachina, one of the most powerful of all kachina dolls. It's supposed to protect the owner and can rid bad people of evil thoughts." He paused and grinned again. "I have one. It doesn't get rid of *my* evil thoughts."

"Are they valuable?" Ron asked.

"They can be, depending on how old they are, or if they're signed by a famous artist. But most nowadays are made for commercial use, and the Indians sell them to tourists. They're priced at fifty to a couple hundred bucks at the trading posts. Since they're all hand carved and take a lot of time, the tribes aren't making a lot of money on them."

Bob looked at the three dolls, then he and Ron wrapped them back up.

"What do you think?" Ron asked.

"I don't know." Bob shrugged. "You'll have to look online, but I'd guess they're probably not worth a lot."

Ron went back to his sorting.

"Was your aunt a Hopi Indian?" Bob asked.

"Not that I know of," Sabre responded. "But I don't really know her history. Although, I'm beginning to think she was more German than anything."

"What makes you say that?"

"Because she was a member of the German Club and scheduled her memorial service there. Also, I recently found some paperwork and a photograph of someone named Hans Albrecht. I'm not certain yet, but I think he was a relative, maybe even her grandfather."

"I don't think so," JP said, as he entered the house. He walked over and kissed Sabre lightly.

"What did you find out?" she asked.

"Virginia Albrecht, who married William Forney, had two children, Gladys Jeanne and Vivian Marie."

Gladys Jeanne? "Wait a minute." Sabre dug through a box of papers and pulled out a copy of a birth certificate. "Gladys Jeanne Forney has the same birthdate as my aunt. She must have changed her name to Goldie."

CHAPTER 20

Friday Afternoon

S abre watched Ron and JP head out to the backyard to assess the situation. She glanced at Bob, who'd stayed inside to keep looking for antiques. For a moment, she felt overwhelmed with gratitude for the wonderful men in her life.

"Look at this." Bob held up an old pocket watch. "It says *Prazicions Anker-Uhr,* which I think is German for Precision Anchor-Clock."

"So, now you speak German?" Sabre smiled and raised an eyebrow.

"My guess is that *prazicions* means *precision*, but I could be wrong. I know *Anker-Uhr* means *anchor clock* because that's the name of a famous clock in Vienna, Austria, which was built in the early 1900s. It forms a bridge between two parts of the Anker Insurance Company. The clock is adorned with mosaic ornaments, and during a twelve-hour period, twelve historical figures move across the bridge. It's a real tourist attraction at high noon."

"It's weird, but I love that you know this stuff."

"The point is, I think this is a rare watch. I would have it appraised." Bob handed it to Sabre.

"It's in great shape too." Sabre admired the workmanship.

"It was in a velvet pouch inside a wooden box, so it was well protected."

"Then it was thrown in a box of junk that was worthless." Sabre shook her head. "That doesn't make any sense."

"Goldie may not have realized that it was valuable."

"What do you think it's worth?"

"A few thousand. Probably more."

"Really?"

"A gem among rocks. Everything else in this box would probably earn ten bucks at a garage sale if you're lucky."

Sabre didn't respond. She was focused on a letter she'd just found. She handed it to Bob. "What do you think this means?" she asked.

Bob read the letter and said, "You don't suppose…?"

"Suppose what?" JP said, walking up.

Sabre turned to him. "That article you read. Did it say how long the Incognito Angel had been giving out gifts?"

"The journalist asked for anyone who had received anything in the last five years."

Sabre reached for the letter. "Ten years ago, someone wrote to Langston Blodgett, offering to pay for his college. All he had to do was apply to the university of his choice, then send his acceptance letter to the donor and all expenses would be paid. The donor said he would pay for on-campus housing, tuition, and books. And that he would continue to pay as long

119

as Langston carried a full load, maintained a B average, and led a crime-free life."

"And you think it was the Incognito Angel?" JP squinted, unsure.

"It's signed with the initials *IA*. There is no name or letter-head, and the response address is a post office box in La Mesa."

"If we want to find out who the Incognito Angel is," JP said, "assuming that's who really sent this, all we have to do is watch to see who goes to that mailbox."

"Yeah, we should do that," Bob said.

JP gave him a glassy stare. "Not *we*. *You* can do it if you want. I'm too busy to chase an angel." JP started to leave.

"Wait," Sabre said. "Here's a letter addressed to *IA* at that address. It's still sealed and was never sent."

"Open it," Bob said.

When Sabre hesitated, Bob grabbed the letter and tore it open before she could object.

"It has a copy of an acceptance to Santa Clara University and a personal letter." Bob read it out loud.

Dear IA,

Here's a copy of my acceptance letter from Santa Clara University.

I accept your offer, thank you profusely, and will follow all your rules.

Langston Blodgett

"But he didn't go?" Bob asked.

"No, he went," Sabre said. "I did a little background work on Goldie's kids before I met with them. Langston went to

Santa Clara and graduated with an MS in marketing. Now he works as a manager at Kohl's."

"As fascinating as this is," JP drawled, "I just came in to tell you we're gonna need a bigger dumpster." He winked at Sabre and headed back out to the yard.

"Do you think the Incognito Angel paid for it?" Bob asked, obviously still intrigued.

"I don't think Aunt Goldie had the money."

"But the letter wasn't sent."

"I bet she made Langston rewrite it because she thought his letter was too short or something. That would be just like her."

"But why would she keep this letter?"

Sabre gestured at the piles of junk and rolled her eyes.

"Oh, yeah, she didn't throw anything away, did she?"

They kept sorting through boxes, and didn't notice the woman on the front porch until she was almost inside.

Startled, Sabre stepped toward the door. "May I help you?"

Bob stood behind her, further blocking the entrance.

"I'm Judy Reed, Goldie's best friend."

"Nice to meet you, Judy. I'm Sabre."

"Oh my, how you've grown up. You were a teenager when I saw you last. Your Aunt Goldie was very fond of you." The woman reached for Sabre's hand and cupped it in hers. "I'm so sorry for your loss. Goldie was such a wonderful woman."

"Yes, she was."

"I met your brother the other day, and he told me Goldie had passed. I can't believe it. I know she had health problems, but she was still so full of life."

"Yes, she went way too young."

Judy leaned to look around Sabre, trying to peek at the stuff behind her.

Sabre was done dealing with her. "I better get back to work. And I'm sorry for your loss as well."

Judy took two steps away, then turned back. "Where's Dually?"

"A dog?"

"Yes, Goldie's border collie. Where is he?"

"So, she did have a dog." Sabre sighed. "I don't know. There were no animals here when we first arrived. It's possible the dog got out when the ambulance picked her up."

"You have to find him."

"We'll try. Thanks for the information. We'll start checking with neighbors to see if they know anything. What does Dually look like?"

"He's black and white with a long, beautiful, healthy coat. His ears and face are black, except for a circle of white around his nose with a thin white line between his eyes. He's white all down his front under his chin and all the way down his belly. All four paws are white, and so are his front legs, but his front left leg has some small, black spots on it. His back is mostly black, and his tail is black with a white tip. And he has the kindest eyes you've ever seen."

That was way more detail than she needed. Sabre tried to cut in.

But Judy kept talking. "When Goldie got him, she was told he was a purebred, but he was rather large for a border collie, and that dog loved to eat. Oh, and he has a collar with his name on it."

"And his address?" Sabre asked.

"No, just his name." Judy stood for a few seconds, then said, "I'd be more than happy to give you a hand with the house. I loved Goldie, and since I can't help her anymore, I'd like to help you."

"Thanks, but we've got it covered."

"Are you sure? Because I have lots of time."

"Goldie didn't want anyone else in the house."

"I'm sure she didn't mean me. I was the only one she let in, and I know what she wanted done with certain things."

"Thanks again." Sabre was a little irritated but kept calm. When the woman didn't leave, Sabre added, "My aunt was very specific about what she wanted me to do, and that's what I'm doing. Thanks for stopping by."

Judy hesitated for a few seconds before she turned and walked toward her car.

"Was she pushy? Or am I just on edge?" Sabre asked.

"She was annoying," Bob agreed.

"She lost a good friend, so she might be feeling lonely."

"Or she wanted to get her hands on some loot. Look at all the cash you've found so far. Judy may have known it was here."

"Maybe." Sabre glanced at the back door. "I'll go ask Ron to canvass the neighborhood and ask about Dually. Poor doggie. We need to find him."

CHAPTER 21

Friday Afternoon

S abre called the Humane Society and learned that a border collie had been brought in a few days earlier, but she couldn't get a good description. She turned to JP. "Why don't you help Ron around the neighborhood, while Bob and I run to the pound. It sounds like they're short-handed, and I want to get there before they close."

"Good idea," JP said.

"I'll call you if we find him," Sabre responded.

Sabre and Bob reached the Humane Society with only ten minutes to spare. A young guy with man-bun hair greeted them at the counter.

"My aunt lost her border collie, and I understand one was brought in a few days ago."

"That's right."

"Could we see the dog?"

"Yeah, but I'm pretty busy. First chance I get, I'll bring him out."

They sat down and waited. Nearly ten minutes passed before the young man headed to the back cages, then came out with a border collie on a leash.

"This one's not very big," Bob commented. "Judy said Dually was larger than most of his breed."

"And the white strip between his eyes is pretty wide," Sabre added.

The attendant brought him closer.

Sabre noticed the dog's back legs were black. "That's not him."

"Are you sure?" the young man asked.

"I'm sure," Sabre said.

Ron and JP split up, so they could cover both sides of the street. Ron knocked on the door directly across from his aunt's house. No one answered. He moved on to the next. A man answered and said he had no idea when he last saw Dually. Ron and JP continued knocking on doors and calling for Dually as they walked down the hill and through the neighborhood. They met up at the end.

"I got nothing," JP said. "Most people knew Goldie and Dually, but no one could tell me much more."

"One woman said she saw Goldie drive by with the dog about a week ago," Ron said. "I guess Aunt Goldie used to walk him in the neighborhood, but she stopped a few years ago and started taking him to places he could run by himself."

They rounded the corner to start back up the hill on the next street over. JP's phone rang. "Hey, Kid."

"The dog at the pound wasn't Dually." Sabre sounded a little stressed. "Have you learned anything?"

"Nothing helpful."

"See you in a few minutes."

JP tried calling Dually's name again. As he knocked on the next door, a dog barked in response. He heard a man yell, "Pepper, stop," then the door opened.

"Hi, my name is JP Torn, and I'm looking for a lost dog. His name is Dually, and he lives on the next block over."

"Goldie's dog?"

"Yes. Have you seen him?"

"Not since last Sunday. I walk by her house every day, and she always gives Pepper a dog treat. But she hasn't been there lately. Is she okay?"

"I'm afraid not," JP said. "She passed away."

"Oh, no. Poor Goldie."

"We didn't know she had a dog until today, and we can't find him."

The man swallowed, then said, "When I walked by Goldie's house last Sunday, she told me she had an appointment to take Dually to the groomer later that day."

That's the day she died, JP thought. "Why would she take the dog on Sunday?"

"I asked her the same thing. She said it was the groomer's least busy day."

"So, the dog must still be there. Do you know who the groomer is?"

"No."

JP thanked him and crossed the street. "Ron," he called. "I think Dually is at the groomer."

They started back toward Goldie's house.

"Use your phone and search for a groomer," JP said. "Since Goldie seemed to frequent local establishments, start with the nearest groomers, and only call the ones open on Sunday. I'll call Sabre."

They headed up the hill just as Sabre pulled up.

"I was just calling you," JP said. "Goldie took Dually to a groomer on Sunday. He might still be there, especially if she was a regular customer."

"Do you know which groomer?"

"Not yet. Ron called the closest one, but the dog isn't there. He's calling others now."

Sabre parked and shut off her car. She and Bob started searching for groomers too, and soon all four were making calls.

"I got it," Bob said. "He's at Lots O Love Pet Wash Center. It's two and a half miles from here. Do you want me to go get him?"

"Let's head back to Goldie's house. I'll get back to work sorting, then you take Ron and go get the dog. Ron has my credit card. He can use it to pay for the grooming."

CHAPTER 22

Saturday Morning

S abre pulled up to Adam McCluskey's house for her nine o'clock appointment with the children. Adam's sister, Olivia, greeted her at the door, introduced herself, and invited her in.

"Adam was called in to work for a couple of hours," Olivia said. "I hope that's not a problem."

"It's fine. I'm here to see the children."

"The girls are eating breakfast, and Dale is feeding the goats. Do you want me to get them?"

"Let them finish," Sabre said. "How are the children doing?"

"Good, for the most part. Of course, everyone misses Perry. Adam tries to hold it together, and he manages most of the time in front of the children. But I hear him crying himself to sleep at night."

"Does he talk to you about Perry's death?"

"Some, but then he starts to blubber, as he calls it, and he stops."

"The social worker can get some grief counseling set up for him," Sabre said. "Do you think Adam would be open to that?"

"I'm sure he would. He wants help for how to deal with the children more than anything. He has encouraged them to grieve, and he listens when they want to talk, but he never feels like he's doing enough."

Olivia sat on the sofa and gestured for Sabre to do the same.

"How are the children adjusting to their new school?" Sabre asked.

"I think it's been good for them. The kids have gone to several different schools since the divorce, but this school is where the older kids attended most. They have lots of friends here."

"Good. Have you met the social worker?"

"Yes, she came yesterday. She has therapy set up for Dale, Fayth, and Harmony; they start on Monday. I think Harmony needs it the most. She hardly talks anymore. She was a shy child to begin with, but now she has really withdrawn."

"How are Fayth and Dale handling the loss?"

"Dale gets angry and rides his bike real fast. I'm afraid he might get hurt, but his dad thinks it's okay. Fayth tries to control everything. That's always been her nature. Personally, I think she compensates for what her mother doesn't do. I've tried to relieve as much responsibility from her as I can, but sometimes it's hard to beat her to it."

"What kinds of things does she do?"

"After school, she would get the other kids a snack and sit

them all down to do their homework. When they were done, she would start dinner. She wanted to do it all herself, but I learned to have snacks ready when they get home. And I make them all, including Fayth, go outside and play for an hour before they do homework. Now when they come in, Fayth helps the others with their work, and I start dinner."

"How's she taking the new arrangement?"

"She's adapting, and I think she likes it, to tell you the truth."

Harmony walked in the room but turned to leave when she saw Sabre.

"Harmony," Sabre said, "may I talk to you a bit?"

She walked slowly toward Sabre, and Olivia excused herself and left the room.

Sabre tried small talk with the girl, but got very little back until she approached the subject of their animals.

"Daddy got me a new guinea pig," Harmony said softly.

"Where is he? Can I see him?"

"Come with me."

Sabre followed her to her room. It was sparsely decorated, but it had two single beds with nightstands, two small white dressers, and new pink bedspreads. Sabre wondered if those were Olivia's contribution.

"Who do you share your room with?" Sabre asked.

"Fayth. That's her bed." Harmony pointed across the room. She walked to her nightstand and reached into a cage sitting on top. She pulled out a reddish ball of fur, almost the same color as her hair. The little girl hugged the guinea pig before handing him to Sabre. Then she said, still with no smile, "This is Spanky."

Sabre cuddled the creature for a few seconds, then handed him to Harmony, who seemed anxious to get him back.

They visited a little longer, with Sabre doing most of the talking. All she got out of Harmony was that she was glad to be at her father's house and that she liked Aunt Olivia a lot.

Sabre waited in the room while Harmony went to get Fayth. When they returned, Harmony left.

Fayth rambled on about school and how happy she was to be back with her dad. Sabre wasn't sure how the girl would react when she broached the subject of Olivia, but to her surprise, Fayth seemed very fond of her aunt and respected her.

After about ten minutes, Fayth started to fidget.

"What is it?" Sabre asked.

Fayth pulled her knees up to her chest and wrapped her arms around them. After a few seconds, she said, "I've been trying to remember about the night Perry died."

"Do you mean something specific?"

"The person who was in the bathroom when I wanted to check on Perry."

"I thought you didn't know who it was."

"I thought so too, but it seems like I saw someone." She started to rock. "And another thing. I think Harmony got up." She paused for a few seconds. "I guess I must've dreamed that, because I also remember seeing her asleep. It's just… It's like I should know something I don't know."

Sabre returned to the living room, and moments later, there was a knock on the door. Olivia answered it.

"I'm Detective Vincent DuBois."

Sabre heard his voice and walked to the door. "Good morning, Detective."

131

"Hello, Counselor." DuBois nodded. "As you know, I'm here to question your client, Dale McCluskey."

"Is this about his brother, Perry?"

The detective shifted his feet. "We need to speak privately. Can I come in?"

"Sure," Olivia said. "I'll leave you two alone." She walked toward the kitchen.

"Is Dale a suspect?" Sabre asked after Olivia left the room.

Dubois stepped inside but stayed near the door. "Dale isn't a suspect. Yet. But you need to know his mother and her boyfriend, mostly the boyfriend, are making accusations about Dale. Or at least strong hints that Dale may have hurt Perry."

"What kind of mother would point the finger at her own son?"

"One who thinks he needs help," DuBois said.

"Or maybe she wants to save herself from life in prison," Sabre countered.

"That certainly crossed my mind; nevertheless, I need to talk to Dale."

"I need to be there when you question him."

"Suit yourself."

They went outside and found Dale walking toward the house. They guided him to the picnic table under the magnolia tree, and Sabre introduced Dale and the detective. "He's the one I mentioned who's investigating Perry's death, and he needs to ask you some questions."

The boy swallowed hard, then nodded.

DuBois spoke gently. "I know this is difficult, and you've had to tell so many people already, but I need you to tell me exactly what happened that night."

"Perry wet the bed the night before, and he got in trouble when Mom had to change the sheet."

"What time of the day was that?"

"Just before dinner." Dale sighed. "Mom and Kenny took him to our room, and he got a spanking. But he kept crying and crying, so Kenny went back in the room. Perry cried some more. I don't know if he got another spanking or not. I didn't hear any whacks, but Perry yelled a lot. Then Kenny left."

"Did you go into your bedroom after that?"

"No." The boy shook his head. "Mom threatened all of us and said to leave Perry alone. She said he had to learn not to wet the bed."

"Then what happened?" DuBois asked.

"After a while, Perry stopped crying. Then after dinner, I kept an eye on Mom and Kenny, and Fayth snuck in the bedroom with a peanut butter and jelly sandwich for him. She came out right away and said Perry was asleep. She left the food in case he woke up."

"Did Perry ever come out?"

"No. I went to our room later and played some video games, and he was still in bed. But the sandwich was gone, so he must've eaten it."

"Did you talk to Perry at any time that night?"

"No. He slept the whole time."

"Dale, how do you know he was asleep?"

Dale's eyes widened. "Do you think he was dead already?"

Sabre put her hand on his shoulder to comfort him.

"I don't know," DuBois said. "I'm just trying to narrow the time of death. Anything you can tell us about what happened would help. Did you hear him making sleeping noises? Or did you see him move? Anything?"

Dale sat very still. Then he shook his head. "No."

CHAPTER 23

Saturday Morning

When Sabre arrived at her aunt's house, Ron was already hard at work—with a beautiful border collie at his side.

"Hi, Sis. Meet Dually."

Sabre reached down and petted the dog. "He's gorgeous."

"And very sweet. He minds well too."

Sabre gave the dog a good scratching behind his ears, then looked at Ron. "Don't get too attached, Bro. You know you can't keep him at Mom's."

"I know. She would have a fit. Her allergies are pretty bad. Can you take him to JP's?"

"Yes. I've already talked to him about it. He thinks Louie would like having another dog to play with. I'll take Dually with me when I go home today."

Ron looked at the pile he was working on. "It's already

been an interesting morning. I found a large box of Halloween decorations and three more heart-shaped rocks. One was a bluish color and looked very different. So, I scanned it, and the app said it was larimar."

"What's that?"

"It's a rare mineral found mostly in the Dominican Republic." Ron pulled out a blue heart stone and handed it to Sabre. "If it's high-grade, it can be rather valuable, according to the internet."

"It's very pretty. We'll have it evaluated," Sabre said. "What else did you find?

"Another journal, more books—mostly mystery and self-help—and a shoebox full of old movie tickets. She must've saved every ticket from every movie she ever saw. Why would someone do that?"

"I don't know, maybe for the same reason she would save a gallon-size plastic bag full of fortune slips from Chinese cookies."

"Fortunes? Really?"

"Really. Bob found them yesterday. Each had a date on the back. I presume the date was when she got the cookie."

"Poor Aunt Goldie. Maybe she followed up to see if the fortune came true."

"Who knows?"

"And phone chargers," Ron said. "If I've found one, I've found thirty."

"I guess you can never really know what's going on in someone else's life," Sabre said. "I'm beginning to think her children didn't know her either."

"I can see why she didn't want them in here cleaning up. Look at all the cash we've found so far. They would be fighting over every penny."

"I just wish we could find her trust."

"You don't think it was in the envelope that was stolen?" Ron asked.

"It may have been. And if that's the case, we'll probably never find it. It's possible we could find a copy, or find the lawyer who drafted it. Or maybe a copy was in there, and we'll find the original. I'm not locating much else where it's supposed to be, so who knows?"

"Maybe she didn't even write one."

"She claimed she did in the note she left me. And she named me as trustee."

"Yeah, but maybe she just *intended* to create a trust. People often put that sort of thing off until it's too late."

"If I don't find it soon, I'll have to file something in probate court, and that'll be a mess."

"Hello," a voice called from the front door.

Sabre and Ron both looked over and saw Judy Reed standing in the doorway. Ron glanced at Sabre, and she rolled her eyes.

Judy stepped in. "I'm so sorry to bother you, but your aunt had a necklace I loaned her, and I really would like to get it back. It belonged to my mother. It doesn't really have any value, except to me." She sighed. "I hate to be a nuisance, but I wouldn't want one of her kids getting the necklace and not appreciating it. And it means so much to me."

"What did it look like?" Ron asked.

"I have a photo of it on my phone." She showed Ron the picture. "It was in a rather unusual little box. I'm afraid I don't have a picture of that, but I think Goldie would have kept it in there."

"Send the necklace photo to me." Ron gave Judy his phone number. "We'll keep an eye out for it."

"And you'll let me know if you find it?"

"Of course," Ron said. "I'll call you. I'll have your number as soon as you send me the photo."

"Thank you."

"You're welcome. Have a good day." Ron turned away before Judy could offer to help again. His phone dinged a moment later, and Sabre smiled. Judy had sent the photo from the porch. Ron held out the image.

"It's beautiful, and it looks quite old," Sabre said. "Do you believe her?"

"Not sure. But it would be awful if she did loan it to Goldie and couldn't get it back."

"I'll need more proof than a photo and her word before I give away anything that might belong to the estate."

"Getting a little cynical in your old age, Sis?"

"Hazard of the job."

They both went back to sorting.

A while later, JP showed up with Conner and Morgan.

"Wow!" Morgan said, looking around. "This is despicable." Then she petted Dually and hurried down the narrow path to see the rest, with the dog following.

"Be careful, Munchkin," JP called after her.

"Is *despicable* her word for the day?" Ron asked.

"Yep," JP said. "After she heard us talking about this place, I think she learned a word that meant something bad. She wanted to be prepared."

"The word fits, for sure." Ron looked a little burned out.

"I see the dumpster was delivered," JP said. "That should make things a lot easier."

"Yeah," Ron said. "There's so much stuff we need to just toss and get out of the way. Even more in the backyard, most of which has been ruined by the weather." Ron picked up a box of junk and headed out to the dumpster.

"I'll get Conner started in the back," JP said.

"Make sure he doesn't throw anything away without checking with one of us first," Sabre said.

"You sure? There's a lot of trash back there."

"Like what?" Sabre asked.

"Old tires, lawn furniture that is totally destroyed, old weather-beaten umbrellas that are in shreds. Lots of stuff that's easily recognizable as trash."

"Okay. Have him focus on all that. Thanks." Sabre held up an envelope. "Another birthday card for Dené."

"Does it have money like the others?" JP asked.

Sabre opened it. "Another fifty-dollar bill. This card isn't as childish as the other three, so maybe it's more recent. And it's signed *With Love from Oma.*"

"Is that a name?"

"It means *grandma* in German," Ron said, coming back inside with an empty tub.

Sabre and JP both turned to him.

"Grandma?" Sabre said.

"I have some German friends who have grandchildren, and they go by Oma and Opa, grandma and grandpa."

"Do you think Aunt Goldie had a grandchild?"

"Looks that way," Ron said. "Or at least, Goldie felt like a grandma. How old is this kid?"

"We don't know." Sabre thought for a second. "I've found four birthday cards so far, so she must be at least four. But the card for her one-year birthday was with other mail that was at least ten years old."

"So, somewhere between four and ten, or so. Are any of her kids old enough to have a ten-year-old?" JP asked.

"The girls are thirty-four, so they're certainly old enough. Langston and Travis would have been eighteen ten years ago, so they're possibilities. Chase is too young, unless he got a girl pregnant when he was twelve."

"But as far as you know, none of them have children?" JP asked.

"No." Sabre pursed her lips. "But if they do, I need to know. Dené may be an heir. Not that Goldie has much of an estate. She had this house, of course, plus a little cash amongst the junk, a few pieces of jewelry, a car, and maybe a few treasures we'll find in this mess." Sabre sighed. "But if I can't find the trust she spoke about, I won't even know how she wanted it divided."

"You do have the will," JP said.

"But it was written long ago, and it divides everything among her children and grandchildren if she has any. I really don't think that's what she wanted now. She didn't even want them around her stuff. Then there's all that cryptic stuff about carrying on her work. There has to be another document. We've got to keep digging until we find her latest wishes."

Morgan returned with the dog. "Did your aunt *live* here?"

"She did," Sabre said. "But she had some real problems."

"I thought about being a hoarder once, because I don't like to throw things away. I keep a lot of stuff I probably don't need." Morgan's eyes tick-tocked, as they often did when she was excited or confused. She had a condition called nystagmus, which made her eyes move repetitively. To focus, she tipped her head to the left and a little forward. "But this is awful and a little scary." She looked around. "Where's Conner?"

"He's out back," Ron said. "Come on, I'll take you to him."

"Okay." Morgan stepped toward the door. She looked back, eyeing the two pathways through the mountain of junk. "It's like a labyrinth." She looked at Ron. "That's the right word, isn't it, Uncle Ron?"

"That's a good word for it."

Sabre smiled. It was the first time she'd heard Morgan call Ron *Uncle*. No one had told her to. They were becoming a real family. It both excited and worried Sabre.

CHAPTER 24

Saturday Late Afternoon

Ron held up an unopened box for Sabre. "Look, another kachina doll in the original package. I wonder what that obsession is about."

"Beats me." Sabre shrugged. She was tired after a whole day of sorting. "What time are you picking up Mom and Harley from the airport?"

"I have to leave in about a half hour."

"I guess you're stuck telling her about Aunt Goldie."

"It's okay. Mom will be all right."

Sabre went back to sorting and reading through paperwork. She heard Ron mumble, "More coasters. And phone chargers. And matches." After a moment, he said, "What's this?"

Sabre turned and watched him cut through the tape on an old shoebox.

"Maybe it's money," Sabre said.

"If so, it's all paper bills, because it's not very heavy."

He opened the box, lifted a scarf, and chuckled. "Aunt Goldie was a real fruitcake."

"What is it?"

Ron set the box on the floor and gave it a little push toward her.

"Eww!" Sabre stared at a shriveled, leathery body. "Is that a lizard?"

"A bearded dragon. He was probably a pet. Look at the nice scarf she wrapped him in." Ron waved a piece of silky fabric.

Sabre did a double take. "Let me see that."

Ron handed it to her, and Sabre checked the label. "Holy crap!"

"What?"

"This is a Kim Hilton original."

"And that means what?"

"About a thousand dollars. That's what. Who wraps a dead lizard in a thousand-dollar scarf?"

"Someone who doesn't know it's worth that much."

"Or really loved their lizard."

Ron looked in the box again. "And there's a note."

"Of course there is." Sabre cringed. "It better not be addressed to me."

"It's not. It just says: *Bart Forney, a sweet, lovable pet. I'll miss you falling asleep on my lap as we watched Law and Order, Special Victims Unit.*"

"That's sad. She must have been so lonely." Sabre looked at Ron. "We should've done better by her."

"You're right, Sis, but we didn't know."

"We should have known."

Sabre reached into the container she was working on and

pulled out more cards. "Here's another birthday card for Dené." She opened it. "With another fifty-dollar bill."

"How many does that make?"

"Seven birthday and four Christmas. And two Easter cards, but they didn't have money."

"It's awfully strange," Ron said. "If Dené is actually Goldie's granddaughter, why wouldn't she give her the cards? Unless she didn't have any real contact with her." Ron paused. "Is Dené a girl's name? I've been saying *she*, but I guess it could be a boy's name. You know, like René is a common boy's name in France."

"Yeah, it could be a boy." Sabre waved her hand. "I'm going with girl. But I think you're right. It appears Aunt Goldie didn't have contact with her, but we still need to find her. If that will ends up being the only one we have access to, Dené may be entitled to an inheritance. Goldie left everything to her children and grandchildren. At the very least, Dené should get these cards."

"How are you going to find her? All you have is a first name."

"I know, but JP will start searching soon." Sabre placed the cards in a smaller bin. "Dang, we need to find the trust or the lawyer who drafted it. Everything could get real nasty with those kids if we don't have something definitive to work from. They keep calling me, and so far, I've managed to dodge them, but I can't do that for much longer."

Ron looked at his watch, pushed aside the box he was sorting, and turned to Sabre. "I need to run. It's time to pick up Mom at the airport."

"Get going. JP and Conner can help me move these containers. Give Mom my love and tell her I'll come see her in a day or so."

Ron took off, and Sabre continued to sort papers. She picked up a bright pink notepad with Goldie's beautiful handwriting and glanced at the note. "Oh my God!" Stunned, she read it again.

I think someone is trying to kill me. They all hate me, so I'm not sure which one.

CHAPTER 25

Sunday Morning

J P got up before six o'clock, made coffee, and fired up his computer. Sabre was still sleeping, which was unusual. She had stayed up late sorting paperwork. She'd been looking for guidance on her aunt's estate and/or evidence that backed up the note that someone was trying to kill Goldie. JP seldom beat Sabre out of bed, but he wanted to get a jump on his search for Dené—before they went to the house for more cleanup.

Louie sat at his feet. Dually was in Morgan's bedroom. Conner had wanted the dog too, but he'd given in when Morgan had looked so sad. They'd decided to swap off every other night. JP knew what that meant. Conner would give in again if Morgan really wanted the dog. So far, Louie appeared to be jealous and hadn't taken to Dually. They all hoped that would change because if none of Goldie's kids wanted him, he would likely be staying right where he was.

JP googled everything he could think of to find Dené but was unsuccessful. He checked Facebook for Goldie and each of her children. They all had accounts, but no one had a *friend* named Dené. Without being their FB friend, he couldn't see much of what they'd posted. He tried Twitter with similar results. His lack of proficiency on social media frustrated him. He gave up and called his friend, Tuper.

Tuper was an old guy who lived in Montana, had a proclivity for guns, gambling, and women, and seemed to know everyone in the state. He was an old friend of Ron's. JP had met him a few years back when Ron had gotten into some trouble. Tuper had really come through for them.

"Hey, Tuper, it's JP."

"Well, I'll be darned. How you doin'?"

"I'm fine as cream gravy."

"Good to know."

"You got a minute?" JP asked.

"Always for you."

"Do you still have that woman working with you? The one who can find anything and everything on a computer."

"I do. Whatcha need?"

JP started to give him the information, but Tuper stopped him.

"I got no way to write any of that down. How 'bout if I talk to her, and one of us will call you back."

"That would be fine," JP said. "How are things in Montana?"

"Not so good."

"What's wrong?"

146

"I lost my dog." Tuper answered with his typical short response.

"Ringo?" JP didn't know why he'd asked the name since it was the only dog Tuper had, but he was saddened to hear it.

"Yes."

"I'm so sorry. What happened?"

"Hit by a car and left to die alongside the road." Tuper cleared his throat but started to choke up. "No call or nothin', just left him there to die."

"I don't know what to say. Ringo was such a sweet dog. When did it happen?"

"A few weeks ago." Tuper took a deep breath. "I'd like to get another dog, but I know I'll never find another Ringo." His voice cracked. "Call ya later."

JP hung up and scratched Louie's ears. He felt bad for Tuper. He knew how awful it would be if he lost Louie.

Around eight, Sabre walked in, dressed and ready to go. "Good morning, sweetheart."

JP admired her morning cheeriness. When he woke up, he didn't want to talk to anyone until he'd been awake for at least half an hour and had downed caffeine. Sabre seemed to get out of bed ready to take on the world.

"Want some pancakes?" she asked. "I'm making some for the kids."

"Sure. It's going to be a long day."

"Can you get the kids up? I'll have breakfast ready by the time they're dressed."

"Will do." JP smiled at the sight of her. He loved her so much and was so happy with their family. He knew the kids would only be with them temporarily, but he had come to love their living situation. For a second, he thought about what it would be like to have a child of their own.

147

"Let's take two cars," Sabre kissed his cheek. "I need to see my mother later today, and it would be silly to drive back here first. It'll save me a little time if I go straight from Goldie's house. Morgan can ride over there with me, and you can bring Conner and Dually. He's so at home in that house."

When JP came back to the kitchen, the table was set, and Sabre was stacking the pancakes she'd cooked. The kids came in shortly after, said good morning, and sat down to eat. Sabre's phone rang. She looked at the screen, then clicked it off and let the call go to voicemail.

"A secret admirer?" JP asked, raising his eyebrows.

"Hardly. It was Micki, one of Goldie's twins. That was her third call in two days. I answered the first one, but I'm not up to talking to her this morning. She just wants to know when things will get 'wrapped up.'" Sabre made air quotes. "They all want answers I don't have."

"So, the others have called too?"

"They've all called at least once, except Chase. I haven't heard from him."

Sabre's phone beeped, indicating she had a message. She listened to it.

"Was that from Micki?"

"She says she has a will dated last year."

"That might change things a bit," JP said.

Sabre called her back and left a voicemail. "Hi Micki. Please make a copy of the will and send it to me so I know what we're dealing with."

They finished breakfast, and JP said, "Conner and I'll go get started on the house."

"Thank you." Sabre stood too.

"Get Dually," JP said to Conner. "We're taking him with us."

Conner smiled and hurried off, then JP's cell phone rang. It was a Montana number, so he answered it even though it wasn't Tuper's.

"JP Torn."

"Hello. This is Clarice. I'm a friend of Tuper's. He wanted me to call and take down some information for him."

"Are you the one who does the computer work?" JP asked, as he headed for his desk, where he could check the file.

"No. But I'll pass on the information. She's not big on talking to strangers. Tuper explained that you can be trusted, but that's just the way she is."

"No problem."

"I'm ready," Clarice said. "What do you want her to research?"

"Sabre is handling an estate for her aunt, Goldie Forney. That's F-O-R-N-E-Y. Her given name at birth was Gladys Jeanne, but she changed it legally to Goldie. We're trying to find a child named Dené. We don't know her last name. Goldie married Edward Nogard, Bill Blodgett, and Norm Perkins, in that order." JP stopped and spelled their last names. "We have reason to believe Dené is between seven and twelve years old, probably closer to twelve, and that she is Goldie's granddaughter. Goldie has five children, and we don't know which one is Dené's parent. Or if any of them are."

"That's pretty sparse. Do you have anything else?"

JP gave her the names, birthdates, and addresses of Goldie's children, plus a few other details he knew about Goldie.

"That might help. I'll pass it on."

"Do you think your computer whiz can help?"

"Oh, Lana will find what you're looking for." Clarice chuckled. "It's just a matter of time."

CHAPTER 26

Monday Morning

After getting the kids to school, JP sat down at his desk. A moment later, his phone rang, and he glanced at the number. He smiled, picked up, and said, "Hi Toop."

"Lana got that information for you."

"Great. What did she find?"

"I'll put her on, and she can tell you, so's I don't mess it up."

"Thanks."

"This is Lana. Sorry I took so long."

She was young, he realized. A kid. "So long?" JP chuckled. "It's only been a few hours. It took me an hour to figure out that Dené wasn't a friend of the family on Facebook."

"For me, it seemed like ages. Mostly because children are difficult to track down. But here's what I found. Dené is Goldie's granddaughter, and her father is most likely Travis

Blodgett. He and Dené's mother dated in their senior year, but they broke up just before graduation. Travis isn't named on the birth certificate, and as far as I can tell, he hasn't had any contact with the child or paid any support. Dené is twelve, and her mother's name was Tanya Dumas."

"Was?"

"Unfortunately, she passed away two weeks ago. September seventeenth to be exact."

Right before this all started. "Where is Dené now?"

"She's in Polinsky, waiting for a foster home placement. There's a juvenile dependency case pending. But here's the thing. I hacked into Tanya's email and found some legal documents naming Goldie Forney as Dené's guardian. But neither the juvenile court nor the Department of Social Services seem to know that."

JP wondered how Lana knew what the DSS and court documents contained, but he didn't ask. Tuper claimed she could get into anything. Apparently, he was right.

"So, Tanya must've been in contact with Goldie. Or at least she knew about her. But why wouldn't Tanya name someone in her own family as guardian?"

"Tanya grew up in foster care after her parents' rights were terminated when she was about six, but she never got adopted. She was in two different placements with adoptive parents, but they both fell through. Basically, she grew up a legal orphan. She had two younger half-siblings, who were both adopted. I started to trace them, but then realized I was getting off on a tangent that probably wouldn't help. So, I let it go. Essentially, she has no family."

"But Goldie's dead too, so where does that leave Dené?"

"I don't know, but I bet Sabre could tell you."

"How did Tanya die?" JP asked.

"She had cancer."

"So, it wasn't sudden?"

"Yes and no. She apparently had it far longer than she realized. By the time Tanya was diagnosed, she went fast. According to her medical records, she discovered it only a few months ago. I can have Clarice email you the medical records."

"That would be great. Thanks."

"You know you can't use them in court or tell anyone where you got them."

"I know. We won't."

"I'll also send you the legal document Tanya had drawn up for Dené's placement with Goldie. I don't know if it'll help, but I'll send it anyway. In the meantime, I'll text you the name of the attorney who drew up the guardianship in case you want to contact her."

"Thanks," JP said. "Lana, could you do me one more favor?"

"Sure, if you think it'll help this kid."

"Could you check Goldie's phone records and see who she was in contact with the last month?"

"Landline or cell or both?"

"Cell. She doesn't have a landline."

"Easy, peasy."

JP gave her Goldie's phone number and thanked her again. He was about to hang up when he heard Lana say, "I forgot to tell you. There's a dependency court hearing today at Juvenile Court on Meadowlark."

"What time?"

"This morning, so it might already be over."

"Thanks, Lana. I have to go. Sabre's at court right now."

JP hung up and called Sabre. When she didn't answer, he

left a message telling her that Dené's case was on calendar. He tried texting her. Still no response. He did the same for Bob and got nothing.

He called Sabre again and left another message: "I'm on my way to Meadowlark. Please call me so I can explain what I learned. If I don't hear from you, I'll keep driving and find you there. There's a lot more you need to know."

∽

Sabre and Bob finished their first two cases in Department Four and walked out into the hallway.

"Judge Hekman is in rare form this morning," Bob said. "By the way, what were you saying before we were called in the courtroom?"

"I found more birthday cards for Dené, a bunch more Hopi Kachina dolls, and another box of jewelry for you to go through. I also found a note from Goldie that someone was trying to kill her."

"Really? Do you think it's real or was she just paranoid?"

"She obviously had problems, but as far as I know, she wasn't delusional. And she died of a heart attack. So even if someone was after her, that's not what caused her death."

"Are you sure?"

"What do you mean? That's what the doctor listed as cause of death."

"Maybe she was poisoned, which can produce a heart attack."

"Now, you're just being weird. Sometimes a rock is just a rock."

"And sometimes it's kryptonite."

"Why would anyone want to kill Goldie? It's not like she

had anything of real value."

"She owns a house in La Mesa," Bob said. "Even some equity could mean a hundred grand or so. And she lived there a long time. Of course, she could have a second mortgage on it. You really need to check out the mortgage or property title."

"Technically, I don't have any legal right to do anything yet. I need to either find the trust or file in probate court to get things rolling. And according to the will I have now, everything is divided amongst all five children and possible grandchildren. When you split it five or more ways, that doesn't leave a very big chunk for any one person."

"Hardly enough to kill someone over, I suppose."

Sabre thought about the scarf. "And we found a dead lizard named Bart, wrapped in a Kim Hilton scarf in a shoebox. Look." Sabre took out her phone to show him the photo and noticed JP had been trying to reach her.

"Wow. Two voicemails and a text from JP. I'd better call him."

"Hi, Kid," JP said when he answered. "Did you get my message?"

"I saw that you left two, so I called."

"Dené has a case on calendar this morning. Her last name is Dumas."

"Delinquency?"

"No, dependency." JP sounded like he was driving. "In a nutshell, her father is your cousin, Travis Blodgett, who doesn't appear to have any contact with his daughter. Her mother, Tanya Dumas, passed away very recently, leaving papers for Goldie to take care of Dené."

"What—" Sabre started to interrupt with questions but stopped herself.

"Tanya grew up in foster care and has no family except for

two half-siblings who were adopted. Her parents' rights were terminated for all of them."

"And in turn, Dené has no family. Poor girl." Sabre walked toward the information desk, signaling with her head for Bob to follow.

"Her mother made Goldie her guardian. You'll have to sort out what that means, but it seems that DSS doesn't have that information, and you don't either—legally." JP paused. "You can't reveal how you got any of this information. But I have the name of the attorney who produced the guardianship papers, so we should be able to get them."

JP gave her the attorney's name and phone number.

"That's a lot of information. Thank you so much."

"I'll call you back if I think of anything I missed."

"What is it?" Bob asked, as they approached the desk.

"JP found Dené. She has a case on calendar this morning. I hope we're not too late."

Patricia Leahy, a Spanish interpreter, was working the desk. "What do you need, Sabre?"

"The court calendar, please."

Patricia handed it to her and walked away to help someone else.

Sabre unclipped the papers and gave half to Bob. They both started perusing them.

"Here it is," Bob said, a few seconds later. "She's in Department One."

"Who's her attorney?"

"Richard Wagner."

"Good." Sabre clipped the documents back together and stuffed them under the counter from the inside. "Let's go."

"I have another case, so you go ahead. And don't worry about being too late. It's Wagner. He's probably still surfing."

CHAPTER 27

Monday Morning

"Hey, Wags." Sabre spotted Richard Wagner just before he entered Department One.

He stopped and pivoted. "What's up, Sabre?"

"Do you have the Dumas case?"

"I was just about to attend that hearing. Are you on it?"

"No. But I have information that might be helpful. Dené is my cousin—at least I think she is."

He looked taken aback. "There isn't anything in the reports about any living relatives. Her mother just passed away, and her father is unknown."

"I have reason to believe her father is my first cousin, Travis Blodgett."

"Do you have an address for him?"

"And a phone number," Sabre said. "I may also have more information for you in the next few days."

"Do you know Dené?" Wagner asked.

"We've never met."

"Does she have other family? Because right now, foster care is the only thing in this child's future. I would love to find family members for her."

"If Travis is the father, Dené also has two aunts and two uncles. But I don't think any of them would be suitable, or even interested, in taking care of her. The girl's grandmother, my aunt, passed away a week ago yesterday, and I'm handling her estate. I'm learning a lot of new things about this family."

"The grandmother died a few days after the mother?"

"That's right," Sabre said. "Can you get a continuance and try to get her alleged father into court?"

"Does the father know he has, or might have, a kid?"

"I have no idea."

"Did the grandmother know?"

"She was aware of a grandchild named Dené, but I don't think she had an address or contact with the child in the beginning. Goldie left behind quite a few undelivered birthday cards with Dené's name on them."

"At some point, we'll make sure she gets those."

"Have you met Dené yet?" Sabre asked.

"I saw her yesterday for the first time. She's a cute kid, and smart as a whip."

"How old is she?"

"She'll be twelve in November, I think." He checked his file. "Yeah, the tenth."

"Thanks, Wags."

"The judge will have to continue this hearing if for no other reason than to give notice to the father. How long do you need?"

"Just a few days. The sooner we determine if Travis is the

father, the better."

"Keep me posted." Wagner entered the courtroom.

Sabre sat on the bench and called the number JP had given her.

"Doyle Law Group," a young voice said.

"I'm Attorney Sabre Brown, and I'm trying to reach Attorney Doyle."

"What is this regarding?"

"Goldie Forney and Tanya Dumas."

"One moment please."

Less than a minute passed before someone answered. "This is Rose Marie Doyle." Her voice was strong and professional. "May I help you?"

"I hope so. My aunt, Goldie Forney, recently passed away, and—"

"I'm sorry to hear that."

"Thank you."

"What do you need from me?" Doyle asked.

"I understand that you drafted the paperwork for Tanya Dumas, making Goldie Forney the guardian for her daughter Dené. Tanya passed away a few days before Goldie, and now the child is facing foster care. I need a copy of the document."

"No problem. Just email or fax something establishing that you're the trustee or executor of the estate, and I'll get it right over to you."

"Unfortunately, we're still looking for Goldie's trust. She left a note saying I was her trustee, but so far I haven't been able to find the actual trust."

"I'm sorry. I wish I could help."

"It's okay. A juvenile dependency case has been filed on Dené, and I'll let DSS know they can contact you. I was just trying to skip a few steps. Thank you, anyway." Sabre hung up.

A moment later, Bob walked up. "Did you find Wagner?"

"He's in there getting a continuance right now."

"See, I told you there was plenty of time."

The courtroom door opened, and Wagner came out. "The hearing was continued until Thursday."

"Thanks. There's something else you should know." Sabre handed him a note with Doyle's name and number. "Apparently, Dené's mother had a document that made my Aunt Goldie the guardian. I don't know if that matters now that Goldie is dead, but you should contact the attorney and get the paperwork just in case. At the very least, it shows that Tanya believed Goldie was Dené's grandmother."

"I'll let the social worker know. It'll be easier for her to get the documents." He smiled at Sabre. "You sure know how to complicate a simple case." Wagner shook his head and walked off.

"Want to go to lunch?" Bob asked.

Before Sabre could say yes, her phone rang. She answered it without checking the caller ID. "Hello, this is Sabre Brown."

"This is Rocki. We need to meet."

Sabre rolled her eyes, wishing she'd let it go to voicemail. "Why?"

"I have a will that Mom gave me last year. You need to see it."

Another one? "I can be at my office at five o'clock today. Will that work?"

"See you at five."

Sabre hung up, then called Micki and asked her to be there too. When Sabre called Langston, he also said he had something to show her, so she told him to meet her as well. Sabre left messages for both Travis and Chase—and didn't tell any of the siblings that the others were invited.

CHAPTER 28

Monday Afternoon

S abre walked into her aunt's house and found Ron working in the living room. He'd cleared another foot of space on the path toward the kitchen.

"How was Mom?" Sabre asked, leaving the door open to let in fresh air.

"She looked great," Ron said. "She couldn't stop talking about the trip. I'm really happy for her."

"Harley has been good for her. It's about time she started enjoying life again. I plan to stop by and see her tomorrow after court."

"She's looking forward to that."

"Find anything exciting today?"

"Three more kachina dolls, six heart stones, and a psychological evaluation for Langston. I just glanced at it, but it looks like he had a lot of problems as a kid." Ron pointed to a bin of papers. "It's over there if you want to see it."

Sabre picked it up, sat down on a folding chair, and began to read.

PSYCHODIAGNOSTIC ASSESSMENT

PATIENT: Langston Blodgett
AGE: 12 years, 4 months
GRADE: 6th
EXAMINER: Dr. Heller

REASON FOR REFERRAL: Langston has been seeing a therapist since this past winter. He had a psychiatric consult with Dr. Martinez. The doctor felt that Langston might be suffering from a depressive disorder, but wanted to rule out the possibility of attention-deficit and/or learning disabilities. Therefore, Langston was referred for a psychodiagnostic assessment.

ASSESSMENT PROCEDURES included Forer Structured Sentence Completion, Bender Memory, Bender-Gestalt Visual Motor Test, Kaufman Assessment Battery for Children, and Rorschach Ink Blot Test.

Sabre put the evaluation aside, realizing it would take too long to read. She would tackle it later tonight. She shuffled through the box of paperwork, setting aside projects and essays Goldie's children had done in grade school. She separated electric bills, bank statements, and several unopened letters from PNC Mortgage that were ten years old. Sabre had come across more PNC mail, but had just tossed the envelopes into a bin for later. She was deep into Lowe's receipts when she heard a knock.

Sabre and Ron both looked up and saw a mailman standing in the doorway.

"Sorry to intrude, but I couldn't help but notice a change going on here. Is Goldie all right?"

Sabre shook her head. "I'm afraid not. She passed away a week ago."

"I'm so sorry. She was a delightful woman. Loved to talk and always had water and treats for all the dogs in the neighborhood."

"That was my Aunt Goldie," Sabre said.

"What should I do with her mail? Just keep leaving it here?"

"Yes, please. I'm handling her estate, and there's a lot of sorting out to do yet."

"Here you go." He handed Ron a stack of mail and a package. "I think that's some kind of subscription, because it comes every month. You might want to check on it."

"Thank you," Ron said. "We will."

Ron handed the mail to Sabre. The thick letter on top was from PNC Mortgage. Sabre opened it.

"What is it?" Ron asked.

"A coupon book with envelopes for sending mortgage payments." Sabre felt hesitant.

"So, she still has a mortgage on the house. I'm not surprised."

Sabre glanced at the section marked *Loan Information*. "It's for a house on the four-thousand block of Acacia."

"That's two blocks over. Almost directly behind us."

"It shows a loan balance of $34,202."

"Do you think she has a rental?"

"It would explain those Lowe's purchases." Sabre dug through the receipt bin. "Here's one for a washer and dryer delivered to that Acacia address."

"Well, I'll be darned. Maybe Aunt Goldie had more money than we thought." Ron pulled out his phone and keyed in the address. "Redfin shows an estimated value of $566,090. That's a hefty bit of equity."

"I wonder if her kids know about the rental," Sabre said.

"Maybe that's why they keep calling you," Ron said. "Divided equally, that's another hundred thousand each. But nobody has said anything, right?"

"Not a word. Speaking of which, I'm meeting with them all again this evening at five. I'd like you there with me again."

"I love fireworks."

"Hello there!" A man's voice called from the porch.

Ron stepped toward him. "Hello. What can I do for you?"

"I'm Urban Scobba. My friends call me Red." He pointed to his hair. "I heard you were selling this house, and I wondered if you have an agent yet. I know the neighborhood, and I'm sure I could get you a good price. I'd be glad to discuss it with you if you're interested."

Ron stepped back. "Sabre, you can field this one."

"Why do you think we're selling the house?" Sabre asked.

"I heard the woman who lived here passed on. I'm so sorry for your loss, by the way."

"Thank you," Sabre said. "How did you hear that?"

"Full disclosure." He tipped his head. "My friend made the referral. She told me Goldie Forney had died and the house was not yet on the market."

"And full disclosure—who is your friend?"

"Micki Nogard. She said her mother had recently passed away, and the house needed to be sold, but the lawyer—I'm guessing that's you." He gave Sabre a half smile. "The lawyer hadn't listed the house for sale yet. I volunteered to offer my services."

"Thank you, Urban," Sabre said.

"Red."

"Thank you, Red. I'll add your card to the other ten or fifteen that have been dropped off here. When, and if, the time comes to sell the house, I'll decide who to use. I appreciate the personal touch. Have a good day."

CHAPTER 29

Monday Late Afternoon

Micki was the first to show up, arriving fifteen minutes early. Sabre was still in the lobby. Micki skipped the niceties and went straight to her point, waving the document. "This will names me as executor and leaves something to each of us kids. So, you don't need to be involved anymore. I'll take care of everything."

"May I see it?" Sabre asked.

Micki reluctantly handed over the paper.

"It's dated last September seventeenth," Sabre noted.

"I know, so it has to be more recent than what you have."

"It is," Sabre said. "But it's not valid."

"I know that's her signature."

"That's not the problem. It needs to be witnessed."

Rocki walked in, and Micki yelled, "What is she doing here? I thought we were meeting alone."

"I never said that," Sabre corrected. "I invited all your siblings."

Micki huffed. "I guess they might as well know who's in charge now anyway."

"That's right. I am." Rocki handed a document to Sabre.

Before Sabre could look it over, Langston walked in, followed by Travis. Ron came in the back door and joined them. "Sorry I'm late, Sis."

"No problem." She gave Ron a warm smile. "Let's all go into my office." Sabre headed to the back, and the others followed, bickering as they went. Ron stayed behind to make sure they all ended up in Sabre's office.

Rocki launched the first bomb. "Mom made me executor and left everything to me, except for a thousand dollars to each of my siblings."

"My will says the same thing," Travis said.

"Mine too." Langston nodded.

"See?" Rocki gestured with both hands. "I'm in charge."

"No, you idiot," Langston countered. "Mom named me executor and beneficiary." He shook his head. "Apparently, she gave us each one, and I bet they're all dated September seventeenth."

Micki's face turned red with anger, and she released a string of colorful words.

"Please take a seat, and we'll talk about this." Micki continued to wave her document in Sabre's face. Sabre moved behind her desk, and Ron herded the group toward their seats. Sabre stayed silent until they finally sat down.

"None of the wills were witnessed, correct?" Sabre asked.

"Mine wasn't," Travis said nonchalantly.

"Mine either," Langston said. "That's why I knew it wasn't valid."

166

"That's not true," Rocki argued. "I googled it, and some wills in California do not need to be witnessed. I think this is one of them."

"Only holographic wills," Sabre said. "They have to be handwritten and signed, all in the testator's handwriting."

Rocki and Micki both started shouting. Finally, Travis yelled, "Stop!" They both gave him dirty looks but quieted down.

"She played us all." Langston chuckled. "Well done, Mom."

"What happens now?" Micki stood and bellowed, "Why don't you just get that house sold and give us our money?"

"I want to ensure that I have the most recent documents before I proceed. And I need to know the full value of the estate before anything can be done. In addition, there have been some complications."

"Like what?" Micki asked. Without waiting for a response, she started lecturing. "Just put the house on the market. You haven't even done that. Just sell it. It's not like she had a lot of assets. How complicated can it be? Get it sold, and we can all get our money, including you. Then we'll get out of your hair."

"Why does she get money?" Rocki asked.

"She gets paid for 'handling the estate.'" Micki made air quotes. "It's not like there's much to handle."

"I only get paid for my time."

"So, there it is." Micki crossed her arms. "The more time she puts in, the more she gets paid. That explains it all." She plopped back down with a huff.

"It's a little more complicated than that," Sabre said. She was interrupted when Chase walked in.

"Am I late?" Chase asked in an energetic voice, unlike his demeanor the last time.

"You're always late," Langston muttered.

"What did I miss?"

"Did you get a will from Mom leaving you everything?" Langston asked.

"If that's why you're in such a good mood," Micki cut in, "the will isn't valid. She didn't have them witnessed, and she gave us each one."

"I know," Chase said. "She told me."

"What do you mean? Why would she tell you?"

"Because she liked me best," Chase said, starting another round of bickering, as he sat in the empty seat between Langston and Travis.

Sabre noticed they sat in the exact order they had the last time. Micki sat on the end, probably because she felt like it gave her power, like a lead dog. And Rocki always stayed close to Micki. Langston and Travis tried to keep their distance from each other, and Langston, being heavy, probably preferred the end seat. Chase, being late, just took what was left, with Travis as his protector. Sabre couldn't help but wonder if those were the same dynamics they grew up with. She knew from experience that it was hard to change family patterns once they developed.

"Enough!" Travis shouted over the bickering. "Let her speak."

"As I was saying, it's more complicated." Sabre hesitated, trying to figure out the best way to approach the subject. "Did you know your mother was a hoarder?"

"What are you talking about?" Micki snapped. "She was not a hoarder. Why would you say something like that? Never mind, I know. It's your way of dragging this out so you can make more money."

"Yeah," Rocki joined in. "Why else would you say that?"

"She had a lot of stuff," Langston acknowledged. "But I wouldn't call her a hoarder."

The three had more to say, but Sabre tuned it out. She noticed Chase and Travis whispering to each other. They didn't seem to share the others' indignation.

Finally, Travis spoke up in his booming voice. "Sabre's right. Mom was a hoarder." The three dissenters turned on him, getting louder with each criticism. Travis waved his hand, dismissing them. "When was the last time any of you were in Mom's house?" When no one answered, he said, "I mean it. Micki, when were you there last?"

"I don't know." She shrugged. "Ten, twelve years ago, maybe."

"Rocki?"

"The same, I guess. I was there with Micki."

Travis turned toward his twin. "How about you, Langston?"

"Ten years, I suppose. Chase was still living at home."

"Didn't you ever wonder why Mom didn't invite you over? Why she didn't have us get together as a family for dinner?"

"I just thought she didn't want to cook anymore," Rocki said in a soft voice.

"But a hoarder?" Micki rolled her eyes. "Really? Isn't that a little dramatic?"

"Ask Chase if you don't believe me." Travis nudged his younger brother.

Micki stared at Chase, trying to intimidate him, but he glanced at Travis and then spoke up anyway. "Mom had already filled your bedrooms by the time I left home," Chase said.

"Lots of people use extra bedrooms for storage," Micki said. "That's no big thing."

"Wake up, Micki," Travis said. "Mom had not been able to get to her kitchen for years now."

"How do you know?"

"Because I went to check on her." Travis stood and looked from sibling to sibling. "Apparently, it never occurred to any of you to do the same." He turned to Sabre. "Thank you." Then he walked out, with Chase following close behind.

Langston stood. "I guess we're done here."

The three abruptly left as well, without acknowledging Sabre or Ron.

CHAPTER 30

Monday Evening

Sabre tucked Morgan in, then sat on the sofa next to JP, bracing for another round of sorting papers. But she had concerns she needed to discuss with JP. "Dealing with Goldie's kids today left me feeling uncomfortable. Do you think there's anything to what my aunt said about someone trying to kill her?"

"I suppose it's possible, but your aunt was very odd. I expect paranoia isn't that unusual with hoarders."

"You're right. I did some research on the disorder, and I also spoke to a psychiatrist I know. He said that hoarding is often the final pathway of an obsessive-compulsive disorder. Or that it can come from fear of theft and poisoning in paranoid delusions."

"There you go." JP gave her a look. "What he said."

"Yes, but you know the old saying. *Just because you're paranoid doesn't mean someone's not out to get you.*"

"Would you like me to investigate?"

Sabre thought for a minute. "Maybe you should. Could you meet with each of her children and see what you can find out. There has to be some reason she made a bogus will for each of her kids. Maybe she thought she could put them off for a while."

"But if someone was trying to kill her, why give them an incentive to do it?"

"Good point. The problem is that so much of what she wrote isn't dated. We know those wills were from September of last year, but we don't know when she wrote the note to me."

"I'll see what I can learn."

"Thanks. And ask if anybody wants Dually."

"Good idea. I'd hate to see him go, but I'm not sure how much longer Louie will put up with him."

Sabre picked up the top paperwork in the bin, Langston's psychological evaluation, and read through it.

PERTINENT HISTORY: Langston is the result of an unplanned pregnancy, born a few minutes before his fraternal twin brother, Travis. Mother married their father while the twins were in utero. Two months later, the father took his own life. Delivery occurred by natural childbirth and was unremarkable. Both boys were deemed healthy.

Mother described Langston as an extremely colicky baby who cried most of the night. The twin brother, Travis, was a much easier infant. When the boys were born, Mother had three other children, an eight-year-old son,

Michael, and identical twin girls, six years old, a product of Mother's first marriage.

Mother explained that Langston liked to be cuddled and ate far more than his twin brother. When Langston was two, his brother Michael was killed in a motorcycle accident, along with Michael's father. Mother blames herself for Michael's death, although it appears that isn't warranted. The incident made her feel inadequate as a parent, and she feels that way to this day.

The next section covered Langston's early school years. Sabre speed read through it, noting that in kindergarten Langston was already competing with Travis, *a better-behaved brother,* and was *thirty pounds overweight by the end of second grade.*

Third through fifth grades continued in a similar pattern, and he had gained the title of "class clown." He had friends, but was never the social butterfly his brother was, and Langston seemed to both resent and admire Travis for it. At home, his mother found him to be increasingly draining, claiming he argues with her about everything and always believes he is right. She states that he is moody and whiny, increasingly losing his temper, and often states, "I want to kill myself."

Mother explained that her own mother was an alcoholic, and a maternal great aunt suffered a psychiatric disturbance that was unknown. Mother, herself, admits to considerable depression. For example, she has low energy, cries easily and spontaneously for little reason or purpose, overeats, and does not sleep well. It is notable that despite this description, Mother placed no blame for her own problems on the fact that she was raising five children and had little time for herself. Instead, she considers herself an inadequate parent.

BEHAVIOR OBSERVATIONS AND TEST RESULTS: Langston was extremely friendly, energetic, and attentive the entire evaluation process. He engaged me in conversation with appropriateness and spontaneity. Langston's positive demeanor was in contrast to the attitude described by Mother. Langston's excessive weight may border on obesity. While he was not overtly self-deprecating, his approach to the various tasks revealed him to actually be hard on himself. Despite his meticulous approach, he demonstrated considerable disorganization, poor use of time, and poor sense of judgment as to what was required in order to be successful on task. Langston's teachers rated him as being excessively inattentive and somewhat impulsive. He often didn't turn in classroom and homework assignments, but still got A's on most of his tests, and when called on in class could almost always give the correct answer in spite of his apparent inattentiveness.

Langston's abilities approach the superior range of intellectual functioning. His scores do not reflect any formal learning disability, and his intelligence level is quite high.

Langston's cognitive profile is not consistent with attention deficits. However, his teachers consistently reported Langston's inattentiveness and occasional bursts of anger. Therefore, it is probable that the explanation for this notion lies in Langston's emotional profile, which is consistent with a depressive disorder. Indices are clear that Langston suffers from low self-esteem, from painful emotions that emerge regarding his self-image, and from disorganization due to increased perceived stress. Increases in inattentiveness, impulsivity, poor reality testing, and poor judgment are likely the result. When Langston compares himself with others, especially his twin brother, he believes himself to be inadequate.

The above feelings and notions about his self-worth are in direct contrast to the fact that Langston's personality structure contains a narcissistic-like tendency to overvalue his personal worth. He often carries himself with a sense of entitlement. These opposing self-opinions are quite uncommon and indicate the presence of a serious conflict regarding self-image and self-value.

In summary, Langston appears to suffer from a depressive disorder and underlying anger issues. He harbors considerable painful emotions. His weight, perhaps, is a manifestation of these tremendous withholds. Much of the pain he harbors involves issues around self-esteem and self-worth, which is in direct contrast to his posture that he is always right, which, in turn, exacerbates his mood disturbance even further.

RECOMMENDATIONS: Any psychotropic intervention should concentrate on the depressive symptoms. Individual treatment might address self-esteem issues. Unfortunately, given Langston's tremendous abilities to disguise his pain—even from himself—treatment around esteem issues will be difficult, but necessary. Without intervention and treatment, these tendencies can escalate in adulthood and result in more extreme lashing out, most likely on loved ones and those he blames for his pain. Family treatment will need to focus on the behaviors Mother finds distasteful at home as well as developing

Langston's self-worth. Langston cannot be expected to correct these issues on his own, so he needs supervision and close monitoring as he approaches manhood.

Should further questions arise regarding Langston Blodgett, please do not hesitate to contact me.

Dr. Heller, Ph.D., Licensed Clinical Psychologist

When Sabre finished, she handed the evaluation to JP. "You may want to read this before you see Langston. When he was young, he had depression and anger issues. He may still have them. I know from other paperwork that Langston had a drug problem in his teen years. He went to a treatment center and to outside therapy for nearly a year."

"Did it help?"

"From what I can tell, it did. He went on to college and is the only one who got a degree. So, he was functioning well enough to do that. And now he's a manager at Kohl's. You might check his work history there. But I'm still concerned about the psychologist's statements that his behaviors may escalate in adulthood and he may lash out."

CHAPTER 31

Tuesday Morning

JP started early on the computer, searching for information about Goldie's children. He started where he was most familiar—law enforcement encounters. Chase was the only one with a criminal record. When he was nineteen, he'd been arrested for drug possession. He'd hired an attorney who got him probation, so he didn't serve any time. JP wondered if Goldie had paid for the attorney, but he had no way of checking.

JP searched school and work histories next, jotting down notes. He also checked social media accounts, where Micki and Rocki seemed to spend a great deal of time. Travis was on Facebook, but not real active. JP couldn't find Langston or Chase on any social media. He continued to search, wanting as much background as possible before meeting with them. The more he had, the easier it would be to navigate the conversations and elicit new information.

At nine o'clock, JP called and made appointments with Travis and Langston, both for that afternoon. Chase didn't answer, so JP left a message. He didn't contact either Micki or Rocki, fearing they would show up together, and he wanted to speak to each alone. He decided to drop in and hoped he caught them at their homes. They lived only a few blocks from one another.

He headed outside, planning to drive to Micki's house, when his phone rang.

"JP, this is Zack. Can you meet for a cup of coffee?"

"Now?"

"If that works."

"Sure, I can do that. Where?" JP climbed into his truck.

"There's a place called Brew Coffee Spot on Lake Murray. Or if you'd rather go to a Starbucks, there's one in the same area."

"Brew Coffee Spot will be great. I can be there in ten."

"I'll see you then."

JP and Zack sat outside on the small patio, coffee in hand. "Thanks for meeting me," JP said.

"It's really nice to see you again. I've thought about you often and told myself I would get in contact with you, but I never did. So, I'm glad you called, even if it was about my brother."

"Me too."

"By the way, I spoke to DuBois, so I know what this is about. I can't believe a little boy is dead." Zack's chin dropped, and he avoided eye contact. "I pray to God Kenny didn't have anything to do with it."

JP understood the man's shame. "I know what it's like to have family members who have caused harm. I have a brother and a father in prison right now."

"My father should be, but I don't know that he is. I haven't spoken to him since I became a cop."

"I'm sorry to hear that."

"Here's the thing," Zack said. "Like I told DuBois, I haven't seen or talked to my brother in about six months, so I don't know anything about the family he's with now. All I can tell you is that Kenny had it rough when we were young." Zack paused and sipped his coffee, his eyes far away. "Dad used to beat him, and sometimes torture him. Kenny protected me so Dad never did anything to me. Several times he tried, but Kenny always stepped in. He'd burn Kenny with cigarettes or make him stand for hours in a corner. He'd also beat him real bad when he would stick up for me. But that never stopped Kenny from protecting me."

Shameful. JP never got used to child abuse. He didn't know how Sabre handled it. "Are you aware of any incidents of Kenny being violent as an adult?"

"I didn't see him all that much. I know he got into drugs pretty heavy, so he never wanted his brother, the cop, around. I didn't particularly enjoy his company either since he was high all the time. I never had any reason to think he'd hurt a kid, until one day he called me to get him out of trouble."

"What kind of trouble?"

"He'd hooked up with a woman who had a young boy about five. After a while, she kicked Kenny out and accused him of molesting her son. I'm pretty sure he never did that, but I found out that he was pretty mean to the little boy."

"Did you help Kenny?"

"I felt like I owed him, so yeah. But I wouldn't have if the molesting allegation had rung true. The mother admitted to me that she made it up, but claimed Kenny had spanked the child and left bruises. He was never arrested so there's no record. It bothered me that the next woman he found had a son around five years old. That seemed to be the age he liked to beat on. That woman didn't last very long. They never even lived together."

"Did you know about his relationship with Ellie?"

"No. I've spent less and less time with Kenny. In retrospect, I wonder if there was something I could've done to save little Perry's life."

"You think Kenny killed him?"

"I don't know." He took a deep breath. "I believe it's possible. Kenny learned a lot of awful things from Dad."

"Where was your mom when all this was going on?"

"She left when I was two, and Kenny was five. I hadn't thought about it before, but maybe that's why Kenny wants to hurt five-year-olds. I don't know." Zack shook his head, distressed. "I don't like the kind of man my brother became, but he sure took care of me growing up. I'll always be grateful to him for that, but this is too much. If he killed that little boy, he needs to be locked up."

"You've told DuBois all this?"

"Most of it."

"And you haven't talked to Kenny?"

"No, and he hasn't called to ask for help. I'm pretty sure it's because the last time I told him I wouldn't help him if he hurt women or children. I was there for him during drug treatment, but this is different. It's inexcusable and unforgivable."

JP reached out to shake Zack's hand. "It was nice to see you again. I'm proud of you."

"You're part of the reason. I learned so much from you when you were my training officer. And not just the tricks of the trade. You had integrity. Now when I'm in an awkward situation, I often ask myself—WWMD? Then I always know what path to take."

"What the heck is WWMD?"

"What would McCloud do?"

"McCloud?" JP frowned. "Really?"

"That's what everyone called you. DuBois started it. He was also the only one with the nerve to do it to your face. I wasn't about to call you that since you were my trainer, and I didn't want to give you reason to fail me."

"DuBois still calls me that. I expect it from him, but you don't get the same license." JP smiled. His mood turned serious, and he spoke with emotion. "You were a good student, Zack, and your integrity is built in. I'm just glad I was able to reinforce it."

CHAPTER 32

Tuesday Morning

J P walked up to the door and knocked. Micki opened it
and said, "You're that private investigator for Sabre,
aren't you?"

"Yes, ma'am. JP Torn. Can you talk for a few minutes?"

"Why ain't she here?"

"Sabre has court this morning, and I'm trying to help out. I
won't take much of your time."

"What the heck? Come on in." Micki stepped inside, and
JP followed. "Have a seat." She pointed to her sofa, then sat
down in a recliner across from it.

JP scanned the room. The one-bedroom apartment had
modest furniture and was clean and orderly, quite unlike her
mother's home. "This is a nice place," he said, taking a seat.
"You keep it tidy and clean."

"I try. The house I grew up in was always a mess. I guess with five kids, it wasn't easy, but Mom never threw anything away."

"Micki, you seem to be the leader of this clan. There's always a pecking order in families. Sometimes it's the oldest who calls the shots. Sometimes not. But in your case, it seems as though you have that role. That's why I'm talking to you." He was laying it on thick, appealing to her ego.

Micki sat up straighter. "The others have always expected me to make the decisions, so I guess you're right."

"You probably know all the family gossip as well?" JP said with a wink.

Micki's serious tone didn't change, nor did she smile. "This family is a mess. I do my best to hold them together, but the boys are just impossible."

"How's that?" JP asked.

"Travis was always the popular one, and he still thinks he's the cat's meow. Chase is a druggie, and Langston is just a jerk. He thinks he's so much smarter than the rest of us. Just because he has an education doesn't make him smart. But he acts all intellectual around us, trying to use words we wouldn't understand. He thinks he's a big shot because he's a 'manager'"—she made air quotes—"at Kohl's. Big fuzzy deal."

"I take it, you and Langston aren't too close."

"I tried for years, but I finally gave up. He really wasn't that nice even as a kid. He always had to be right about everything—even when he wasn't."

"Do you get along with Rocki?"

"Rocki and I were wombmates. We're tied together forever. Don't get me wrong, we have our disagreements, but if she's in pain, I'm in pain. One time, when we were about eight, Rocki broke her arm, and my arm hurt even before I knew about it. We're that way with a lot of things."

"Are Langston and Travis like that?"

"Not so much. They're pretty different, and maybe it's because they aren't identical like we are. I'm not sure they even like each other."

JP decided to give her an opportunity to talk about herself, which seemed to be her favorite subject. "Where do you work, Micki?"

"I'm a bartender at the Dragon Bar in San Diego. There's another one in La Jolla where we work sometimes, but mostly the one in San Diego because it's closer."

"Who's we?"

"Rocki works there too, but different shifts. She likes days, and I prefer nights because I can make more tips. But we cover for each other a lot. Some customers think there's only one of us. It's fun playing with their heads, especially after a few drinks."

"You've never married?"

"No. Men are just too difficult to put up with." Her lips turned up slightly, but not quite in a smile. "No offense."

"None taken. And none of your siblings are married, right?"

"Right. Mom was pretty disappointed in all of us. She sure wanted some grandkids."

"Did you ever want children?"

"Not really. I guess I don't have much of a maternal instinct."

"It's not for everyone," JP said. "I'm just curious, if you and Rocki get along so well, why don't you live together? I mean, rent is so expensive in this town. It just seems it would be easier."

"I like my privacy, if you know what I mean." She tipped her head and looked up at him, an awkward coquettish attempt at flirting. "Rocki would like to share a place, and we did for years, but I finally had to get my own apartment. She took it hard, but we're good now."

"What about Chase? Do you see much of him?"

"Not really. He used to ask me for money, but he finally quit since I never gave him any. I took him in a few times and fed him, but I refuse to give him drug money."

"How bad is he?"

"He's been in rehab a couple of times—three, I think. When he gets out, he's good for a few months, but it doesn't seem to hold."

JP expected her to take offense at all the questions, but he soon realized that as long as he asked things that allowed her to paint herself in a good light, she was happy. "How well did you get along with your mother?"

"We were pretty close. We talked a lot on the phone, and we'd get together for lunch occasionally." She paused and seemed to be in deep thought. "I think the boys were jealous because she seemed to like me and Rocki the best."

"Did you visit her much?" JP asked.

"She didn't want us to come over, so I haven't been there in years. But she'd spend holidays with me sometimes." Micki hesitated, then added, "I don't know if the others even knew."

"Which holidays?"

"Christmas Eve, Christmas Day, Thanksgiving, the big ones."

"Recently?"

"Yeah. I called her a lot too. We spoke three or four times a week."

She was trying too hard. "Did she ever bring Dually with her?"

"Who's Dually?"

JP decided to see just how much she knew about her mother, especially since he didn't believe her story about the holidays. "Did she have a cat?"

"Oh, Dually, her cat? No, I don't like cats."

"Do you like dogs?"

"I don't like most animals."

What a surprise, JP thought. "Did your mother ever say anything about having health issues?"

"Nothing unusual. Just colds and stuff. Nothing lately."

"Micki, you seem to have a pretty good pulse on the family." JP said, in an effort to encourage her to keep talking. "Tell me, how did the others get along with your mother?"

"Not well. Rocki was good with her, but even she wasn't as close as I was with Mom. The boys were real bad. I know Travis likes to claim he saw her more, but I think he's making it up, and I'm sure Chase only went to her when he needed money. Mom and Langston never really got along, even when he was young. She spent a lot of our money on drug programs and therapy for Langston. I personally don't think it improved his disposition any."

"You said *our* money? What do you mean?"

"You know, money that should have gone to the family."

"Did you have to do without a lot when you were a kid?"

"Not that much. We always had food and clothes, but there weren't any extras. And our clothes were mostly from thrift stores."

"Do you know if your mom had much money?"

Micki swallowed and asked, "What do you mean by *much money*? Does she have money I don't know about?"

"I don't have any idea what she has. It doesn't seem like your family was wealthy or anything. I just wondered if she had anything besides the family home?"

"No, we never had anything special. That's why I didn't go to college, because there wasn't money for it."

Yeah, that's why, JP thought.

CHAPTER 33

Tuesday Morning

JP approached Rocki's apartment and saw her through the front window, talking on her cell phone. When he knocked, she hung up and invited him inside. He guessed the caller had probably been Micki, but he'd expected that.

While they talked, Rocki didn't seem as guarded as Micki, and she even smiled from time to time. JP asked mostly the same questions, but often got different responses.

"I understand for the last few years your mom spent the holidays with Micki."

She looked surprised. "Well, both of us," Rocki said indignantly. "We just met at Micki's house."

"Did the boys come over?"

She shook her head. "They do their own thing."

"Do you get along with your brothers?"

"We do all right. Travis is nice enough, but Chase is a lost soul."

"You didn't mention Langston. What about him?"

"Langston is Langston. We don't talk much."

"But you and Micki get along well, right?"

"Yeah." Rocki rolled her eyes. "She's pretty bossy, but other than that, we're good. We're better now that we don't live together. I had to move out. She never wanted me bringing guys home. Don't get me wrong, it's not like I'm a slut or anything, but a girl has needs." She winked at him. "I'm sure a handsome guy like you understands."

"Uh, thanks." JP was always embarrassed when someone flirted with him. He was pretty sure that's what she was attempting to do, and if it was, she wasn't much better at it than her twin.

"Micki never even dates. She would get jealous when I did, but I think it was more about me spending less time with her than anything else."

JP shifted to a different tack. "Do you know anything about your mother's finances?"

"Not really." Rocki shrugged. "We always had mostly what we wanted growing up. Mom was a real bargain shopper. She bought a lot at thrift stores."

"Did it bother you to wear used clothes?"

"Mom knew what brands were good, and she dressed us in nice things. Micki was the only one who took issue with it. She wanted 'store bought' stuff, and sometimes Mom would indulge her, even though she was pretty frugal most of the time."

"More currently, did your mother ever seem to be without?"

"I don't think so. She never said anything."

And it never occurred to you to ask or check on her. JP wondered how Goldie raised such selfish children. "How well did you and the others get along with your mother?"

"When we were young, Travis, Chase, and I pretty much did what she told us to do. We didn't argue with her like Micki and Langston did."

"What did your mother do for a living when you were young?"

"I'm not sure. She took care of some apartments or something, I think. She was gone a lot."

"Did you see much of your mom in the last years?"

"Not really."

"How often did you talk to her on the phone?"

"Maybe once a month."

"Micki said she called your mom three or four times a week. Did you know that?"

Rocki's eyes shifted. "I suppose. Whatever she says. I wasn't around Micki all the time, so she probably did."

JP got the impression she didn't really believe her twin but was backing whatever Micki said. "When was the last time you were at your mom's house?"

"Probably ten or more years."

"Did you know she was a hoarder?"

"I know she kept everything, and that the closets were always full. But that doesn't make her a hoarder, does it?"

"The situation is far worse than full closets." JP stood. "Did you know your mother had a dog?"

Rocki shrugged. "She always had some kind of animal—dogs, cats, birds, lizards. She loved them all."

"Would you be interested in taking her dog?"

"I would, but I can't have one in this apartment." She

glanced around the small room. Then, as what seemed like an afterthought, she added, "Sorry."

～

JP drove toward the shopping mall. Langston had agreed to meet with him before his shift at Kohl's. On the way, JP called DuBois to see if he had anything new on the McCluskey case. All he got was, "Nothing I can share with you right now." JP knew that meant he had something.

He parked at Starbucks and spotted Langston sitting at a table in front of the coffee shop. Langston didn't get up or make any attempt to greet JP when he approached. JP sat down without invitation.

"Is that the Kohl's you work at?" JP nodded at the nearby department store.

"That's why I picked this place."

"How do you like working there?"

"It's fine. But you didn't come here to talk about my job, and I don't have a lot of time. What do you really want to know?"

"How well did you get along with your mother?"

"Goldie and I had our battles. I gave her some grief growing up, but she helped me a lot. She put me in a drug program, which I hated at the time, but it was good for me. I stayed clean after that."

"Who got along with her best, you or Travis?"

"Travis was spoiled. He never had to work for anything the way I did. That's all I have to say about that."

"Did your other siblings get along with your mother?" JP asked.

"Chase was pretty close to Goldie. He'd probably still be

living at that house if not for his drug problem. She couldn't tolerate that. She tried everything. Finally, Goldie had to go the tough-love route, but he just can't seem to stop."

"Have you tried to help him?"

"Why would I?"

"Oh, I don't know. He's your brother, and you've been down that road. I just thought maybe you could get through to him." JP realized he was being condescending, but this guy was starting to irritate him.

"Chase doesn't like me. He wouldn't listen to me if I tried." Langston shook his head. "It's not my problem."

No brotherly love here. Time to move on. "What do you know about your mother's finances?"

"Not a whole lot." Langston seemed to play it down, but his eyes narrowed.

"You know something," JP said.

"I know she was very thrifty, and she worked hard. I think she saved more than she let on." Langston gave him a hard stare. "What do *you* know about my mother's finances?"

"Very little," JP said, noticing that, for the first time, he called her "mother" instead of Goldie. *Maybe the idea of money made her more endearing,* JP thought. "Sabre is handling that."

"So, there *is* something to handle?"

"Sabre is still sorting through piles of paperwork. She doesn't have the full picture yet."

"Are we done?" Langston looked at his watch. "Because I have to get to work."

"Do you want her dog?"

"No."

"Do you think any of your siblings would try to kill your mother?"

His eyes widened. "Are you saying Goldie was murdered?"

"No. But Goldie thought someone was after her."

"Why would any of us want to kill her? What would we have to gain?"

"I was hoping you could tell me."

Langston stood, looked directly at JP, and said, "Goldie was paranoid."

JP's last stop was at Travis' place on Mt. Helix. The house was small but had a large backyard and a great view. They stood on the back patio, with Travis still in work clothes and sweat on his face.

Travis opened the mini-fridge built into his deluxe grill. "Would you like a beer?"

"No thanks," JP said. "I'm still working."

"Well, I'm not." Travis popped open a bottle of a dark microbrew.

"This is a nice place. Great view," JP said. "Do you own it?"

"I bought it five years ago, and I've done a lot of renovations. Like this whole deck. It's a nice place to entertain, although I don't do as much as I used to."

They both sat down in cushy patio chairs. "It's a nice backyard for a dog too," JP said. "Would you like your mother's?"

Travis gave a sad smile. "Dually is a sweet dog, but I can only be around him for a few minutes. I have awful allergies. Mom loved animals, but we couldn't have cats or dogs when I was a kid because of me. So, she always had reptiles or birds. Those I could handle."

"I'm sorry to hear that." JP paused, then changed the

subject. "What did your mother do for a living when you were young?"

"She managed a small property management company. She was quite adept at it. She did a lot of the repairs and painting. She could fix almost anything. When I was a kid, she'd take me with her sometimes to help replace a washer or dryer or something. I remember how strong she was. I was about sixteen before I could outlift her."

JP was impressed with the way Travis spoke about his mother. It was quite the contrast to the way the others described her. "What do you do for a living?"

"I work for a construction company."

"Do you like it?"

"For the most part. It keeps me outdoors, which I like, and the pay is pretty good."

They chatted for a few more minutes, and JP decided Travis was the most likable of the bunch. At least, he put on the best front.

"Do you know if your mother was having financial trouble?"

"She was not."

"You know that for certain?"

"Mom had plenty of money, she just didn't want anyone to know about it."

"What does 'plenty' mean?' How much did she have?"

"I don't know for certain, but she owns a couple of rentals. That's how I learned about construction, from working on her properties."

"She told you she owned them?"

"No, but she set me up with a company. I worked there for years before I knew anything about the owner. It seemed odd that they treated me so well, even when I screwed up. At first,

I was kind of lame and irresponsible, but I kept getting chances to prove myself. Eventually, I grew up and actually became halfway decent at my job."

"What makes you think your mother had anything to do with it?"

"I learned that by accident. I was dating the foreman's daughter, and everything was fine until I broke up with her." Travis paused. "To be honest, I cheated on her. She was furious and started yelling at me. She called me a loser and accused me of only being able to keep the job because my mother owned the business. When I questioned her, she shut down and walked away. So, I started checking."

"Were you able to verify that it was Goldie's company?"

"Not for certain, but if I had to bet on it, I would. I confronted Mom, and she denied it. But I know the conversation made her very uncomfortable. So, I assume she had some stake in it."

"Maybe a good friend owned the company and saw to it that you had work?"

"I thought about that, but I know Mom had more money than she let on. I used to offer her money to help pay her bills, but she never would take it. One day I saw a bank statement that had over thirty thousand dollars on it, so I figured she was doing okay."

CHAPTER 34

Tuesday Late Afternoon

Sabre sat with her mother in the kitchen, while Harley left to run some errands. Sabre was happy for her mother and her new love interest. Her mother had never thought she'd find anyone after Sabre's father died. Sabre felt a little guilty that when she was growing up, she secretly hadn't wanted her mother to be with anyone else. Now, seeing her so happy made Sabre realize how selfish she'd been.

Beverly insisted on feeding her something, so Sabre gave in and agreed to cheese and fruit. Her mother put together a platter, and as they ate, they chatted about Beverly's trip. She flipped through her phone, showing Sabre the photos she'd taken, explaining each one. Eventually, they got around to the dreaded subject.

"How are you holding up?" her mother asked. "Are you taking care of yourself through all this?"

"I haven't had time to run as much as I'd like, and I really need to," Sabre said. "I feel so bad about Aunt Goldie."

"I know, Sabey. She was far too young." Her mother reached for Sabre's hand. "Ron said she called you for help. That couldn't have been easy. I checked my phone messages, and she tried to call me too. I wish I could've been here for both of you."

Sabre told her about the hospital visit and Goldie's letter, then described the condition of the house. "It's just awful. She must've been living like that for years and years. It's really sad."

"She was a lonely woman, who carried a lot of guilt." Her mother nodded sympathetically. "And those kids... well, you know."

"They're quite a bunch."

"I'm kicking myself for not making a greater effort lately. I had only seen her once since I met Harley, and that's because she insisted. We've just been so busy." She shook her head. "But that's no excuse. I should've made the time."

"Don't beat yourself up. None of us knew how bad things were. She always seemed so jolly when we talked."

"I know."

"Did Aunt Goldie tell you that the Incognito Angel paid for Langston's education?"

"What?"

"We found a letter, which appears to be from the Angel, offering full payment. And a reply that was never mailed. I'm not sure what happened, but Langston went to college and graduated with a master's degree, so I'm pretty sure he took the money."

"She never said a word." They sat in silence for a few minutes, then Beverly said, "You're handling her estate?"

"I'm trying."

"Wait here. I have something for you."

Her mother left the room, returned a minute later, and handed Sabre a notebook. The cover read: *The Vincent Law Group, Estate Planning Portfolio.* "You'll need this."

Sabre opened the notebook. There it was, the trust she needed, nearly an inch thick. She ignored the sticky note and flipped through until she found the page listing the trustee. She wasn't sure she wanted to be named. Her instinct was to help Aunt Goldie, but she knew what a headache it would be.

The current acting trustee is GOLDIE FORNEY. If she should cease to act as the Trustee for any reason, she shall be succeeded by SABRE O. BROWN as the successor Trustee. If she fails to qualify or ceases to act, RONALD BROWN shall act as the alternate successor Trustee.

Sabre sighed. There it was in official language: *First Trustee, Attorney Sabre O. Brown.*

"At least now I can get the job done without so much hassle," Sabre said.

"You think?" Her mother raised her eyebrows.

Sabre laughed. "You're right. It'll still be a lot of hassle, but at least I'll have legal authority to back me up."

Her mother patted her arm. Sabre closed the trust binder and looked at the sticky note on the front. It read:

There's an envelope I keep near my chair that says "My Trust" on the outside. It's a decoy. I left it there for bait when I gave the real trust to your mother. If that envelope isn't there, that means someone has been in my house and found it.

I knew Beverly would keep the real trust safe, and none of them would know where to look for it. If any of my children saw the real trust, they would destroy it. I don't think any of them know what I'm worth, but the truth is, I don't really know what they know or don't know.

"Mom, do you think Aunt Goldie was just paranoid?"

"I don't know, Sabey. You've seen the kids a few times now. Are they really that bad?"

"It's hard to tell. JP interviewed all of them today, and I'll get his assessment tonight. But I've witnessed a lot of resentment toward their mother and each other. And I'm finding more assets every day."

"Like what?"

"She kept quite a bit of cash in the house, and we've found a couple of bank statements totaling over fifty grand. Now that I have the trust, I'll be able to access her accounts. She also has a rental with several hundred thousand in equity, so she's definitely worth more than we initially thought."

"And you're thinking that if her kids knew, they might believe there's financial gain in her demise."

"Exactly."

CHAPTER 35

Tuesday Evening

I t had been a long day, and Sabre didn't feel like cooking.
JP apparently felt the same and ordered pizza. After dinner,
Sabre helped the kids finish their homework, then she and JP
finally had a chance to sit down and talk.

"How did it go with Goldie's kids?" Sabre asked.

"I didn't see Chase. He didn't answer his phone or return
my call. I went to his apartment, but he wasn't there." JP
leaned back on the couch and stretched out his legs. "But I saw
the rest of them. Interesting bunch."

"Did you learn anything new?"

"A little. Micki and Langston are both pretty angry at their
mother and the world in general. They both like to bully the
others around and don't get along with each other. Rocki pretty
much does what Micki says, at least when they're together, but
Rocki also seems to resent her twin, which conflicts with this

whole bond thing they supposedly have going. Travis is the nicest of the four, or at least the most normal." JP glanced at Sabre. "Oh, and no one wants Dually."

"That's too bad." The dog was in Morgan's room at the moment. "Do any of them know that Goldie has more than just the house?"

"Travis seems to think she owns the construction company he works for."

"What?"

"He's done work on her rentals, and he's seen a bank statement, which makes me think Travis visited her."

That was all surprising to Sabre. "Did he tell his siblings?"

"It's hard to tell. The girls acted like they thought their mother was just getting by. I think Langston, on the other hand, knows a great deal. He's smart, he's suspicious, and he's shifty. I think he's done his homework."

"Do you think any would go so far as to try to kill her?"

"Rocki, Micki, and Langston don't seem to like their mother much. According to them, Travis and Chase were the closest to her. From what I can tell, they saw her more often and treated her better. But Langston doesn't even call her Mom. He calls her Goldie."

"That's odd."

"They're all odd, except maybe Travis." JP gave a heavy sigh. "And Micki claimed that Goldie came to her house for the holidays the last few years."

"What holidays?"

"She mentioned Thanksgiving and Christmas." JP looked over at her again. "Didn't you say your aunt spent them with you?"

"She did. Goldie would go to my mom's early on Christmas Eve, spend the night, then have Christmas dinner with us. She didn't go home until late when I left. There is no way she was at Micki's. Goldie came for Thanksgiving as well."

"I asked Rocki about it, and she went along with what Micki said. I also think Micki lied about calling her mother three or four times a week. Why would she lie about that?"

"Probably to make herself look better. Or maybe she feels guilty. I don't know."

"So, your mom had Goldie's trust. That's good, right?"

"For sure."

"Have you read the distribution yet?"

"No, I was about to."

Sabre picked up the trust, glanced through some boilerplate clauses, and flipped to the important page: *Article VI, Disposition of Trust. 6.F. Distribution at My Death*. She read the text aloud so JP could hear.

On my death, the Trustee shall hold, administer, and distribute the trust fund, as then constituted, plus any additions thereto as a result of my death, as follows:

(1) The Trustee shall distribute such items of my tangible personal property in accordance with any written instructions left by me, and the remainder of such personal property to my living children as determined by the Trustee.

(2) My residence shall be put in trust for my son, Chase Perkins. Once it is cleaned up, he can use it for his home. The furniture and appliances shall remain with the house. Should Chase choose not to live there, the house will remain in his trust and be used as a rental, with all profits to go back into his trust. Chase's trust will remain in effect until he reaches the age of forty AND has

randomly drug tested clean for five consecutive years, at which time Chase will become the Trustee of his own trust. Should he not be drug-free at age forty, the trust will remain as is.

(3) The Trustee shall sell all other real property (listed in Appendix F) whose title is held in my personal name and distribute the proceeds accordingly:

(a) 15% shall be divided, free of encumbrances, equally among my children, Michelle Nogard, Rochelle Nogard, and Langston Blodgett.

(b) 5% shall be put into the trust for my son, Chase Perkins, to be distributed according to his daily maintenance needs, until he meets the age and conditions outlined in Section 2. In the event one or more of the above-named children are not living at the time of my death, the Trustee shall distribute his or her share to my other living children.

(c) 5% shall be distributed, free of encumbrances, to my good friend, Judy Ingrid Reed.

(d) 75% shall be put in trust for my granddaughter, Dené Dumas. In the event Dené is no longer living at my death, the Trustee shall distribute her share to her then-living issue, by right of representation, outright and free of trust, unless they are minors. If she has no issue, her portion reverts to my trust, and is divided equally amongst the remaining heirs.

JP cut in. "She left out Travis."

"Hold on. I see his name in the next paragraph." Sabre read it out loud.

Tegbold Construction shall be put in trust for my son, Travis Blodgett, according to the provisions in Appendix G.

JP sat up, looking surprised. "Well tie me to a pig and roll me in the mud. Travis was right. His mother does own Tegbold Construction. I wonder what else he knows."

"And I wonder if the others know." Sabre turned back to the trust and scanned ahead.

"What's in Appendices F and G?" JP asked.

"I don't know. I'll look that up later." Sabre glanced at the next paragraph. "But get this." She read it to JP.

All properties in Yenrof Corporation shall be sold and donated to The Silent Thunder Charity Trust to be managed by Attorney Sabre O. Brown as Head of the Board and Ronald Brown as CEO.

"What the heck is all that?"

"I have no idea. I haven't seen any paperwork on either of them." Sabre frowned. "Let's see what other surprises she has."

All assets and property listed in Appendix H shall be distributed according to the instructions in that appendix.

"So, in summary," JP said, "Yenrof Corporation, whatever that is, goes to a charity trust. Travis gets the construction company, and Chase gets her home, plus five percent of her other personal real estate. The three other kids will split fifteen percent of her personal real estate, which includes at least one rental house. Five percent goes to Judy Reed, and seventy-five percent goes to the granddaughter, Dené."

"That's what it looks like. Well that and whatever is in Appendix H. The trust has the standard language declaring that if anyone contests the distribution and loses, they get nothing. Goldie also had a rather unusual clause." Sabre read it again.

If anyone makes an attempt on my life or commits any crime against me, they lose any and all inheritance.

JP snorted. "That greedy group will be madder than the snake who married the garden hose."

CHAPTER 36

Wednesday Morning

S abre met Bob in front of Department Four to discuss the upcoming jurisdiction hearing on the McCluskey case.

"Your client isn't setting this for trial, is he?" Sabre asked.

"Nope. He's fine with jurisdiction. It makes it easier for him, and even though he's the non-offending parent, he doesn't mind taking a parenting class. Timing might be a little difficult, but he'll manage." Bob checked his watch, then continued. "Adam wants the kids in therapy, and he can't afford it on his own. So, all in all, he's good with it. But I'm sure the mother will want to go to trial."

Sabre noticed Ellie's attorney approaching. "Is that right, Mr. Oakes?"

"What?"

"Are you asking for a trial?"

"We are," Oakes said. "And my client wants Dale in therapy. She thinks he needs serious counseling."

Sabre got right to the point. "Does she think Dale killed Perry?"

Oakes took a second before he spoke. "She thinks it's a strong possibility, since he was the only one in the room with Perry that night."

"And she wants him convicted," Sabre said. "Don't you think that's an odd position for a mother to take?"

"It's not that. She wants him to get the help he needs. She's sure it was an accident, but it will haunt him the rest of his life if he doesn't get help."

"It just feels like she's shifting blame. Anyway, you can tell her that Dale is already in therapy."

"My client loves her son," Oakes said, sounding defensive. "Ellie's not a monster, you know."

"Unless she *is* the monster who killed her own son," Bob countered. "Or she knows her boyfriend killed her son and is willing to let another son take the fall for it."

Oakes turned to Bob, his eyes blazing. "I really don't believe that." He looked back at Sabre. "She's concerned because Dale has been known to have blackouts."

"That's the first I've heard of it," Sabre said.

"Ellie didn't want it known because she was trying to protect Dale, but she realizes he has to deal with the psychological ramifications if he did kill Perry."

"How many blackouts?" Sabre was skeptical.

"Let me get my client, and you can question her." Oakes started to leave but turned back. "Only about the blackouts."

"Of course."

"Is there somewhere we can talk a little more privately?"

Sabre pointed to the door leading up to the mezzanine. "We

can go upstairs. There are some chairs up there and very little traffic."

"We'll be right up."

With little time left before the hearing, Sabre hurried up the stairs. Within minutes, Ellie and her lawyer arrived. Oakes explained that Sabre would ask her some questions, but they'd be limited to Dale's *condition*. Sabre found that an interesting choice of words.

"Mr. Oakes said you expressed a concern about Dale's mental or emotional state. Is that correct?"

"You mean his blackouts?" Ellie looked nervous.

"Yes. How many has he had?"

"Maybe three."

"When did they start?"

"About two months ago, Dale had an accident on his bike. He was pretty scraped up, and so was his bike, but he said he couldn't remember what happened. I figured he'd been doing something he wasn't supposed to and didn't want to tell me."

"Did he get medical attention at that time?"

"No." She was a little defensive now. "I checked him over, and he didn't have anything broken, and his bruises weren't that bad. I bandaged his scrapes, and he seemed fine."

"And he's had two other blackouts since that accident?"

Ellie glanced at her lawyer. When Oakes nodded, she continued. "I saw Dale sitting on the sofa holding his head. I thought he was watching TV, but then I saw his eyes were closed. I shook him to wake him up. When he finally woke, he seemed confused."

"And the third time?"

"I had made the kids popcorn, and we all sat down to watch a Disney movie. About fifteen minutes later, Dale got up and left. I thought he was going to the bathroom or something, but he didn't come back, so I went to check on him. He was sleeping, and when I woke him up, he couldn't remember how he got to his room."

"And you thought he blacked out?" Sabre struggled to sound calm. This woman was either a liar or had failed to get her son necessary medical attention. *She must know that Kenny is abusive.* Sabre wanted to question her about Kenny, but that wasn't within the scope of what they had agreed to, and she knew Oakes wouldn't let her go there.

"He must have, because he couldn't even remember that we were watching a movie. I was going to have him checked, but then this whole thing with Perry happened. But Dale needs to see a doctor and get into therapy."

"How long ago was that incident?"

Ellie swallowed. "Just a few days before Perry died."

"Have you told any of this to the social worker?"

"We will," Oakes said.

CHAPTER 37

Wednesday Afternoon

After Sabre finished at court, she grabbed a quick lunch and drove to her office. She sat down at her desk to research Silent Thunder Charity. She needed to get more information on Yenrof Corporation as well, but right now she would focus on the charitable foundation of which she basically knew nothing. She had almost two hours before the McCluskey kids were out of school and she could talk to them.

Sabre checked the state registry, which listed Goldie Forney as the founder of Silent Thunder, a nonprofit with a mission statement that read:

The purpose of this foundation is to provide relief to the poor or distressed. Notwithstanding anything herein to the contrary, the purposes are limited exclusively to exempt

purposes within the meaning of Section 501(c)(3) of the
Internal Revenue Code.

That was all she could determine from the registry. She needed to find bank statements or annual reports to see what the foundation was worth and exactly what it did. Sabre moved on to Tegbold Construction, which was incorporated as a for-profit entity. It wasn't publicly traded, so she couldn't determine a real value, but the company was larger than she'd expected. She decided to pay them a visit. She still had time before her appointment with Dale and Fayth. Sabre jotted down the address, made a copy of the trust statement, and left her office.

On the way to her car, she called Ron. "Are you at Goldie's house?"

"Yes. Is there something else I should be doing?"

"You're good. I just want you to focus on Aunt Goldie's room. The most recent paperwork came from around her chair. Maybe you'll find something that gives me a better idea of her assets."

"Are you looking for something in particular?"

Sabre told Ron about the nonprofit foundation in Goldie's trust. "I'm looking for bank statements, annual reports, anything with Silent Thunder on it. Any recent mail, mortgages, loan documents, that sort of stuff. The same thing with Yenrof and Tegbold Corporations. Also, keep an eye out for the necklace Judy Reed told us about."

"Do you think it's hers?"

"I have no idea, but I'd hate to keep it from her if it is."

～

Sabre parked at Tegbold Construction in La Mesa. The small office in front was dwarfed by the warehouse in back. As she walked in, the receptionist welcomed her.

"My name is Sabre Brown, and I'd like to see the manager."

"May I ask what this is regarding?"

"It's about Goldie Forney."

The receptionist left and returned quickly. "KC will see you now."

She led Sabre down a short hallway to a sparsely decorated office. A woman about five-eight with jet-black hair stood and walked over to offer her hand. "I'm KC Loring. Have a seat." Her piercing green eyes were friendly, but businesslike. She wore a red t-shirt with the Tegbold logo, jeans, and L.L. Bean work boots. "Please excuse the way I'm dressed, but I'm going out on a job today. I try to wear office clothes when I can, but sometimes I have to get dirty."

"No problem. I envy you. I get tired of wearing suits all the time. I dress down every chance I get." She took a seat. "I'm Sabre Brown, by the way."

"Goldie's favorite niece," KC said with a sincere smile. "I've heard a great deal about you."

"You have an advantage over me. I knew nothing about you or this company until a few days ago."

"Goldie said I would meet you someday." Her friendly smile suddenly faded. "But that means something has happened to Goldie, hasn't it?"

"I'm afraid so," Sabre said. "She passed away just over a week ago." Sabre handed KC a document.

"What's this?"

"It's a copy of the trust, the section showing I'm Goldie's trustee."

"She told me you would be. I'm going to miss her. She was one of the most fascinating women I've ever met. She had an incredible head for business and a frustrating personal life." KC walked to the window and looked out where trucks were loading. Then she took a seat behind her desk. "The only time Goldie felt adequate was when she was conducting a business transaction. She felt like a complete failure as a mother, but I don't think she was nearly as bad as she thought." She paused for a second and then added. "You're probably wondering how I know such personal things about Goldie. She didn't generally tell much about her life, and she seldom drank, but occasionally, we would share a bottle of wine and she would open up. I think she trusted me because she knew I kept her business secrets, and we had different social circles."

"Do you know her kids?"

"Just Travis, and he's not so bad. He was an eighteen-year-old punk when he started working here, but he's grown into a halfway decent man. He's still a big flirt and a little egotistical, but he's become a good worker with a decent head for business. Not as sharp as his mother, but decent. And most of the guys respect him. A couple of older guys have trouble taking orders from a twenty-eight-year-old, but they're like that with me too."

"Travis is more than just a laborer?"

"He's worked his way up to foreman on his crew, and the last two years he filled in for me when I took a vacation. And he did a good job. He'll eventually be able to fill my shoes."

"How long have you worked for Aunt Goldie?"

"We celebrated my twentieth anniversary two months ago. Goldie came by after work with a bottle of wine, and we had a celebratory drink. That woman really knew her wines. I don't think she drank much, but I got the feeling she was a collector of fine wines."

And coasters, kachina dolls, and a lot of other stuff, Sabre thought. "You must've been pretty young when you started working here."

"I was twenty-three. I grew up in Connecticut, working in my father's construction company. I went to college, got my degree in business, and went back to work for my father. But I didn't like the role of boss' daughter, so I moved to California and got my contractor's license. I heard from friends that this woman was looking for someone to help out with a couple of rentals. I thought it would be good part-time work until I got something better." KC suddenly chuckled. "I'll never forget the interview I had with Goldie."

"What was it like?"

"She asked me a few questions about construction that only someone with experience would know. After I answered those to her satisfaction, she said, 'Imagine this scenario. You're in charge of my building full of expensive materials and equipment. You and another employee are in the building. It catches fire, and the other employee is pinned down. You have just enough time to save the building or your co-worker, and you have to choose. What do you do?' Then she sat quietly waiting. I thought that if she was ruthless, she might expect me to save the building. I really needed the job, so I wanted to get the answer right."

"What did you say?"

"I decided to go with the truth. I said, 'I'd get the worker out of the building, call the fire department, and pray like hell that you had insurance.' Goldie started to laugh, then said, 'You're hired.' That was the beginning of our relationship."

Sabre smiled. She was seeing a side of Goldie she'd never known "How big was the company then?"

"She only had two rentals. I started out painting, fixing plumbing, and laying tile. Then we remodeled one of the houses. The plan was to sell it, but she decided to rent it again. Then she bought another to remodel and flip, but the same thing happened. She decided to rent it as well. She seemed to have trouble letting things go."

You have no idea. Sabre smiled again. "When did she form the Tegbold Corporation?"

"Ten years ago, just before Travis came to work for us. I think she had hopes that someday Travis and Langston would run the business, but Langston never had any interest. Of course, neither knew she owned it. I was supposed to be the only one who knew the owner. I had a man working for me who figured it out and told his family. When Goldie found out, she insisted that I let him go. She was big on loyalty and didn't tolerate anything less. Since then, no one else has been told." KC gave a wry smile. "She named the business Tegbold because it's Blodgett spelled backward."

Sabre wrinkled her brow. "But it isn't."

"You're right. The original papers mixed up the *B* and *D* and left off the second *T,* and Goldie decided to leave it. She said it sounded better anyway."

"Aunt Goldie was an interesting woman," Sabre said. "Are the rental houses part of Tegbold?"

"After the sixth house, we added a property management division. I ran that too, but I hired someone to do the books. Shortly after, Goldie formed Yenrof—Forney spelled backward—and put all the houses and property management into that corporation. So, Tegbold doesn't own them, but we do all the maintenance and remodeling for them."

"How many houses are in Yenrof?"

"Ten, I believe."

"If they were sold, would Tegbold survive?"

"Absolutely. We have twenty-two employees, and we do more outside work than we do for Yenrof. Actually, it would be a blessing."

"And you wouldn't have to cut back any employees?" Sabre was thinking of the trust instructions to move Yenrof into the charity.

"No, we'd just have to cut back on some overtime."

"And you'll continue working here?"

"Hold on." KC stood and retrieved a document from a safe. She handed it to Sabre. "Here's the agreement Goldie and I signed. She had it drawn up by an attorney, so it's all legal."

"What's the gist?" Sabre asked, glancing at it.

"I agreed to stay on as manager and president of the corporation, in full control of decision-making, for up to ten years after Goldie's death. I choose when I leave and with a nice retirement package. There are a few contingencies about physical and mental health, profit margins, and such, but I've always been able to meet those."

"Do you have any idea what the value of Tegbold is?"

"Goldie and I recently came up with a number around two million."

CHAPTER 38

Wednesday Afternoon

Reeling from what she'd learned about Goldie's assets, Sabre called JP the minute she got back in her car.

"Tegbold Corporation is worth about two million. And Yenrof Corp owns ten houses. If we estimate each house at five-hundred thousand, that's another five million. And that's conservative because it's almost impossible to find a house in San Diego for half a million. But she probably has mortgages, so our estimate likely balances out."

"You're up to seven million?"

"And that's not counting her residence and the other rental we got the mortgage bill for. That was in her name, not the corporate name. And there may be others like that. Then there's the charitable foundation. I have no idea about the value of that. Plus, who knows what else."

"Do you think any of her kids know what she was worth?"

JP asked. "Because I sure didn't get that vibe from any of them. Only Travis seemed to know about the construction company, but I doubt he understands the value. And Langston may have some suspicions. I don't trust that guy."

"I'm just flabbergasted. How does a woman live like Goldie did, be a multimillionaire, and no one knew it?"

Sabre sat with Dale under the magnolia tree. They talked about school, and she learned he was struggling, but Fayth and his Aunt Olivia were helping him when he needed it. He was glad to be back with his old friends, and he liked living with his father.

"I hear you started counseling," Sabre said. "Do you like your therapist?"

"He's pretty cool. He has lots of animals in his office."

"What kind?"

"A snake, a turtle, a rabbit, and a parrot."

"Wow. That's impressive."

"And he lets me hold one for part of the session. But not the parrot. He'll sit on my shoulder, but I can't hold him."

Just then, Ivory ran up with Olivia behind her. "I'm so sorry." Olivia picked up the little girl and hurried off.

"Dale, have you ever blacked out?"

"I'm not sure what you mean."

"Have you been in a situation where you can't remember something that happened? Or suddenly, it's later in the day, and you feel like you missed a section of time?"

"No."

"A few months back, did you have a bike accident?"

"Yes."

"Do you remember how it happened?"

Dale sighed. "I rode my bike to the park, and I was doing tricks. I wasn't supposed to ride that far, and I wasn't supposed to be on the ramps."

"Did you tell your mother you didn't remember how you got hurt?"

He looked down at his feet. "Yeah. I didn't want to get in trouble for going there."

"Are there any other times recently when you told your mother you couldn't remember something? Either because you didn't want to get in trouble, or you blacked out?"

"No. Just that time with the bike, and I didn't blackout. I lied."

"Do you remember a few weeks ago when your mom made popcorn and you all watched a Disney movie?" When Dale wrinkled his brow, Sabre asked, "What's wrong?"

"Mom never makes us popcorn, and she hasn't watched a movie with us since Kenny came around."

Sabre wondered if Dale actually *had* blacked out, or if his mother made the incident up. Or maybe she'd embellished a minor thing to make herself sound like a better mother. But one of them was lying.

When they finished talking, Dale went to get Fayth, who came out wearing her bathing suit.

"Are you going swimming?"

"As soon as you leave, I can go in the pool."

She wasn't being snarky, just stating the truth. Sabre appreciated this girl's candor. Sabre smiled. "I just have a few questions." She knew how protective Fayth could be, but she also had to get to the point. "Have you ever known Dale to have blackouts?"

The girl gave it some thought. "No." But she looked stressed.

Sabre touched her hand. "What are you not telling me?"

"It's nothing."

Sabre was silent, waiting her out.

Finally, Fayth blurted, "Dale loved Perry. He'd never hurt him."

"I didn't say he did. I just asked if Dale ever had a black-out. Did he ever seem disoriented or like he didn't remember something?"

"He forgets things sometimes, but we all do." She looked Sabre directly in the eyes. "Can I go swimming now?"

"Just a few more questions," Sabre said. "Did you watch movies with the other kids at your mother's?"

"Yeah. Every Thursday was Disney night, and we took turns picking the movie. Perry always wanted to watch *Happy Feet*." She made a face.

"Did your mom watch them with you?"

"Only when we all lived here. Dad would make popcorn, and we'd all sit down together. We always picked something that didn't scare the little ones, so it kind of ended up becoming Disney night."

"Did you carry on the tradition with your mom and Kenny?"

"Not with them." She sighed, sadness in her eyes. "I would make popcorn, and us kids would watch, but it wasn't the same. Mom was too busy with Kenny." Fayth brightened a little. "We still do it here with Dad though on Saturday nights."

"Sounds fun." Sabre had to keep pressing for the truth. "Did your mom watch a movie with you in the last few weeks that you lived there?"

"No." The girl scoffed. "Mom didn't have time to do

anything with us. She was always with Kenny. Kenny needs this. Kenny needs that."

Sabre decided it was time to stop. "Are you ready to go swimming?"

Fayth didn't jump up as Sabre had expected. Instead, she took a deep breath and blurted, "I remember who was in the bathroom the night Perry died."

"Who?"

"Mom. I remember peeking through the door and seeing her as she went in. That's when I got in bed. I was going to wait until she came out, then take Perry to the bathroom."

"But you fell asleep?"

"Then I woke up and saw Harmony walk out the bedroom door. I was just so tired, I couldn't make myself get up. Do you think maybe she saw something?"

"Do *you*?" Sabre asked.

"I dunno. She won't hardly talk anymore. And she won't talk about Perry at all. It's like Harmony doesn't want to remember him. How could she do that?"

CHAPTER 39

Wednesday Evening

Sabre had so much preparation to do for hearings that she didn't get back to Aunt Goldie's documents until nearly nine o'clock. JP shut down his computer and joined her at the dining table, where several piles of paperwork awaited her perusal. But the trust came first. Sabre picked it up and turned to Appendix F. She read through it, then summarized it for JP.

"She listed two rental properties; one we already knew about. The other is a house in La Jolla. The zip code alone means it's probably worth close to a million. Of course, we don't know how much equity she has in it."

"What's in Appendix G?"

"It's all about Tegbold. The company is held in trust for Travis, but he must continue to work there. KC remains in control with the same contract she has now, and it apparently includes a profit share of twenty percent. Goldie got the remaining eighty percent, which will now go to Travis."

"That explains why she didn't include him in the division of her personal real estate."

"Exactly. This company is very profitable, so he'll have cash available right away."

"And the profit share stays that way indefinitely?" JP asked.

"No." Sabre read the conditions.

1. *KC Loring is to remain as manager and run the company as sole decision-maker until her death, or she chooses to retire, or ten years after my death, whichever occurs first.*
2. *Upon KC Loring's retirement, she will receive, in addition to her 401K, profit-share of 20% for five years or until her death, whichever comes first.*
3. *Upon KC Loring leaving the company for whatever reason, Travis Blodgett will become the trustee, at which time he can dissolve the trust, and Tegbold Corporation will be his in its entirety.*
4. *In the event Travis is no longer living at my death, Tegbold Construction shall be held in trust, and profits distributed to my remaining living children, with the same conditions set out above.*

"What kind of profit are they making now?"

"According to KC, about two-hundred grand annually, but she says it'll be even better once they transfer Yenrof. She claims the landscaping division is a drag on Tegbold, and they only kept it because of Yenrof. I have an appointment next week with the accountant so I can get specifics. I need every-thing for a full accounting of the trust."

"Travis is making out pretty well. Why do you think she favored him?"

"Really?" Sabre gave him a look. "Maybe because he's the only tolerable one of the bunch? And you said yourself that he actually spent time with her." Sabre read Appendix H, then said, "Maybe he didn't do any better than the others. Goldie has a few more assets."

"Like what?"

"Dragon Incorporated."

"What does that spell backward?"

"Oh my God. You're right. It's Nogard, the girls' last name."

"I was kidding, but I'm not surprised. Your aunt was queer as a football bat." JP paused. "Wait a minute. Dragon is the name of the bar where Micki and Rocki work. Do you suppose Goldie set it up for them like she did for Travis?"

"Let me see." Sabre read further, then summarized it out loud. "Yep. Micki is set to manage the Dragon Bar in La Jolla, and Rocki will be in charge of the one in San Diego. And Goldie wants Langston to run Dragon Incorporated, but she set it up so they have to work together and show certain profits for any of them to get anything."

"Obviously, she was determined to provide for those kids." JP shook his head. "But why wouldn't she do more before she died? She had so much money, and yet she lived like they were poor."

"I don't know. She was obviously a sick woman. She couldn't throw anything away and lived in squalor, eating junk food—all while building multimillion-dollar companies. And Goldie was so lonely. I just don't get it."

CHAPTER 40

Thursday Morning

Sabre spotted Travis sitting in front of Department One and walked over. "Hello, Travis."

He looked up from the report he was reading. "Hi." His eyes narrowed. "I don't mean to be rude, but why are you here?"

"This is where the majority of my cases are."

"Sorry, I didn't realize that. I guess you know how this all works then?"

"I do."

"What happens now?"

She wanted to ask him what he knew but resisted. "Has an attorney talked to you yet?"

"Just the social worker. She came to my house and said I have a twelve-year-old daughter I know nothing about. She mentioned asking the court for a paternity test. How do I do that?"

"You'll be appointed an attorney who will explain the process to you, but I'll tell you this much." Sabre sat next to him. "In court this morning, the judge will order a paternity test if you ask for one. Actually, this judge will probably order one whether or not you ask for it. Then she'll set the hearing over until she gets the results. In the meantime, Social Services will look for relatives to take Dené, so she doesn't have to be put in foster care. From what I understand, the mother had no family at all. So, if you're the father, they'll look to you or your family."

"I wouldn't wish that on any kid. Can I stop them from putting her with my family?"

"Maybe. But nothing will happen until they determine if you're her father. Let me find out who will be appointed to represent you, then he or she can explain it. I would explain further, but since I'm handling your mother's estate, I have a potential conflict."

"Thank you."

Sabre hurried to the attorneys' lounge. She checked the detention list and saw that Russell Miller was on with the public defender and would be Travis' attorney. She tracked Russ down near Department One and explained the situation.

"The alleged father is waiting to talk to you," Sabre said.

"Let's go."

They walked to where Travis waited at the other end of the courthouse, and Sabre introduced the men.

"You're in good hands," Sabre said. A few minutes later, she found Wagner, Dené's attorney.

"Hey, Sabre, just who I wanted to see." Wags held up a file. "I got the documents stating that Goldie Forney was

Dené's legal guardian. I think you should attend the hearing and see what the judge wants to do with it."

"I'm not sure Travis would want me there," Sabre said.

"I don't care. He's still the *alleged* father. He has no real standing yet, and I want you there on behalf of the minor."

Judge Hekman called the hearing, then both County Counsel Linda Farris and Russell Miller introduced themselves. Wagner stood. "Richard Wagner for the minor, Dené Dumas, who is not present in court." He looked at Sabre, who sat in the back. Wagner continued, "Attorney Sabre Brown is here as well, Your Honor. I'll let her explain her connection to the case."

Sabre stood. "Your Honor, I'm the cousin of the alleged father, Travis Blodgett. I'm also the trustee of his mother's trust and executor of her estate. His mother's name is Goldie Forney." Sabre spoke slowly, knowing how complex it sounded. "Dené's mother, Tanya Dumas, left a guardianship naming Goldie Forney as guardian for Dené. Unfortunately, Goldie passed away just a few days after Tanya. I'm not sure what the court wants or needs to do with this information, but I thought it prudent that you be made aware."

"I'm not sure either, Counselor," Judge Hekman said. "But thank you."

After a moment, Russ Miller stood. "My client is requesting a paternity test, Your Honor."

"Granted," the judge said. "Where is Dené now?"

"She's in Polinsky," County Counsel said.

The judge turned to Travis. "Do you have any siblings or other relatives who might be an appropriate place to detain this child?"

"No," Travis said quickly.

"Does that mean you don't have any, or they wouldn't be appropriate or available for placement?"

"I have four siblings, none of which would be a good placement, Your Honor."

"Do you have a relationship with this child?"

"No, Your Honor."

"Ms. Brown, are there any paternal relatives you would recommend?"

"Not at this time, Your Honor. From what I know, I'd have to agree with Travis."

"Very well," Judge Hekman said. "I'm ordering an expedited paternity test. This little girl has had enough loss, and she needs love and structure back in her life as soon as possible. We'll hold off on any relative evaluations until we know whether Mr. Blodgett is the father. I'm setting the jurisdiction hearing over for two weeks." Hekman took a breath. "If the paternity test comes in sooner, I expect the minor's attorney to put it on calendar immediately. All other orders remain in full force and effect. This hearing's adjourned."

After they all left the courtroom, Travis approached Sabre. "My mother knew about Dené?" he asked.

"She did," Sabre said, noticing his distress. "But apparently Goldie didn't share that information with you."

"Do you know how long she knew?"

"Probably from the start. I'm not sure that she knew where she was or if she had any contact with her, but Goldie was aware that Dené existed and knew her name. A few months ago, they must have connected, because that's when Tanya had guardianship papers drafted. That's about all I know."

Travis wasn't his normal, cheerful self, but he remained

polite. "Thank you for not asking for home evaluations on my siblings."

"I did what I thought was best for Dené."

"Either way, I'm grateful. None of them would make good parents. I just feel so overwhelmed. If I am the father, I know I should consider raising her, but I feel so unprepared. I guess I shouldn't be judging my siblings." He sighed. "I'm no prize either."

"You don't have to make that decision yet. You have time to let it sink in while you wait for the test results."

"Thank you. By the way, Chase would like to have Dually."

"Do you think he can parent a dog?"

"I don't know. He could sure use the company, and I'd see that he has food for him."

"I'll see about getting him to Chase."

"I'd take Dually to him, but I can't have him in the car that long. And it would take weeks to get rid of his hair."

Sabre finished her cases and walked out of juvenile court. Outside, she called JP and told him that Chase wanted Dually.

"Can he take care of him?"

"We'll see. Can you find the time to take the dog over? If the situation looks too bad, don't leave him."

Sabre hung up. A moment later, Bob joined her and asked, "Want to have lunch?"

"Thanks, but I'll just stop at a drive-through because I don't have a lot of time. I have an appointment at one with my Aunt Goldie's accountant."

"It's hard to believe she's worth millions. I wonder what else she owned that you're not aware of."

"I should have a better idea after this meeting." Sabre had a nagging worry she couldn't let go of. "Goldie left a big chunk to her 'granddaughter, Dené.' What happens if the paternity test proves Travis isn't the father? What do I do then?"

"If you don't give her the money, I would expect Wags to hire someone on Dené's behalf to contest the trust," Bob said. "And you know the other heirs will fight to keep it all."

"This could be an even bigger nightmare than I imagined."

"Yup." Bob's cell phone rang. "Excuse me," he said, then took the call.

Sabre stepped away, allowing him some privacy.

A minute later, she heard him say, "She's right here. I'll tell her." Bob hung up and turned to her.

"Tell me what?"

"That was Adam McCluskey. Dale has been arrested for Perry's murder."

CHAPTER 41

Thursday Afternoon

Sabre walked over to Juvenile Hall and attempted to see Dale, but they were still processing him. She checked the time and realized she was running late, so she drove to her appointment with Goldie's accountant.

The first thing she noticed were the dozens of Legos figures around his office. The accountant smiled and said, "I'm a bit of a Legos enthusiast. I've always been drawn to solving puzzles. I guess that's why I chose accounting. Legos require an added dimension of creativity and physical aptitude. I've been building them since I was a kid, and these are some of my favorites."

Sabre walked around, getting a closer look. "Very impressive."

"They keep me from going mad."

"I understand. I'm a runner, and sometimes it's the only

thing that keeps me sane." She turned back to him. "Sabre Brown."

He stretched out his hand. "I'm Ward Bond." He stood about five-ten, and she guessed him to be in his early fifties, even though his thick, white, wavy hair made him look older. He had a slight paunch that showed through his oxford shirt and blue jeans. "That's my favorite." He pointed to a wagon train.

"It's beautiful."

"But you're too young to appreciate the joke." He smiled.

Sabre didn't know what he was talking about, and it must have shown on her face.

"There was an old western on television in the late fifties and early sixties," Ward explained. "My mother was a big fan, and she named me after the wagon master, an actor named Ward Bond."

Sabre smiled politely, as she took a seat. She explained who she was and that her aunt had died.

The accountant rubbed his mustache. "I'm sorry to hear that. Goldie Forney was one of a kind."

"I'm learning that more every day." She gave Ward a copy of the document showing she was the trustee. "I've recently discovered that Goldie owned several companies. I know you do the accounting for Tegbold, but do you handle her other companies as well?"

"I have other clients, but your aunt has kept me busy over the last ten years." His bright-blue eyes smiled when he spoke, making Sabre feel very comfortable. Ward went on to summarize his responsibilities. "Tegbold has a subsidiary corporation called Yenrof, and I also handle Dragon Incorporated. I not only do the accounting for all of them, a staff member here handles the bookkeeping. I did not handle any of Goldie's personal accounting, nor do I know if she has other companies. She employed a woman named Corina Christiansen, who took care of her personal finances, so she would know the full extent of Goldie's ownership."

"Were you with her from the start of the businesses?"

"I was for Tegbold and Yenrof, but Dragon was already in existence when we met." A reflective look came into his eyes. "The interview with your aunt was fascinating. After she quizzed me about my accounting background, she asked a very strange question."

"Was it about a fire?"

"No." He chuckled. "But it was equally puzzling. She looked me straight in the eye and said, 'Be truthful now.' She paused, and I had no idea what was coming. Then Goldie asked, 'Mayonnaise or Miracle Whip?' I almost laughed, then said honestly, 'Mayonnaise, of course.' She hired me on the spot."

"So, you gave the right answer," Sabre said. "I wonder what she would've done if you preferred Miracle Whip."

"That's what I wondered at the time, but over the years as I got to know Goldie, I realized she was just yanking my chain. I'm quite certain she had already decided to hire me." His face lit up at the thought of her. "But I'm sorry, I digress. What else would you like to know?"

"I'd like to know an estimated value of the companies and have access to the financial reports."

"Your aunt was an incredible businesswoman. Even though she was very tuned in to what was going on, she hired good people and stayed out of their way. She required three things of her employees: loyalty, honesty, and efficiency." He clicked a few buttons on his computer keyboard. "I can give you a quick overview, then I'll put together a portfolio for each company so you'll have it for the job you need to do."

"Perfect."

"Dragon makes an annual profit of around a half-million, but it also owns the real estate that both bars sit on. Off-hand, I would say conservatively the value is around five and a half million, maybe six."

"I had no idea Aunt Goldie was that wealthy. She always seemed to be struggling."

Ward stroked his mustache as he talked. "Tegbold was initially created to service the Yenrof properties, but between Goldie and her manager, KC Loring, they had it making a profit by the second year. They expanded until it was a great business on its own." He clicked another button. "Tegbold shows an annual profit of approximately two-hundred thousand. With equipment, other assets, and the real estate, it's worth close to three million."

"That's counting Yenrof?"

"No." He smiled. "Goldie added a new house to Yenrof every year, and a hundred thousand of Tegbold's annual profit went to pay down the mortgages. All the rent money went back into Yenrof to pay the mortgages as well. She never took anything out of Tegbold." Ward looked around his monitor at Sabre. "About six years ago, Goldie also bought a small shopping mall in Pacific Beach. Its three retail spaces have remained rented to a donut shop, a law office, and a used bookstore. Yenrof's value is about sixteen million, less the mortgages."

"How much does she owe?"

"About nine million."

"Leaving seven million in equity."

"Yes, but if you sell the properties, you'll have to account for a huge tax bill. She never planned to sell anything though. She talked about donating Yenrof to a charitable foundation, which I think she started herself."

"Silent Thunder Charity?"

"I don't know, but her personal accountant could fill you in."

Sabre felt overwhelmed. "In short, the companies you do the accounting for are worth about fifteen and a half million."

"Conservatively."

"You'd never know that by the way she lived."

"I know." Ward swallowed and looked out the window. "I had to take Goldie some papers a few years back. She was sick and couldn't leave her house. The condition was shocking. She swore me to secrecy, but she knew me well enough to know I'd never tell anyone."

"She must have really trusted you."

He chuckled. "That didn't stop her from having outside audits of the businesses every two years. She was nothing if not shrewd."

CHAPTER 42

Thursday Afternoon

An attendant brought Dale to the interview cubicle where Sabre waited. He looked so young and vulnerable—a skinny, little kid with no street smarts. *Fayth would survive in juvenile hall better than Dale would*, Sabre thought. She had to figure out what had happened and move this detainment along quickly if possible. Based on the time she'd spent with Dale, she believed that if he had killed Perry, it was an accident.

"I don't like it here," Dale said first thing, as he sat down across from her, a plastic window between them. The tiny room felt like a confessional. Sabre made a mental note to request a different location next time. She'd been able to get face-to-face interviews with clients in the past.

"I know this place is terrible for you," she said with empathy. "And I'll do everything I can to get you home as soon as possible. But to do that, I have to ask some very specific questions. And I need you to be completely honest with me. But first, tell me exactly what you said to Detective DuBois, or anyone else who interrogated you."

"Not much. That detective asked me several times if I hurt or killed Perry, and I just kept telling him I didn't." Dale looked scared, but he made eye contact. A good sign. "He asked me about the fight Perry and I had the night before, and I told him what happened."

"What fight?"

"It was more of an argument, really. Mom had bought chicken from KFC. I got the drumstick, but Perry grabbed it off my plate and took a big bite. It made me mad, so I yelled at him. That's it." He paused, looking upset. "Mom yelled at me to stop and didn't say anything to Perry. That made me mad too. Fayth gave me her drumstick, but I was still upset with Mom. She always spoiled Perry." He drummed nervously on the window between them.

"That's what you told the detective?"

"Yes."

"This is the first I heard about the fight. How did Detective DuBois know?"

"He said Mom told him." Dale lowered his eyes, seeming troubled. "I felt really bad the next day when Perry got in trouble and had to stay in his room. But I had already said I was sorry."

"What did Perry say?"

"He didn't care, cuz it wasn't a big deal. But I sure wished I had a drumstick to give him when he was being punished." Dale started tapping the glass again.

"I know you've told me before, but I need you to tell me again about the night Perry died. And don't leave anything out."

His shoulders slumped. "I hate talking about this. It won't bring him back."

"I know. I'm sorry. But I'm trying to help you."

"Okay." He sighed. "Just before dinner, Mom discovered that Perry had wet the bed the night before. She pulled him into the bedroom, and we heard him crying. When Mom came out, Perry was still crying. Then she sent Kenny in."

"Did you go into the room after that?"

"Not until bedtime."

"Did you talk to Perry?"

"I tried, but he didn't answer. I thought he was asleep."

"And you never talked to him again?"

"No. He was still sleeping when I got up." Dale swallowed. "I thought he was. But later when Mom sent me to get him up, Perry was dead."

Dale's tapping got louder. Sabre smiled and asked him to stop.

"Sorry."

"No problem," Sabre said. "Did you see or hear anyone come into your room that night?"

"No. But I don't wake up very easy. I sleep through alarms and stuff. Fayth always wakes up, but I never do."

"Has Kenny ever hurt any of you kids?"

"He mostly ignores us, and we just stay away from him. Perry was afraid of him though."

"Why is that? Did he ever do anything to Perry?"

"He yelled at him a lot, but I never saw him do anything else."

"And Perry never said anything about it?"

"No, but I think he would've been too afraid to tell if he did."

Sabre tried to think what else she could ask. She needed to

trigger an answer that she could build on. She believed Dale, but she had little to go on that might help him.

Dale finally asked in a soft voice, "Why do they think I killed Perry?"

"Partly because you originally told people it was your fault."

"But I just meant that I should've watched him better, not that I hurt him."

"I know, but as far as we can tell, you were the only one in the room with him."

Dale looked down, and his voice shook. "Do you think I blacked out and hurt Perry?"

"Probably not. And I will do everything I can to find out what really happened. Then I'll work harder than anyone to get you back home."

JP called Chase, but he didn't answer. It was the third time he'd called, with no answer and no return call. JP loaded the dog into his truck and drove to Chase's home in La Mesa. His place was a small shack attached to the back of a bar, located less than five feet from the dumpster.

The stench of stale beer, cigarettes, and rotten food filled the air as JP walked up to the shack's door. Dually tugged on the leash, stopping to sniff everything along the way. JP would've preferred to leave Dually behind until he saw how Chase was living, but he didn't want to leave him alone in the truck.

To JP's surprise, Chase answered the door, but he didn't say anything. A strong smell of marijuana floated past.

After a few seconds of silence, JP introduced himself and added, "I'm the investigator for Sabre Brown."

Chase looked blank.

"The attorney who's handling your mother's estate."

"Oh, yeah, okay, come on in." They were inside the apartment before Chase noticed the dog. "Dually!" He hugged him and scratched behind his ears with both hands. "You brought Dually." The dog licked his face. "Thanks."

JP looked around the tiny L-shaped studio. A small table with two chairs sat in one corner. Next to them was a gas stove with a microwave above it and a small refrigerator. Across from the kitchen area was a door, which JP presumed led to the bathroom. The other side had a narrow bed, an old bike, and a flat screen atop a tall dresser. Nothing hung on the walls, and other than some clothing lying around, there was little else in the room.

"I'm not criticizing," JP said, "but Dually's a pretty big dog. Do you think you have room for him?"

"Sure." Chase nodded. "I can take him for walks, so he gets his exercise."

"Travis said he would help with dog food. I'd take him up on it if I were you. Dually's a big eater."

"I get scraps from the bar too. He'll be well fed." Chase seemed to pull out of his fog. "I'm sorry, have a seat." He led JP to the table in the corner. "Would you like a beer?"

"No thanks," JP said. "Do you have a job?"

"I work at the bar."

"Doing what?"

"I wash dishes, clean tables, take the trash out, that kind of stuff. The owner's a good guy. He pays me a little and lets me live here. It's not bad."

"Chase, I'm really sorry about your mother."

"Me too," he said softly. "She was a good woman."

"Did you know she was storing all that stuff in her house?"

He made a grunting sound. "You don't need to sugarcoat it. She was a hoarder. She had all the extra bedrooms filled before I ever left home."

"When was the last time you were at her house?"

"About a month ago."

"Did she let you in?"

"Yeah, sure. I knew how bad it was, so she didn't have any reason to keep it from me."

"Do you know anything about her finances?"

"Not really." He shrugged. "I know she had plenty of money."

"What do you mean by *plenty*?"

"She didn't have to live the way she did. She was always giving stuff to people. Helping others out. She gave me cash, twenty or so, every time I saw her. Sometimes, I didn't want to go because I didn't want her to think I just wanted the money." He paused. "Who the hell am I kidding? Most of the time, that's exactly why I went. I wasn't a very good son." His eyes filled with tears. "I miss her though. I never realized just how much I would."

"Again, I'm sorry for your loss." JP stood, not totally comfortable leaving Dually. He and the kids were already attached to the dog. But Chase needed him more. JP just hoped it was the right decision for Dually.

After her meeting with Dale, Sabre walked back to court through the tunnel. As soon as she stepped into the courthouse, her phone beeped. Bob had left a message that just said: *Call*

me. She hurried through the lobby and toward her car, calling Bob on the way.

"Fayth and Harmony didn't come home from school," Bob said, cutting right to the point.

"No word from them?"

"Not yet. Their father is in a panic. I'm on my way out there now to help look for them. They should've been home two hours ago, and they've never done anything like this before."

"Has anyone called the police?"

"They're already on it."

"I'll get JP and join you."

CHAPTER 43

Thursday Afternoon

A s they drove toward the McCluskey home, Sabre received a text from Bob: *Meet us at the school.*

Sabre got directions on her phone, JP turned around, and minutes later, they pulled into the school parking lot. Four police cars sat near the front. As they exited the car, Bob waved and hurried over, followed by Adam McCluskey.

"Do you know anything yet?" Sabre asked.

"Some kid saw Fayth go up to the bus, but she didn't get on." Bob spoke rapidly. "The principal contacted the bus driver who said that Fayth stepped into the bus, looked around, then suddenly took off running. He waited a while, but when she didn't return, he left. Adam told the cops about the pending murder investigation, and Detective DuBois is on his way."

"Look!" JP pointed across the schoolyard.

A policewoman and a young girl were walking toward them. The little girl started to run.

"That's Fayth," Sabre said, relieved.

The girl dashed toward her dad, who was already running to her. Sabre, JP, and Bob hurried to join them.

"Daddy," she sobbed, clinging to her father. Her clothes were disheveled, and her face bruised. Her left arm was scratched and bleeding.

The policewoman said, "She ran toward me calling for help. Then she spotted her dad and took off, so I didn't get a chance to question her."

"I can't find Harmony," Fayth said. "I saw him, but I couldn't stop him."

"Who did you see?" The policewoman asked.

"I don't know," she cried out. "Just a man."

Adam hugged Fayth. "Calm down, sweetheart. We'll find your sister."

Detective DuBois walked up and knelt in front of Fayth. "Do you remember me?"

"Yes."

"Take a deep breath and just tell us what happened today."

The girl breathed in and blew out slowly. "Harmony wasn't here when I came to get on the bus. Then I saw her over there." Fayth pointed toward some trees near the playground. "Someone had her." She choked on her tears.

"Could you see his face?" DuBois asked.

She shook her head. "He was too far away, and he wore a dark ski mask. But I ran after them, and I caught him. I jumped on his back and started hitting him. He held onto Harmony and tried to shake me off, but I wouldn't let go." She glared at DuBois and sobbed. "You gotta find her."

"We will. But you need to tell us what happened next, so we know where to look."

"The man backed up real fast and slammed me into the tree. It hurt bad, and I couldn't hold on to him. I fell on the ground, but I saw that he had let go of Harmony. So, I yelled at her to run. That's when he kicked me in the head." Fayth rubbed her bloodied forehead. "I don't know what happened after that. He was just gone, and so was Harmony. I got up and saw the policewoman, and then I saw you, Daddy." She turned to DuBois. "Please go find her. We can't lose Harmony too."

"Put out an APB and call for a helicopter," DuBois said to an officer. Then he looked up at the dark sky. "They need to search before it rains." Then he turned back to Fayth. "Did you ever see his face?"

"No."

"What was he wearing?"

Without hesitating, Fayth said, "A black t-shirt and jeans— and the ski mask."

"Could you see any of his hair?"

"It was all covered."

"How about his eyes?"

She shook her head. "I was on his back, then on the ground."

"Is there anything else you remember?"

She wrinkled her nose. "He smelled like cigarettes."

A crowd was gathering to help with the search. The officer in charge gave people instructions for how to spread out and search in a grid pattern. Other cops were already searching the school and the woods.

Sabre saw Bob, Adam, and Fayth standing off to the side. Sabre scooted over and squeezed Fayth's shoulder. "You were very brave, and you did everything right. We'll find her."

The girl nodded silently.

Sabre led Bob away to speak privately. "Aren't you and Adam going to search?"

"We're waiting for Olivia to pick up Fayth. She refused to stay behind, and Adam doesn't want Fayth with him if they find Harmony... just in case it isn't good."

"Smart."

Sabre thought about the last conversation she'd had with Fayth and decided to share it with DuBois. She approached him, and JP tagged along. "There's something you should probably know," Sabre said.

"Tell me," DuBois said.

"The night Perry died, Fayth says Harmony got up and left their room. Now, Harmony won't talk about Perry at all. I'm wondering if Harmony witnessed something. Or worse, that someone saw Harmony."

"It could have been Dale, you know," DuBois said.

"Dale is eleven and in juvie. It's not likely he sent someone to kidnap his sister."

"Good point," DuBois said. "That leaves Kenny, the mother, the person who was seen in the backyard by the neighbor, or some random perp who found the door open. It doesn't get us any closer."

Sabre, JP, and Bob joined the search party. The police department provided flashlights, and teachers brought sandwiches and sodas for the volunteers. They were separated into groups. Some searched the hills behind the school, while Sabre's team knocked on doors in the neighborhood. At one point, Ron joined the search too.

Eventually, it became too dark to be safe, even with flashlights. But Adam McCluskey wouldn't give up, so Bob stayed out with him and a skeleton crew of officers.

Sabre, JP, and Ron stood in the parking lot, not knowing what to do next. "He must have gotten away with her in a vehicle," JP said. "It's unlikely that Harmony is still in the area."

"Which means she could be anywhere by now." Sabre shuddered.

"Do you want to go home?"

"I don't think I can." Sabre swallowed. "I hate to think about what that poor little girl is going through. If she saw who killed her brother, and now that person has kidnapped her, she must be terrified that he'll kill her too—if he hasn't already. Even if it's some random pervert, she's going through hell."

"I know," JP said, putting his arm around her. "But I'm not sure there's much more we can accomplish here. And I really should check on Conner and Morgan."

"Go ahead. I'll stay here with Ron, and he can bring me home later."

"I'll feed the kids and make sure they've done their homework, then I'll be back."

It began to sprinkle, but Sabre stayed for nearly another hour. By then, the rain was falling hard, and they had no gear. JP showed up with rain ponchos and umbrellas for Bob and Ron, then finally convinced Sabre to go home.

CHAPTER 44

Friday Morning

Sabre got up at six and dressed in jeans, a long-sleeved shirt, and tennis shoes. She wished she was dressing for a good, hard run instead of searching for a missing child. *Maybe tomorrow.*

In the kitchen, JP had already made a thermos of hot tea for her and one with coffee for himself. Neither ate anything.

"You don't have court this morning?" JP asked.

"I only have one case on calendar, and it's a review. Regina Collicott is on the case, and I've already left her a message to submit on the recommendations for me, or if there were any complications, to continue it. I don't expect any problems."

Conner wandered into the kitchen, looking sleepy.

"You and Morgan will have to get your own breakfast this morning," JP said. "We're going back out to look for Harmony."

"No problem." Conner opened the cupboard and grabbed a box of Cheerios. "I could go along and help."

"I appreciate your offer to skip school," JP said dryly, "but not today. Do you mind driving Morgan and yourself to school?"

Conner's eyes widened, and he fought back a smile. "I think I can manage."

"Sabre and I decided you can take her car. If we need it before you get home, we'll stop by the school and pick it up."

"Thanks, Uncle Johnny. And Sabre." This time he couldn't contain the smile as he strutted off.

As they picked up their thermoses to leave, Sabre's cell phone rang. She didn't recognize the number but thought it might be the police. *It better not be one of Goldie's kids,* she thought. "Sabre Brown."

"My name is Gabe Armstrong. I found a little, red-headed girl in my backyard, and she had your business card in her pocket."

Relief washed over Sabre. "Oh my God. Is she okay?" Sabre put the phone on speaker and headed out the door. JP followed.

"She hasn't said anything. My wife and I tried to get her to talk, but she won't or can't respond."

"What is your address?" Sabre climbed into JP's truck.

The man told her but added, "I've called an ambulance. I think she needs to be examined."

"That's good. Do you think I could talk to her?"

"She's weak and very skittish. She flinches if I get close, but she's been better with my wife."

"Have your wife ask her if her name is Harmony."

"Hold on."

While they waited, JP asked, "Where are we going?"

"For now, keep heading toward Lakeside."

A minute later, Gabe came back on the phone. "She nodded when my wife asked if her name was Harmony."

In the background, Sabre heard sirens nearing Gabe's house. "Put your phone on speaker so Harmony can hear me. She might feel better if she hears a familiar voice."

"Okay. I'll give the phone to my wife. Go ahead."

"Harmony, this is Sabre. Can you hear me?"

"Yes." Her weak, little voice was barely audible.

"Sweetie, you are safe now. Those nice people are taking care of you. Soon, you'll get a ride in an ambulance to the hospital. The doctors will make sure you're not hurt. I'll meet you at the hospital. Okay?"

"Okay."

"I'll call your daddy so he can come too."

"Okay."

"Don't be scared. You're safe."

"The ambulance is here," Gabe said. "I'm sure they'll take her to Sharp Grossmont because it's the closest. I'll ask and call you back if I find out differently."

"Thank you, Mr. Armstrong. This little girl went missing yesterday, so her family will be very happy. I'm so glad you found her."

"Actually, my dog found her. He wouldn't let up until I followed him outside to her."

"We're all very grateful to you, your wife, and your dog," Sabre said. "I need to alert the police, so they can stop the search. I'm sure they'll contact you shortly."

"Hold on," he said.

Sabre heard talking and moving around, then he came back on. "My wife says they're taking her to Grossmont. The girl is very afraid of the men, but one paramedic is a woman, and

Harmony is sticking right by her side. The poor girl screamed when she first saw me. I had to call my wife to come out and carry her inside. She wouldn't let me get near her. I hate to think about what she may have endured."

"Me too." Sabre hung up and called Bob, so he could call his client with the good news.

∽

Sabre and JP sat in the ER waiting room, sipping from their thermoses. Ten minutes later, Bob walked in. "How is she?" he asked.

"We don't know much." Sabre stood to stretch. "Harmony has some bruises, and she was wet and cold when they found her. But Mrs. Armstrong got her warmed up before putting her in the ambulance, and Adam is in there with her now."

"Has she said anything about what happened?" Bob looked tired.

Sabre felt it too. They'd all been up late. "I saw her for a few minutes, but she's too weak or too scared to talk. I didn't press her. The cops have to question her, and the poor girl doesn't need any more stress than necessary."

They sat in silence until Adam McCluskey came out of the emergency room.

"How is Harmony?" Sabre asked.

"She's going to be fine. She has bruises on her legs and arms, but the most she would say about them is 'I fell.'" Adam glanced away and hurried through the rest. "No evidence of sexual assault, but she won't let any men touch her other than me. A female detective asked Harmony if the man touched her private parts, and she said, 'No.' She didn't recognize him either. Other than that, she's hardly uttered a word, except to say, 'The doggie kept me warm.'"

Sabre sighed in relief. "What are they doing now?"

"Keeping an eye on her for a few hours. Then she'll go home."

"If it's okay, I'll come by the house tomorrow and see her," Sabre said.

Adam looked at Sabre. "Thank you for finding her." He furrowed his brow. "How *did* you find her?"

"She had my business card on her. I gave it to her the first time we met. Actually, Harmony asked for it. I guess she kept it with her."

CHAPTER 45

Friday Afternoon

"I've been so busy, I almost forgot about these other storage units," Sabre said.

"Me too." JP parked the car near unit fourteen, and they got out. "Last time, we went inside twelve, didn't we?"

"That's right." Sabre glanced at her list. "She also has sixteen, twenty-three, and twenty-five."

JP unlocked the padlock and raised the door. The space was more orderly than the last unit they'd looked at. The front held several ladders, a table covered with paint cans, a lawn mower, and several weed trimmers. Electric cords and various tools, such as rakes, hoes, and a cement mixer took up the space under the table. To the side was a stack of cardboard boxes, all marked.

"Open that box marked *PVC* and see what's in it," Sabre said.

JP pulled the box down and cut the tape. "Yup, it's PVC. I expect the one marked *Hoses* is probably hoses."

"Please check it."

He opened the second box, and it was filled with garden hoses. "There's one marked *Small Yard Tools* and another labeled *Electric Cords*. Do you want me to open them?"

"Not now." Sabre didn't care about yard stuff. "Could you just move them so I can see what's behind?"

JP made room for her to access the center of the unit, where she found a bookshelf. On it sat a briefcase similar to the gold one she'd found in the first storage space. This one was slate blue and considerably more worn.

Sabre clicked it open and glanced at the paperwork. "Wow."

"What now?"

"It has the mortgage for the Tegbold property, the contracts with KC Loring, the articles of incorporation for Tegbold, and several other legal documents."

"Anything for the other corporations?"

"These all pertain to Tegbold, but I bet if we keep looking, we'll find other briefcases."

They spent the next hour moving things around and searching boxes. "I don't think there's any other paperwork in here," Sabre said.

"It all seems to be construction stuff. Want to try another unit?"

They left the door open and moved to the adjacent unit. The content looked much like the last one, with more yard equipment, but it also had two stoves, three washers, a dryer, a dining table, and more boxes, most of which were marked *Dishes* or *Pans*. Blankets and baskets had been tossed onto stacks of junk that needed sorting, much like Goldie's home.

For an hour, JP moved things around, while Sabre searched through boxes. Against the back wall sat a small antique table covered with bedding. JP set the pillows and blankets aside. "Look at this," he said, sounding surprised, as he removed the bubble wrap from around the mahogany drum table exposing a leather top with an intricate design. "It looks really old."

"It's beautiful." Sabre thought it might have value too. "Let's load it. I'm taking the jewelry to get appraised tomorrow, and Bob knows someone who assesses furniture."

"We should probably lock up and get going. It's starting to get dark."

Sabre checked the time on her phone. "And they close in five minutes."

JP pulled the desk from the wall. "Look here." He lifted an aluminum case and handed it to Sabre.

"Oh, good." She opened it and riffled through the paperwork. "This one has all the contracts and mortgages for Yenrof. I'll look at them when we get home."

As JP dragged the table away, Sabre spotted an old wooden box covered with blue-green leather and enhanced with gold leaf. On the lid was a wiseman in meditation, holding a pilgrim's staff and surrounded by writing she didn't recognize. In the corners, monkeys dressed in vendor clothes played musical instruments. Sabre opened the box and found it lined with beautiful blue silk. On the fabric sat a pearl necklace with what looked like emerald stones, along with a note in Goldie's handwriting.

This necklace belonged to my great grandmother, Xaviere Lisette Ganeau, who was French. According to legend, it was given to her by Baron Gaston Legrand when she was sixteen. The piece has been in the family for over 150 years. I want the necklace to go to my granddaughter, Dené, when she graduates from a four-year college or turns twenty-five, whichever comes first.

Sabre pulled out her phone and searched for a recent photo. "This is the necklace Judy Reed claimed was hers."

JP glanced at the image. "So, at some point Judy had to have seen the necklace, even took a picture of it, and decided she wanted it for herself," he said. "I wonder what it's worth."

"I don't think it's costume jewelry, so I bet it's worth thousands," Sabre said. "That would explain Judy's interest in helping with the house. She probably thought she could get her hands on it, and we'd never know."

"I thought she was a friend who helped Goldie out."

"Apparently, they spent time together, and Goldie referred to her as a friend in the trust. Aunt Goldie also left her five percent of the rental properties. Maybe Judy thought Goldie owed her something for everything she'd done for her. Apparently, she didn't know she was getting something in the will. People do strange things when they feel entitled."

CHAPTER 46

Friday Evening

"I'm glad you and Bob could come over. It was such a last-minute invitation," Sabre said. She and Marilee were in the kitchen getting condiments and drinks, while JP and Bob grilled the hamburgers.

"Anytime I don't have to cook is a good day," Marilee said. "Besides, CJ was excited to see Morgan." Just then, the couple's ten-year-old son chased Morgan through the house and out the sliding door.

"I think she missed him too." Sabre laughed. "I really want Bob to have a look at a few things we've found. Do you know much about antiques?"

"I used to have a vintage store, and I can spot them pretty well, but Bob is more of an expert than I am."

They carried everything outside and chatted with the men.

Conner sat with them as well. "Uncle Johnny, can I go to the batting cages after dinner? Aiden will be there."

"Is your homework done?"

"It's Friday, so I have all weekend."

"Sure, you can go."

"One more thing," Conner said sheepishly. "Can you take me? Or if you're busy, I could drive myself. That's if I could use the car."

JP looked at Sabre, and she nodded.

"You can take Sabre's car, but don't go anywhere else. And don't take Aiden anywhere. You know the law about having another teenager in the car."

"Thanks, Uncle Johnny. Thanks, Sabre." He looked at the hamburgers stacked on a plate. "Are these ready?"

"They are."

Conner glanced at her again. "Do you want me to wait and eat with the family?"

"You go ahead," Sabre said.

JP grabbed a paper plate and transferred two burgers. "Eat them and get out of here. And have fun."

When Conner left, Bob asked, "Do you worry about him when he's out?"

"We both do," JP said. "But so far, he has always gone where he says he's going."

"How do you know?"

"Because Sabre has a tracker on his phone." JP nodded toward Bob. "And, Counselor, if you're worried about privacy issues, Conner knows it's there. He's not allowed to turn it off, or he can't take the car the next time."

As they ate their meal, Sabre realized how much she enjoyed the life she and JP had created. She was happy, even though things were crazy with her aunt's estate and her case-load. Tonight was a good break.

"Let's see the items you want me to look at," Bob said.

They went inside. While JP went to get the small table, Sabre showed Bob the blue, heart-shaped paperweight. "Ron thinks this is larimar."

"It looks like it to me." Bob held the stone in his hand, feeling the weight. "If so, it would probably cost about eight hundred."

"For a paperweight?" JP said, coming back in with the table. A moment later, he set it down.

"Wow," Bob and Marilee said at the same time.

"Sweet, isn't it?" Sabre commented.

Bob looked it over carefully. "That's an English drum table. And it's in great shape and looks authentic. I can't be sure of the value, but I'd guess between five and ten thousand dollars."

"For a tiny little table?" JP said.

"It's a *very old*, little table. I'd say early nineteenth centu-ry." Bob turned to Sabre. "What else do you have?"

She showed him several pieces of jewelry, and he esti-mated most at a few hundred dollars. Saving the best for last, Sabre took out the blue box.

"That's beautiful." Bob handled it gently as he examined it. "See the cartouche." He pointed to an area above the wiseman. "That's Sanskrit. It most likely signifies the name of a pharaoh. It's French, probably made in the mid-eighteen-hundreds. I have no idea what the box is worth."

"Wait until you see what's inside," Sabre said.

Bob carefully opened the lid and stared at the necklace. His mouth hung open as he turned it over in his hands. "I think this is really valuable."

"Are the stones emeralds?"

"Better," Bob said. "They look like grandidierite, which is quite rare."

"My aunt left a note saying it had been in the family for a hundred and fifty years."

Bob took a closer look. "Maybe I'm wrong about the stones. Grandidierite wasn't discovered until 1902 in Madagascar."

"Goldie said it was a gift to her grandmother from Baron Gaston Legrand."

Bob and Marilee both laughed.

"What?" Sabre asked.

"Baron Gaston Legrand is an expensive wine," Bob explained. "So, it sounded funny. I suppose the wine was named after a real baron."

"Can you take the necklace to your friend tomorrow and have it appraised?"

"No." Bob laid the necklace back in the box, and pulled back his hands, as if he didn't want to touch it. "One of you can bring it and meet me there. I don't want to be responsible for it. What if those stones are grandidierite? That means it was discovered prior to 1902, which could make this necklace even more valuable."

After some cajoling, Bob acquiesced. "Okay, I'll take the necklace. But if I'm right, this is worth more than anything I've seen so far."

"More than the table?" JP asked.

"Probably ten times more ... at least."

JP shook his head. "That woman had enough money to burn a wet mule."

~

After their friends left, Sabre sat with Morgan, and they told each other about the best part of their day. Then Sabre tucked the girl in, said goodnight, and started to leave.

"Do you think Louie could sleep with me tonight?" Morgan asked.

"I'll bring him in. I'm sure he'll stay for a while."

"Thanks, Sabre. I miss Dually."

"Me too. But Dually is with someone he knows, and that's a good thing." Sabre hoped that was true.

She called Louie, and he jumped on the bed with Morgan. "Goodnight, you two."

Sabre returned to the living room and sat down on the sofa next to JP. He wrapped his arm around her. She snuggled up to him and laid her head against his shoulder, trying to let go of all the chaos.

"This is nice," Sabre said. "It's been a rough few weeks."

"I know."

Sabre stayed there for about two minutes. But her brain wouldn't shut down. Abruptly, she sat up straight. "My aunt sure had a lot of money, and those kids had to know, or at least suspect it. What if one of them *did* try to poison her?"

JP's expression was grim. "I think it's a real possibility. But we have no evidence to support it. The poison in her system could easily have come from food, and considering the way she lived, that's very likely. And your aunt's notes about someone trying to kill her aren't enough to go to the police with."

"I know." Sabre sighed. "I just hate the thought that someone killed her, then benefited from her death. Is there anything we can do?"

"I'm meeting DuBois for coffee in the morning. I'll run it

past him. Maybe he can suggest some things we should be looking for."

CHAPTER 47

Saturday Morning

"So, McCloud, what can I do for you?" Vinny asked, as they sat drinking coffee at a local coffee shop near the police station.

"Have you made any progress on the Perry McCluskey case?" JP focused on the priority case first.

"Nothing substantial. I can't help thinking Harmony witnessed something, and the perpetrator was trying to shut her up. Otherwise, it's just random chance that she was kidnapped, and I'm not much for coincidence, as you know."

"I keep thinking the same thing. Did Harmony say anything when she was questioned?"

"She won't talk about what happened. The girl denies seeing the guy's face, but that's the most we got out of her." Vinny sighed. "I don't know if that's the truth or if she's just too scared to say anything."

They sipped their coffee in silence for a moment, while JP figured out how to bring up the new subject.

"You have that dumb, I-have-another-question look on your face," Vinny said. "What is it?"

JP explained the whole story, keeping the background brief, then focused on the strange notes Goldie had left and the botulinum toxin found in her blood.

"Was that the cause of death?"

"It's listed as a heart attack. She had some symptoms of food poisoning, so the ME ran some tests."

"But he didn't think the botulism killed her?"

"No, he said it was insignificant."

"But you think, because of her hefty estate, one of her kids poisoned her?"

"It's a possibility. They all act like they don't know her net worth. And in all fairness, she did keep as much from them as she could. She didn't want any of them involved in distributing her estate; she even drew up fake wills to throw them off. And then there's this." JP showed him the first photo of the area around Goldie's chair. "See that envelope that says *My Trust* on it?"

"Yeah."

JP showed him the second photo. "See this one? We took it a couple days later."

"The envelope's not there."

"None of us were in the house between those photos."

Vinny studied the images and scowled. "There's also a fast-food wrapper missing. Did someone take it too?"

"It had to be the same person who took the envelope."

Vinny shook his head. "If we had the leftover food or the packaging, we could test it for poison, but what you have isn't enough. But you already knew that." He downed the rest of his coffee. "Here's what you do. Keep your eye out for other evidence. It sounds like Goldie was a clever woman. Maybe she left clues or evidence of past behavior by one of her kids that might be incriminating. It's possible she's had previous attempts on her life. Otherwise, all I can say is that you and Sabre need to be careful."

Sabre met Ron at Goldie's house to help him sort. He'd been there all week while she had court, and he'd made enough room to open the front door all the way and had stacked bins against one wall. Sabre couldn't believe they were still working in the living room. She'd really underestimated the project.

"Another kachina doll," Ron said, lifting it up for her to see.

"How many does that make?"

"Twenty-three. But that's nothing compared to the one hundred and sixteen heart-shaped rocks."

Sabre saw movement at the front door and spun toward it.

A disheveled Dually trotted toward her, panting. "What are *you* doing here?" Sabre asked in a soft, sweet voice. She scratched his ears, feeling his dirty, tangled fur.

"He looks exhausted," Ron said. "I'll get him some water." He returned with a bowl full that Dually eagerly lapped up.

"Is there any dog food here?" Sabre asked.

"I'll get it. I know exactly where it is."

Sabre petted the dog until Ron came back with the food, and Dually quickly switched bowls.

"What do you suppose happened?" she mused.

"Why don't you call JP and see if he knows."

"He should be here any minute." Sabre looked out at the street. "There he is now."

Seconds later, JP walked in. "What's Dually doing here?"

"We were hoping you would know," Sabre said.

"I took him to Chase two days ago. Did Chase bring him back here?"

"If so, he didn't stop to let us know. Dually just wandered in."

"Is he okay?" JP's face was tight with anger.

"He's hungry, thirsty, and tired," Sabre said. "But other than that, he seems all right."

JP turned around and stepped outside.

"Where are you going?" Sabre called after him.

"To see Chase. I want to know what the hell happened."

Sabre followed him as he headed to his truck. "What's the point? Chase either dropped him off because he didn't want the dog, or he didn't watch him, and Dually got away. I assume you don't plan to take him back there?"

"No." JP stopped on the sidewalk. "I should've never left him there in the first place. My gut told me not to, but I felt sorry for the guy."

"Then let it go. We'll find a good home for the dog."

They walked back toward the house just as a white SUV pulled up to the curb. "Who's that?" JP asked.

Sabre hurried inside. "That's Goldie's friend, Judy Reed. I don't want to talk to her."

Ron came out from behind a wall of junk. "Hi, JP."

"Judy Reed is back," Sabre said, rushing her words. "Please go intercept her and get rid of her. I don't feel like talking to that woman."

"Will do."

"And, Ron, don't tell her anything about the necklace."

"What about it?"

Sabre realized he didn't have the latest news. "Just tell her you haven't found it."

"Did you find it?"

"Just go."

Sabre stood near the door and watched Ron interact with Judy. She tried to inch her way forward, but Ron held his ground. Sabre saw Ron put his hand on Judy's shoulder and guide her back to her car. The woman was relentless.

Ron quickly came back in. "She offered to help again and asked about the necklace, of course. Did you find it?"

"We did, but it isn't hers. Goldie left a note saying it was a family heirloom that belonged to her grandmother. Bob took it to an appraiser this morning. He should be here shortly to tell us what it's worth."

CHAPTER 48

Saturday Afternoon

Sabre heard someone coming up the front path. Hoping it wasn't Judy again, she turned and saw Bob come through the front door carrying the drum table and the jewelry box. He set the table down and handed the box to Sabre like it was a hot potato.

JP stepped over from his sorting project and stared at Bob. "You look as frazzled as a cow's hide under a branding iron."

"I am." Bob shook his head. "If you find anything else of value, you're taking it yourself. I'm not doing this again."

"What happened? Did you lose something?" Sabre was suddenly worried.

Bob gave her a look. "Do you have any idea what these things are worth?"

"No. That's why we sent you," JP said.

Bob took a breath. "The table is a mere sixty-five hundred,

give or take. The box is from the Napoleon III era, circa 1860, and is worth about ten grand."

"Just for the box?" JP looked stunned.

Bob nodded, smiling.

"What about the necklace?" Sabre asked.

"Apparently, there's a legend about Baron Gaston Legrand that says he fell in love with a peasant girl named Xaviere Lisette Ganeau." Bob was now in full lecture mode. "The baron gave her the box containing the necklace on her sixteenth birthday. He wanted to marry her, but he already had a wife, so the only alternative was that she be his mistress. That didn't set well with Xaviere's father, so he packed up his daughter, and they left the country. Historians think they went to Germany."

"That's exactly where they went," Sabre said. "I learned that Xaviere married a German, and they had a daughter named Alice, who married Hans Albrecht. They had a daughter named Virginia, who married William Forney. And they had a daughter named Gladys Jeanne, who changed her name to Goldie."

"Seriously?" Bob sounded excited. "You're telling me that Goldie's great grandmother was *the* Xaviere Lisette Ganeau who received the necklace from Baron Gaston Legrand?"

"That's right."

"How do you know?"

"I found Goldie's genealogy records. She had everything verified with hospital records, birth certificates, and church documents from both France and Germany. I don't think there's any question, especially since she has the box and the necklace." Sabre sighed. "How much is it worth?"

"The necklace alone is worth a million."

"Whoa!" JP uttered.

"Wait. It gets better," Bob said. "Having the box and the necklace together almost doubles the value. That makes it worth somewhere in the neighborhood of two million."

"That's some neighborhood," JP said.

"Except," Bob added, "since the stones are actually grandi-dierite, which supposedly hadn't been discovered yet, the value is most likely far greater."

A two-million-dollar heirloom? Stashed in a storage unit with empty paint cans? It took her breath away. But she couldn't focus on that right now.

Sabre checked the time. "I need to go see the McCluskey kids." She touched JP's arm. "Will you take care of the jewelry box and necklace?"

"What should I do with them?"

"Put them in your gun safe for now. I'll get a safe deposit box on Monday morning."

"I can do that," JP said. "Do you think Judy Reed knows how valuable the necklace is?"

"It makes you wonder."

"And can you bring Dually home?" Sabre asked.

"Of course. He and Louie are just going to have to get along."

"It'll make the kids happy."

"Happier'n a preacher's son at a biker-babe rally."

After Sabre left, JP said, "If you boys don't need me in here, I think I'll go work out back."

"Sure," Bob said. He looked at Ron. "Hey, what's that in your hand?"

"An ivory horse, maybe a chess piece." Ron handed it to Bob.

"It sure is, and it looks old. I'll take it to my appraiser."

"I thought you weren't gonna do that anymore," JP said.

"Don't worry. This isn't worth a million dollars. A couple hundred, maybe."

It was all too rich for his blood. "I'm definitely going outside," JP said. "If I had found that, I probably would have tossed it. The stuff in the backyard I know about. I can tell the difference between a snake and a garden hose."

JP had no sooner reached the backyard when his phone rang. The display was a Montana number. "JP Torn."

"This is Clarice again. Lana wants to talk to you."

"Thanks, Clarice."

The younger woman came on the phone. "I checked Goldie Forney's phone records," Lana said with no greeting. "I'll have Clarice email you a copy of the calls as well as the breakdown I did by name and number. But this is what I've learned so far." A paper crackled in the background. "I tracked the numbers for the last three years, screening for frequent contacts that were made or received, and I have the names of the callers. I also have phone records for the last decade, but I didn't analyze anything before three years ago. You can do that yourself, or if you find a number you can't track, let me know, and I'll do it for you. The most frequent number was to or from Judy Reed. Do you know who that is?"

"Yes." JP started to explain.

But Lana was already talking again. "The next most frequent is a number associated with her own phone service, so I can't tell who had the phone, but my guess is her son, Chase Perkins."

"What's the number?" JP asked. Lana gave it to him, and

he checked his contacts. "You're right, that is Chase. How did you know?"

"Because she has calls to all her other children, but not him. So, either they were not in contact at all, or she was paying for his phone. From what I've learned about Chase, the latter seemed most likely."

JP was amazed at how much Lana could learn about people by hacking into accounts without ever meeting them. He found it both impressive and intimidating.

Lana continued. "Goldie made regular calls to several corporations, Tegbold, Dragon, Yenrof, and Silent Thunder, which I'm sure you know she owns. I did some research on each of them. If you'd like, I can give you the rundown." She went on, not waiting for a response. "But as for people, in the last few months, there were a lot of calls between Goldie and Tanya Dumas. They started on the third of July. Before that, there were no calls to or from that number."

"Who made the first contact, Tanya or Goldie?"

"Tanya called first, and Goldie called back. After that, they called each other regularly. Goldie also had recent calls to Doyle Law Group, more specifically, Rose Marie Doyle. There were also calls between Doyle and Tanya, so I'm guessing there's some connection. If there's anything else you'd like to know about Tanya Dumas or Rose Marie Doyle, I did extensive backgrounds on each. By the way, Tanya Dumas recently passed away from cancer."

Lana never seemed to pause, and JP couldn't take notes fast enough.

"Goldie spoke to her son, Travis Blodgett, about once a month, sometimes twice. As for her other three kids, Goldie made more-frequent calls to her hairdresser, nail salon, and dog groomer than to any of them. She talked to Rocki about every six weeks. Langston and Micki communicated with their mother every two or three months, and Goldie almost always initiated the calls."

JP knew most of that. "You said you did some research on the corporations she owns?"

"Yes. They all make a lot of money. She was a smart businesswoman. Silent Thunder is the most interesting. It's a nonprofit foundation, set up for the purpose of helping people. And she does it anonymously. It's handled by the lawyer, Rose Marie Doyle."

JP heard clicking on her keyboard.

"I have to go," Lana said. "If you need more information about the corporations, or anything for that matter, let Tuper or Clarice know, and I'll get back to you. You should be able to get whatever you need on Silent Thunder from Doyle. She's pretty involved with it. Bye."

CHAPTER 49

Saturday Afternoon

As Sabre drove to Lakeside, her mind reeled from the value of Goldie's estate. The necklace alone was shocking, and she wondered what they hadn't yet discovered.

When Sabre exited her car, all three girls ran up to greet her. Fayth did most of the talking, since Ivory was still developing her vocabulary, and Harmony was traumatized.

"When's Dale coming home?" Fayth asked, getting right to the point.

"I don't know yet, but we're doing everything we can," Sabre said. "Right now, I'd like to speak with Harmony alone for a few minutes."

"She might do better with me here," Fayth said. "I should stay and keep an eye on her."

"She'll be just fine. Run along now."

Fayth left reluctantly, and Sabre led Harmony to the picnic

274

table. Sabre chatted about the hospital and being home again, which Harmony seemed to respond to. Hoping the girl was ready, Sabre broached the delicate subject.

"It's very important that you tell me what happened to you at the school on Thursday. If you give us enough information, we can catch the man and put him in jail. That will keep other little girls safe. I really need your help."

Harmony lowered her head and whispered, "I was waiting for Fayth near the bus, and I saw a big, white dog come around the corner. I wanted to pet him. He was so pretty."

"Did you pet him?"

She shook her head. "The dog walked away, so I followed him. When I got around the corner, a man grabbed me and covered my mouth." Harmony stopped, her eyes filled with fear.

Sabre had to keep the conversation going. "You're doing great, Harmony. What happened after he grabbed you?"

"He tried to run, but he almost fell." She started to cry, but kept talking, as if she suddenly had to get it out. "When we got away from the school, he put me down. But he grabbed my hand and made me run. I kept falling, so he slowed down."

"Did he still have the dog?"

"I don't know where it went."

"Had you ever seen that dog before?"

"No."

"Did you recognize the man's voice?"

"He never talked."

That seemed odd, unless he was afraid Harmony would recognize his voice. "Then what happened?"

"The man kept pulling me, and it hurt my arm." The poor girl sobbed.

"I'm so sorry. You're being very brave. Take a deep breath,

and you'll get through this. Remember, the man can't hurt you now."

Harmony inhaled, choking a little, and let it out.

"We're almost done," Sabre said. "Did you see anyone else near the man?"

"I saw Fayth when she jumped on the man's back. Then she yelled at me to run."

"Did you?"

"At first, I couldn't. I was scared for her. But she kept yelling, 'Run. Run.' So, I did, 'cuz when Fayth says stuff, she means it."

Sabre held back a smile. "Did you get away?"

"Yeah. I ran down the street and hid behind a shed. I peeked out once and saw him looking around, so I took off and ran through some other yards. I was tired, so I sat down and leaned against a garage."

Her words were tumbling out now. Sabre had to keep her talking. "Is that where Mr. Armstrong found you?"

"No, because a dog started barking, and I took off. But it was getting dark and raining, so I was even more scared."

"Did you try to get help from anyone?"

She shook her head from side to side. "No. I was too scared to go out in the street. I was afraid the man might see me, so I stayed behind the houses."

"How did you end up in Mr. Armstrong's yard?"

"I dunno. I just sat down somewhere dry. Then another dog came up to me. He didn't bark though. He laid down by me and felt warm."

"Did you stay there the rest of the night?"

"Yeah, Mr. Armstrong was standing over me when I woke up. He scared me, and I screamed, but his wife came. She was real nice and carried me inside and got me warm."

"I'm so glad you're safe," Sabre said, smiling. "Are you glad to be home from the hospital?"

"Yeah, but I wish Dale was here."

"I'm doing what I can to bring him home," Sabre said. "There may be something you can do too."

"What?"

"I need to know if you saw something important the night Perry died."

"I don't want to talk anymore." Harmony jumped up and ran off.

CHAPTER 50

Saturday Late Afternoon

S abre and JP spent the late afternoon at the last two storage spaces. The first unit they searched had been filled with old furniture, so they started on the last one.

"I still hope we'll find something on that charity," Sabre said, opening a box. "I have to meet with Goldie's kids soon, and they'll have questions, especially since such a big chunk goes to Silent Thunder."

"They're getting plenty," JP said.

"But not without conditions, and that's what will make them unhappy."

"Nothing will make Langston or the girls happy. If I were Goldie, I wouldn't have left them a red cent. They had no respect for her, and they treated her somethin' awful. The three of them ain't worth the powder and fuse it'd take to blow 'em up. I'd have given it all to Travis with a trust to take care of

Chase. He's got his drug problems, but he still seems to have cared about his mama. Any kid who doesn't, don't deserve to get what she left behind."

"One thing for sure," Sabre said. "Those three sure think they're entitled."

JP picked up a box full of paperwork and set it near Sabre. "Maybe there's something in here. If not, you have the name and number of the attorney who handled the charity trust."

"I already called her and left a message, but her voicemail said she was out of town and wouldn't be back in her office until Wednesday."

"That's not so long."

"I get a call every day from one of the three greedy kids." Sabre started to sort through the documents. "I'll set a meeting date for Thursday or Friday just to get them off my back." Now that she knew Goldie's net worth, Sabre couldn't stop thinking about the warning notes. "I just wish I had more information about this food poisoning issue. I don't want to dole out anything to someone who tried to kill her."

"You may never know. We haven't found anything yet. Maybe that's because there's nothing there to find."

"You don't really believe that do you?" Sabre looked at him with skepticism.

"If one of them did kill her, my money is on Langston. He knew she had assets, even if he didn't know how much, and he's just not a nice guy. And don't forget what the psychologist said in the psych eval."

"Micki and Rocki are no prizes either, especially Micki. She has no heart." Sabre threw some papers in the trashcan. "And Chase is an addict. Who knows what he might do to get his next fix."

"I agree. The only one we don't suspect is Travis. Because

he's nicer than the rest? Maybe it's all an act. He knew his mother owned the construction company. Although, in fairness to him, he also admitted that he knew it."

Sabre didn't respond. She was studying an old document. "I'll be darned."

"Did you find the charity trust information?" JP asked.

"No. But this is equally interesting." She picked up another paper. "Remember the lawsuit Hans Albrecht had against his father's estate?"

"Yeah, he got a million dollars."

"Apparently, he turned that into three million before he died. His wife had already passed on. He only had one daughter, Virginia, Goldie's mother. She died from an aneurysm when she was twenty-eight."

"So, everything went to his grandchildren, Goldie and her sister Vivian?" JP set down a box and stared at Sabre.

"It did. But Vivian died a year after inheriting the money, also from a brain aneurysm. She died intestate. She wasn't married and had no children, so it all went to Goldie by right of succession."

"That's how she started her empire."

"Looks that way."

"She was a smart lady. She more than quadrupled her initial inheritance, and in a relatively short time."

"Yes, in about twelve or thirteen years." Sabre sighed. "But she sure had a lot of loss in her life. People important to her died at a young age. Her mother, her grandmother, her father, her sister, and her son, Michael."

"Not to mention the husband who hung himself."

Sabre's face flushed. "I don't mention him unless I have to."

"I'm sorry, Sabre. I wasn't thinking."

"That's all right. It was a long time ago." Sabre exhaled. "I feel so bad for all the sadness and loneliness that Goldie endured." Sabre put the documents back in the box. "I'm done here. Let's go home to our family."

CHAPTER 51

Monday Afternoon

I t was nearly three o'clock, and Sabre had just finished at court for the day. The morning had been especially busy. Several departments didn't get finished and had to carry the cases over to the afternoon. Feeling tired, she sought out Bob to let him know she was leaving. She found him outside of Department Two.

"I'm done here," Sabre said.

"I'm waiting on Wagner, but it's my last case. Want to hang around and keep me company? You know how Wags is. I might be stuck here another hour or two."

"You know I'd love to," Sabre said flippantly.

"Sure you would."

"I have an appointment to see Harmony. She had therapy after school today, and the counselor called and said Harmony wanted to tell me something important."

"She wouldn't tell the therapist?"

"Apparently, Harmony said she would only tell me. I'm meeting her at the therapist's office. She thought it would be better than talking to Harmony at home."

Bob's eyes widened. "Don't tell me Adam has done something now. But I can't imagine what it would be. He seems like a very good father."

"I agree. From what the therapist said, I think it's about Perry."

"Well, go then," Bob said, waving his hand dismissively.

Harmony sat curled up on a sofa, holding a stuffed, pink unicorn. Sabre sat close to her, partly so she could hear her soft voice and partly to make her feel safe.

"Your therapist said you have something you want to tell me. Is that right?"

She nodded but didn't speak.

"Could you tell me what it's about?"

Harmony looked down, then at the unicorn, but still no response.

"Why don't you tell the unicorn what you wanted to talk about?"

The little girl glanced at Sabre, then back at the toy. She held up the stuffed animal and whispered, "It's about Perry." She lowered the unicorn to her lap.

"Is it about the night he died?"

Harmony nodded.

"Did you see Perry that night?"

She nodded again.

"Where did you see him?"

The girl held the toy and whispered again. "I went to his room."

"Why did you go there?"

"I had to know he was okay. They beat him in his private parts because he wet his bed."

"Who beat him?"

This time Harmony looked at Sabre before she answered. "Kenny did it, but Mom told him to."

"Did you see what Kenny did?"

She shook her head. "But I went in there after, and Perry told me. He showed me, and it was all red. He said Kenny kept slapping him there."

"Did you see or hear anything else?"

Harmony nodded and continued to look at Sabre.

"What did you see or hear?"

"I was in bed when Fayth came in from outside. I knew she had gone to get vegetables again. She really loves those vegetables." Harmony suddenly let the words flow. "After she got in bed, I snuck out to go see Perry. He was asleep, but I woke him. He had peed in the bed again, and I wanted to help him change the sheets. I was about to wake Dale to help us, but then I heard someone coming. I hid behind the dresser." The girl started to cry.

"I'm sorry, Harmony. I know this is hard for you." Sabre gave her hand a gentle squeeze. "But we need to know who hurt Perry and stop them from ever hurting anyone ever again."

"I shouldn't have hid," she cried. "I should've screamed or woke Dale or something. Then Perry would still be alive. Dale blames himself for not waking up, but I was awake, and I was too scared. It's all my fault, not his."

"Harmony, it's not your fault. Not one bit. You're not the

one who hurt Perry. If you had done anything else, you might have been hurt too." Sabre wrapped her arm around the little girl. "Who came in the room?"

"It was Mom." She sobbed, then caught her breath. "She was mad because the bed was wet. She was saying bad words, and she sounded funny, like how she gets sometimes."

"What do you mean?"

"Sometimes she talks funny. She says things that don't make sense."

"Did your mom see you?"

"I don't think so. She didn't turn on the light, but there was light from the hall, so I saw her."

"What happened then?"

"Mom left the room. But I waited a while. I was afraid she would come right back. And she did. Mom and Kenny both came in." Her little voice started to shake. "This time Mom flipped the light on, but Kenny turned it back off. He said it would wake Dale. They were both angry at Perry, but Mom said, 'You take care of it.' Then she left again."

"But Kenny stayed?"

"He told Perry he would have to be punished. Perry started crying, and Kenny covered his mouth with his hand." Harmony raised her voice in anguish. "I should've screamed."

"You did all you could," Sabre said to console her. But she wanted to keep her talking, feeling sure there was more. "What happened next?"

"Kenny put a pillow over Perry's face and held it down. And Perry stopped making noise. Then Kenny left, but I couldn't move. I tried to make my legs work, but they wouldn't. I finally fell asleep sitting there by the dresser. When I woke up, I snuck out and went back to bed."

"Did you see Perry before you left?"

"I saw him up against the wall. But I didn't know he was...
was...dead."

CHAPTER 52

Monday Evening

"You look exhausted," JP said, as Sabre finally sat on the sofa, leaning against him.

"I am. It's been a rough day for me, but I expect it was a lot worse for Harmony. When I told her how important it was that she tell the detective, she agreed to do it. I offered to set it up for tomorrow, but she wanted to do it right then."

"And DuBois was able to come right over?"

"He was there in twenty minutes. And he was very kind to her."

"Vinny's a good guy. He loves kids. That's one of the reasons he became a cop. He hates it when people hurt kids. He doesn't do well with men who beat women either."

"Sounds like someone else I know."

"Any kind of bully makes me mad as spit on a griddle."

Sabre smiled, sat back up, and picked up one of Goldie's journals.

"A little light reading?" JP asked.

"Yup."

"What time period is this journal?"

Sabre turned to the front page. "Thirteen years ago. I'm in May."

"Let me know if you discover anything new."

Sabre read several pages, then had to stop. "Oh no."

"What is it now?"

"Remember when Aunt Goldie apologized to me in that note, but I had no idea why?"

"Sort of."

"I just found out why. Listen to this." She read from the journal, trying to keep her emotions in check.

I just received an announcement for Sabre's high school graduation. She is such a sweet girl. I know she'll do great things in the future. I only hope my mistake hasn't haunted her all her life. My biggest mistake in life was marrying Bill Blodgett. Of course, he did give me Langston and Travis, and I don't regret that. But for what he tried to do to my girls and what he did to poor little Sabre, I will never forgive myself. Micki and Rocki were lucky because they got away before he really did anything. I just wish they would've told me because I never would've taken him to California. I don't regret his death, except that it was too easy. But I will never forgive him for molesting Sabre. And I'm so sorry she had to be the one to find him hanging from the rafters.

"All that time, she blamed herself. The poor tortured

woman." Sabre's phone rang before she could say more. She glanced at the ID. "It's DuBois."

She took the call, listened for a minute, thanked him, and hung up.

"What did he say?" JP asked.

"They brought Ellie and Kenny in for questioning. They both sang like birds, to quote DuBois. They each corroborated Harmony's account of what happened."

"Are they in custody?"

"Yes. They charged Ellie with child endangerment, and Kenny with second-degree murder." Sabre sighed. "I feel so bad for those kids. They've lost so much."

"What happens to Dale now?"

"I'll set a hearing on calendar tomorrow to get him released. It shouldn't be a problem with the new evidence and charges. He'll be back with his dad and siblings by the end of the day."

Sabre went back to reading the journal but couldn't concentrate. "Did I tell you I have a meeting set up with Goldie's kids to go over the trust distributions?"

"I think so. When is it?"

"Thursday, at five o'clock. Can you be there?"

"I'm afraid I can't," JP said. "I have an appointment at five-thirty in Vista. I can come by when I'm done, if you think it'll still be going on."

"I expect it will be. I don't anticipate a smooth discussion. They bicker so much amongst themselves, meeting with them takes longer than it should. But call or text me before you drive over."

"Maybe I can change my appointment. I'd prefer you weren't alone with that looney bunch, especially Langston. I don't trust that guy."

"I'll call Ron and see if he can be there again."

Ron was available and more than happy to help out. "I want to see their faces when they find out how loaded their mother was. I'm sure they won't be able to contain their sorrow over her passing." Ron's tone was eager and bitter at the same time.

Sabre felt the same. "That will be worth seeing. I don't expect them to be happy with the distribution either," Sabre added. "That reminds me. I need to let Judy Reed know about the meeting. It bugs me that she's inheriting something when I know she was trying to steal that necklace. I wish we could bust her on that."

"I'll be at the house tomorrow," Ron said. "I'm sure she'll stop by as usual, and I'll tell her about the meeting. She comes almost every day. If she doesn't, you can call her tomorrow night or Wednesday."

As soon as Ron hung up, he called Bob. "I need your help."

"Doing what?"

"A sting operation." Ron gave him a general idea of what he planned. "Are you in?"

"You bet. See you tomorrow."

CHAPTER 53

Tuesday Afternoon

"Sabre's not going to like this," Bob said, as he walked in.

Ron was waiting for him in the living room of Goldie's house. "I know, but it ticks me off that this woman who claims to be Goldie's best friend is trying to rip her off. Judy shouldn't get anything from Goldie's estate. And she won't if we can prove she's committing fraud." Ron looked around, hoping he was set up and ready. "I need to do this, and I know Sabre wouldn't agree with it. But if you're not comfortable, I'll do it alone."

"You can't do it alone. Besides, I never said I was uncomfortable. I'm all in. The woman's greed bothers me too, and I didn't even know Goldie."

"I have the recorder all set, and I have this." Ron held up the blue mahogany box from Baron Gaston Legrand.

"You brought the necklace! Are you crazy?" Bob threw his

hands up, palms out. "I'm not touching that. You don't know how desperate this woman could be. If she knows how much that's worth, she might come in with a shotgun and blow us away."

"Relax," Ron said. "I didn't bring the jewelry, just the box."

"That's bad enough. It's worth ten grand by itself."

"Don't worry. Look right over there." Ron pointed to the top of a pile of boxes. "And over there." He pointed to another pile. "I have cameras in there, so if she tries anything, she'll be recorded."

"That won't do us any good if she goes all fifty-one-fifty on us."

"She could go a little crazy, but it'll all be okay." Ron paused. "I think."

"What's your plan exactly?"

"I'll leave the box right here." Ron placed it on top of the pile near the entrance to the next room. He placed some things around it but left it visible enough to be noticed.

"You think she'll steal it."

"I do."

"And then what? How do you get it back?"

"That's where you come in."

"Wait a minute."

"Hear me out." Ron had a moment of doubt, then plunged ahead. "You need to block the front door at all times so she can't get out. There's no way she can go out the back. Both doors are blocked."

"What am I supposed to do? Tackle her if she tries to leave?"

"You won't have to. She'll hand it over after I threaten to

expose her to the cops." Ron looked out at the street. "There she is. Just follow my lead."

It took Judy several minutes to get out of her car and make it to the front door. Ron opened the security screen, invited her in, and introduced her to Bob.

"I see you've made a lot of progress," Judy said, looking around.

"It's slow, but we're getting there."

"Thanks for calling and letting me come inside. I feel connected to Goldie here."

Judy walked down the aisle to the right, where Ron had created a path nearly to the kitchen door. She scanned everything, taking in every detail. "Goldie loved her kachina dolls," Judy said, as she passed one sticking out of the pile.

"She sure did," Ron said, following her. "I've found twenty-three so far. Do you know what that was all about?"

"She said Chase was part Hopi Indian, and she hoped to stir up some interest about his heritage."

"Did it work?"

"I don't think so." Judy moved down the other aisle that led to the next room. "Do you mind if I have a look?" She kept walking through the labyrinth Goldie had created.

"Not at all," Ron said, still behind her. "We haven't done much back here yet."

When they got almost to the end, Judy turned around. Ron wanted to get behind her so he could watch her, but there wasn't enough room. He turned around and started back. After a few steps, he said, "You probably knew my aunt better than anyone." He kept the conversation going, so he had reason to glance back at her.

"She didn't trust anyone else."

"Not even her children?"

"Especially her children."

"Do you know anything about her finances?" Ron turned so he could see her face.

She remained expressionless. "Like what?"

"Did you know she owned some other property?"

"I used to bring the mail in for her sometimes, and I've seen letters from mortgage companies. I asked her about them one day, and she said she had a rental but didn't want her kids to know. Goldie didn't really have anyone else to talk to, so she confided in me a lot."

Right. Ron thought. *She was such a good friend that you feel justified in ripping her off.*

They reached the front room. When they passed the jewelry box, Ron didn't look back. He was blocking Bob's view, so neither of them could see it. A few steps later, Ron looked back, and the box was gone. He nodded at Bob, who positioned himself right in the doorway, leaning back on the security screen.

"I probably should get out of your hair," Judy said. "Thanks for showing me around." She stepped toward the front door, but Bob kept his position.

"I haven't shown you the necklace yet," Ron said. "That's what you came for, right?"

"Of course. I almost forgot. I just feel so sad being here without Goldie." Judy wiped her eye, as if to dry a tear. Her right hand remained at her side. "Where is it?" she asked.

Ron produced a blue Tiffany box. "I couldn't find the photo on my phone, but I thought this might be it." He opened the box for her. Inside was a necklace with emerald-colored stones he'd found with some junk jewelry.

"That's not it." She took another step toward Bob. "Excuse me, I really need to go."

"It's not in that box either," Ron said.

"What?" She sounded uneasy.

"The box you're holding in the folds of your dress. There's no necklace in there either."

Judy's eyes widened and darted from Ron to Bob.

"Open it and see."

"I don't know what you're talking about. I need to go."

Bob remained against the screen, blocking the doorway.

"Please move," Judy said in a loud voice.

"You might want to rethink this," Ron said. "If I report the theft to the police, they'll be looking at you for murder."

Judy spun around. "What are you talking about?"

"Aunt Goldie died from botulinum toxin."

"You said she had a heart attack."

"That's what we thought at first, but blood tests showed poison in her system. The police have a partial hamburger still in the wrapper. It was left by her chair."

"No, it wasn't," she blurted.

Ron and Bob exchanged surprised glances.

"How do you know that?" Ron demanded.

Judy didn't answer.

"You know because you came into the house after Goldie was taken to the hospital, and you removed the evidence."

"I wasn't trying to kill her," Judy blubbered. "I just wanted to get her out of the house for a while. There was just enough poison to make her sick—not to kill her. I was very careful, and I knew she'd call for help. She liked ambulance rides almost as much as she liked stuff. If she hadn't called 911, I would have called for her."

"Why would you poison her? Couldn't you just wait until she left for some other reason?" Bob asked.

"She wasn't going anywhere, and I knew the trust was by

her chair. I had to see what was in it. She promised me she would put me in her will and take care of me, but she didn't."

"You took the trust so no one would see it?"

"No. I took it because I didn't have time to read it while I was here. I didn't want to stay too long in case someone came by. If I was in the trust, I figured I could slip it back in here, or tell *whoever* that she left it with me for safe keeping." Judy fought back tears but sounded angry. "But the trust left everything equally to her children. When I saw that I wasn't even mentioned, I kept it. I hoped she might have an older one that left me something. Goldie promised she'd take care of me. I've been taking care of her for years, and what did I get in return?"

"I understand she did a lot of things for you," Ron said. "She helped you get your new car. She paid for your daughter's wedding, and most recently, dance lessons for your granddaughter."

"That was nothing. The old money bag could've bought the dance studio if she wanted."

"So, you decided to shake us down for the necklace?

"That is mine. I told you I loaned it to Goldie. Just give it to me and let me go."

Ron couldn't believe her audacity. "Why would you loan out something so valuable?"

"We were best friends, and she wanted to borrow it, so I let her. What's the big deal?"

"No one is that good of a friend."

Judy looked puzzled. "How valuable is it?"

"You must think the necklace is worth something, or you wouldn't be trying so hard to get it."

"I know it's valuable because it's my necklace. I had it appraised a few years ago."

"Oh, really? How much did the appraiser say it was worth?"

"About ten thousand. I know that's a lot, but Goldie really wanted to borrow it, so I let her."

"Except it's not yours," Ron said. "Goldie had paperwork showing where it came from. It belonged to her great grandmother, and she left behind all the records we need to prove it."

Judy's shoulders slumped. "I told her all I wanted was the necklace, and she said she'd leave it to me. She also said she'd take care of me when she was gone. But she didn't do either." Tears started to roll down her cheeks. "I looked around for the necklace when I came in that night. She had it in the pouch of her chair just a few days before, but she must've moved it, because it was gone."

Bob held out his hand. "Give me the box."

Judy looked down, then slowly lifted the box and opened it. Suddenly, she raised her arm and flung the box at him.

Bob yelled, "No!" But it was too late.

Ron reached up to catch the box. He stretched out and dove for it, crashing into a wall of junk. Bob dashed toward him as objects fell on top of both of them. They tumbled until they were both lying under a heap. When the debris stopped falling and they looked up, Judy was gone.

"Are you okay?" Ron asked.

"I'm fine." Bob tossed a few things aside and stood up. "How about you?" He pulled a box and several baskets off Ron.

Ron held up his hand. And the baron's box sat in his palm. "I caught it! I guess all that softball practice was worth it."

CHAPTER 54

Wednesday Morning

Sabre met with Travis, his attorney, and Dené's attorney outside the courtroom. The minor's hearing would start soon. Sabre watched Travis' expression as he learned the results of the paternity test. He wasn't his usual confident self as they all walked into the courtroom.

Hekman called the hearing to order, then looked at Russ Miller, Travis' attorney. "The paternity test results show that, by a ninety-nine percent certainty, your client is the father of Dené Dumas. What is his position on the matter?" the judge asked.

"My client would like to explain that to the court, Your Honor," Miller said.

"Very well, Mr. Blodgett."

"I don't know exactly how to react to this news," Travis

began. "I've been thinking about it ever since I was first approached by DSS. I'd like to meet my daughter, but I don't want to turn her life upside down." He paused and cleared his throat. "The truth is I don't know what kind of a father I'll be. There's no way I was fit to be a father when she was born. That's probably why Tanya never told me about the baby. We didn't have much of a relationship. I moved on rather quickly in those days. I've really only started to grow up the last couple of years. I'd like to be a father—a good one—but I don't know if I know how."

"I appreciate your honesty, Mr. Blodgett." Judge Hekman turned to Dené's attorney. "Is the minor aware of her father?"

"No. Her mother told her he left before she was born, and she never saw him again."

"But I understand she knew her paternal grandmother, is that right?"

"The grandmother had her suspicions about the baby when the child was born," Wagner said. "And we believe she saw the child once right after her birth. Dené's mother, Tanya, contacted Goldie a few months back, and the three spent time getting to know one another."

"What would you suggest we do with this, Mr. Wagner?"

"I think we can take jurisdiction, if the father is ready to enter a plea. We can set disposition over." Wagner glanced at Travis. "I'll check with my client to see if she wants to see her father. If so, we can set up visitation and see how it goes."

"That'll work for my client, Your Honor," Russ Miller said. "Travis would love to meet his daughter, but he wants to do it in a way that's best for her."

"What about detention for this child?" The judge looked at her paperwork. "Is she still at Polinsky?"

"Yes," County Counsel said. "However, we are encouraging Sabre Brown to consider detention with her. As you may remember, she is the child's second cousin and the trustee for Dené's inheritance from her paternal grandmother."

The judge looked at Sabre. "Are you willing to have this child in your home, Ms. Brown? For the record, I can't imagine a better placement."

"I haven't yet met Dené, but we have it set up for her to come to my house this weekend and spend the afternoon with my family. My significant other and I have his niece and nephew placed with us through DSS already. I want to see how compatible we all are before I take Dené into our home. I want to make sure she'll be happy there." Sabre tried to sound calm and professional, but her heart was hammering. This was another huge commitment.

"Either way," she continued. "I plan to develop a relationship with her if she wants one. After all, she is my cousin. However, I don't want this child to have to move any more than necessary. From all accounts, she sounds like a wonderful little girl. But as I said, I have yet to meet her. Who knows? She may not like me."

"I doubt that, Ms. Brown, but I think it's a good plan. Would you be willing to supervise visits with the father if the child is detained with you?"

"I don't see a problem with that, Your Honor."

The judged looked at her notes and took the plea from the father, who submitted to jurisdiction of the court. "The minor will remain at Polinsky for now," Hekman ordered. "If Dené were younger, I'd be taking a different stand, but she is a twelve-year-old with no family except through her father. I agree with Ms. Brown that we need to move slowly and create as few disruptions for this child as possible. On the other hand, I don't want to see her languish in Polinsky." The judge issued her ruling. "The department has discretion to detain the minor with Ms. Brown. The father is to have supervised visits at least once a week, more if the minor chooses."

CHAPTER 55

Thursday Evening

S abre sat at her desk, waiting for Ron to escort Goldie's children into her office. Five chairs were lined up just as they had been before, and the heirs took the same seats as last time. Sabre wondered if that was the way they always seated themselves, or if it was just for her benefit.

They were all seated when Dené's attorney walked in. Ron offered to get him a chair, but he chose to stand. "This may take a while," Ron whispered.

"I'll leave if I need to," Wagner said.

"Who are you?" Micki asked.

"Attorney Richard Wagner," was all he offered in response.

"Why are you here?" she pressed.

"I'm representing my client."

Sabre chuckled to herself at Wagner's cat and mouse game. He loved to yank chains.

Micki looked at her siblings. "Who hired an attorney? Langston?"

"No," Langston said. "Not that it's any of your business if I did."

"Then it has to be you, Travis."

"I didn't," Travis countered. "Let's just get on with this."

"Do we need lawyers?" Micki asked, looking at Sabre.

"You are certainly welcome to retain one," Sabre said. "But you don't need one here today. Mr. Wagner is here because his client is a minor." The girls whispered to each other, and Sabre went on. "If you have questions as we go—questions about the trust—feel free to ask, but please keep extraneous comments to yourself. We have a lot of ground to cover. Can you do that?"

Langston said, "Yeah," and made a dismissive gesture. Chase nodded. Micki and Rocki both mumbled some affirmative comment. Travis affably said, "Of course."

"As you know, I was named as the trustee of your mother's estate. I have the sole right and responsibility to manage the trust. That includes buying and selling assets, without input from trust beneficiaries. That said, I will ask for your input on the distribution of certain personal property."

"When?" Micki asked.

"I can start distribution after everything in the house has been thoroughly examined, appraisals have been done, and an accounting of Goldie's assets is completed."

"That shouldn't take long. She didn't have much."

The boys all turned toward Micki. Chase sighed, Travis shook his head, and Langston mumbled, "You're an idiot."

"Don't call me an idiot, you imbecile. I'm just saying, how much can she have?"

"How would you know?" Chase said, rather meekly. "You haven't been home in ten years."

In the time Sabre had spent with Chase, she'd never heard him challenge his siblings. The group seemed equally surprised as they all turned toward him. Micki started to argue, but Sabre shut her down. *It's going to be a long afternoon,* she thought.

"I told you before that your mother was a hoarder," Sabre said. "I'm not using that word lightly. The house is full of stuff from top to bottom with only a small pathway leading from the front door to a chair in her bedroom. You cannot get into the kitchen at all, and both bathrooms are so full the showers and sinks are not accessible. One has a commode she was able to use. The backyard is in the same condition, with a pile six feet high."

"I've been to the house," Micki scoffed. "It looked fine."

"You've been *by* the house," Travis interjected. "It looks fine from the street, but you obviously weren't inside."

Sabre held up her hand, then continued. "In addition to the stuff in the house, she has five full storage units. It will take months to sort through everything, get it assessed, and start distributions. And much of it will end up in a landfill." She looked at Micki, who for once didn't argue.

"In the meantime, you have one hundred and twenty days from the time you received notice of the trust to contest it. You are entitled to a copy of the trust, but I will go through the basics here today. Also, you need to know that if you contest the trust and lose, you get nothing. That also means I won't start distributions until any contested matters are decided by the courts, or the one hundred and twenty days has passed without contest. Any questions about that?"

"Just get on with it," Langston said.

Sabre looked at her notes and began. "The first clause reads as such."

The Trustee shall distribute, free of trust, such items of my tangible personal property as may then be included in the Trust Estate in accordance with any written instructions left by me and the remainder of such personal property to my living children.

"Your mother left certain items to each of you. If you don't want them, they will return to the estate to be distributed equally amongst the other siblings. At a future date, I will tell you individually what those are, but as I stated earlier, I cannot give them to you yet." Sabre looked at the trust. "The next distribution clause reads as follows:"

My residence shall be put in trust for my son, Chase Perkins. Once it is cleaned up, he can use it for his home. The furniture and appliances in the house shall remain with the house. Should Chase choose not to live there, the house will remain in his trust and be used as a rental, all profits to go back into his trust. Chase's trust will remain in effect until he reaches the age of forty AND has randomly drug tested clean for five consecutive years, at which time Chase will become the Trustee of his own trust. Should he not be drug-free at that time, the trust will remain as is.

"What the hell?" Micki blurted. "She gave everything to Chase?" She stood and stepped in front of Chase, only two feet from his face. "The druggie baby's getting everything," Micki said in a mocking voice. Then her tone turned angry. "You made her do that, didn't you? You probably whined and cried that you had no place to live."

Travis stepped between them. "Leave him alone. Mom

didn't give everything to Chase. She had more than just the house."

"Yeah," Langston joined in. "Sit down and shut up, so we can hear what Goldie did with her small fortune."

Micki looked from one twin brother to the other, walked back to her chair, and sat. Travis patted Chase on the shoulder, who said a quiet, "Thanks." Travis took his seat.

Sabre looked at the group. "Let's try this again."

The Trustee shall sell all other real property (listed in Appendix F) whose title is held in my personal name and distribute the proceeds accordingly.

"Appendix F has two rental properties that your mother held title to. I'm having the properties assessed and checking for encumbrances such as liens and tax debt, so I don't have the exact values yet. I know the mortgages are minimal, so there should be a fair amount of equity in those homes."

"What's a fair amount?" Langston asked.

"If there are no liens or back taxes, I'd estimate the equity at about a million and a half."

Sabre watched their faces, curious to see who would be surprised. Chase didn't look up, Travis' expression didn't change, and Langston smirked. But both girls' mouths dropped open, and their eyes widened. They glanced at each other and grinned gleefully.

After a few seconds of quiet, Micki said, "Since Chase got the house, the rentals should be divided between the four of us." Micki's eyes did mental math, and her fingers moved to help with the division.

"Actually, it's not divided that way, so please wait until

you hear everything before you comment on the equity of her choices."

Micki scowled but didn't respond. Sabre continued to read.

15% shall be divided, free of encumbrances, equally among my children, Michelle Nogard, Rochelle Nogard, and Langston Blodgett.

"Fifteen percent?" Micki jumped up again. "That's like… like a hundred and fifty thousand or something. The house mom lived in is worth half a million at least."

"Micki, will you shut up and sit down," Langston bellowed. "And it's not a hundred and fifty thousand. It's half of that." He stared at Micki. "It's seventy-five thousand, since you can't do the math."

"You're okay with Chase getting way more than we do? And what about the other eighty-five percent?"

"Just let Sabre finish," Travis said. "In case you haven't noticed, my name hasn't even been mentioned. You don't see me acting like a brat, do you?"

Micki sat down. Rocki gave her a reassuring pat on the arm.

Elaine opened the door, and everyone got quiet. She walked up to Sabre and whispered something.

"I'll take it in David's office," Sabre responded. Elaine walked out, and Sabre looked at the heirs again. "I need to take a phone call, which I'll do in another office. You can stay here or take a break. If you leave, please be back in five minutes so we can get this done. If anyone wants a bottle of water, let Ron know. I won't be long."

CHAPTER 56

Thursday Evening

S abre returned, and when everyone was seated, she looked at Chase. "Okay, let's get on with this."

5% shall be put in trust for my son, Chase Perkins, to be distributed according to his daily maintenance needs, until he meets the age and conditions outlined in Section 2.

Both Micki and Rocki rolled their eyes. Sabre read the next clause.

5% shall be distributed free of encumbrances to my good friend, Judy Ingrid Reed.

"Are you kidding me?" Micki exclaimed. "She's getting as much as I am."

"That remains to be seen," Sabre said. "There's a clause in your mother's trust that prohibits anyone from inheriting if they commit a crime against her. And Judy Reed has been arrested for such a crime."

"That bitch," Langston uttered. "What did she do?"

"I can't get into that now, but it's public record, so you can look for yourself. As a result, she may not be entitled to any inheritance. I've already filed on behalf of the estate. If she loses, the money will be divided among you five, as per the trust instructions." Sabre took a deep breath. "Remember, we're still just dividing the money from the sale of the rentals Goldie owned." She read the next clause.

75% shall be put in trust for my granddaughter, Dené Dumas. In the event Dené is no longer living at my death, the Trustee shall distribute her share to her then-living issue, by right of representation, outright and free of trust, unless they are minors. If she has no issue, her portion reverts to my trust, and is divided equally amongst the remaining heirs.

This time both Micki and Rocki jumped up.

"Who the hell is that?" Micki yelled. Wagner chuckled, but Micki didn't seem to notice. She turned toward her brothers, pointing her finger from one to the next. "Which one of you has a kid? And why is Mom giving her all our money?"

"It's not *our* money," Langston shot back. "It's Goldie's money, and she can do whatever she pleases with it."

"So, it's you who has a kid. Of course, you don't care. I suppose you'll have control over her money since she can't be more than ten or twelve."

"Do you need a calculator to do the math?" Langston chided.

"You're an ass," Micki shouted.

"At least I'm not a *dumb* ass," Langston said.

Sabre wondered if Langston knew about Travis' child. "Please calm down," Sabre shouted. "I'd like to finish this."

"What more could there possibly be?" Micki asked. "Are you going to divide up the pots and pans?"

"You have no idea what Goldie had," Langston said. "So, why don't you just sit down and shut up so we can get this over with?"

Wagner walked over to Sabre and asked, "Is there anything else I need to be here for?"

"That's it."

"As much as I hate to miss the fun, I have other matters to attend to. Good luck." He smiled all the way out the door.

Sabre read on.

Tegbold Construction shall be put in trust for my son, Travis Blodgett, according to the provisions in Appendix G.

"She owned the company you work for?" Micki bellowed.

Travis didn't answer, and Sabre turned to him. "I'll give you a copy of the appendix, but in a nutshell, you have to continue to work at the company. KC Loring will remain as manager and sole decision-maker until she retires or ten years have passed. Once KC is gone, you will become the trustee and can dissolve the trust to become full owner. However, the profit sharing will continue, as per the contract."

Travis tried to maintain his composure, but Sabre could see

his excitement. Chase looked pleased for him. Micki and Rocki both tried to argue.

Sabre cut them off, talking over them. "Please, just wait until I'm done." She continued to read.

All properties in Yenrof Corporation shall be sold and donated to The Silent Thunder Charity Trust to be managed by Attorney Sabre O. Brown as head of the board and Ronald Brown as CEO.

"And there you have it," Micki said. "I don't know what Yenrof Corporation is, or Silent Thunder, but that must be what you and your brother were after. I plan to hire a lawyer to contest this. Travis got a million-dollar company, Chase got a half-million-dollar house, and the rest of us got a measly seventy-five grand." She pointed at Sabre. "You and your brother got a corporation. I'm not going to stand for this."

"Me either," Rocki said.

"It's a charity, you idiot," Langston said. "They don't get the money for themselves."

"Thank you, Langston," Sabre said. "There's more, Micki."

"I'm not going to sit here and listen to any more." She stood. "Come on, Rocki, let's go."

"No." Rocki tugged at her sister's arm. "We should see what else there is."

Micki shrugged and sat down.

"We're almost done," Sabre said.

All assets and property listed in Appendix H shall be distributed according to the instructions in that appendix.

"Appendix H consists primarily of Dragon Incorporated."

"The bars?" Rocki asked. "Mom owned the Dragon bars?"

"Yes. And she left very explicit instructions. Micki is to manage the bar in La Jolla, and Rocki will be in charge of the one in San Diego. Langston, your mother appointed you CEO of Dragon Incorporated." Sabre stared at the three. "Goldie set it up so you have to work together and show certain profits for any of you to benefit from profit sharing. If you manage the bars as well as they're run now, it'll be very lucrative."

"Does this mean I'll be working for Langston?" Micki spit out the words.

"It means you'll be working *with* Langston."

"He'll try to boss us around. I know him."

"No, he won't," Travis said. "Langston is no fool. He has a good head for business, and he'll do what it takes to make a profit. He's far more interested in that than he is in making you miserable, Sis. It sounds like you guys will have to learn to get along, or none of you will make much money. Mom knew exactly what she was doing. She took care of all of us, and she did it in a way that would bring out the best in us."

CHAPTER 57

Friday Morning

Sabre walked into the Doyle law firm, anxious for her appointment. She'd become quite curious about the charity Goldie was so proud of. A few minutes later, she met Rose Marie in her office and handed her the trust paperwork.

"What do you know about Silent Thunder Charity?" the attorney asked.

"Not a whole lot. I looked up the articles of incorporation, so I know it's a nonprofit that started about fifteen years ago. I know the purpose is to help the poor and distressed, which is pretty vague. Most important, Aunt Goldie is leaving a big chunk of her estate to the trust."

"How big?"

"Somewhere around five million."

"Excellent. That almost doubles it."

"There's already five million in the trust?" Sabre was

surprised, even though nothing about her aunt's estate should surprise her anymore.

"Five point six million," Rose Marie said. "The new funds will keep the trust going for quite a while and increase the disbursements."

"Is the money invested?"

"Goldie worked with an advisor at Merrill Lynch. His name is Raleigh." Rose Marie pulled out a business card and handed it to Sabre. "He's done a good job for the trust. The past five years have averaged around seventeen percent growth. The five years before, around ten percent."

"Is the money invested in stocks?"

"Stocks and bonds, but always with twenty percent liquid. That was one of Goldie's rules. She had lots of rules." The lawyer walked over to a small refrigerator in the corner. "Would you like a bottle of water?"

"Please. I left mine in the car."

She returned with two bottles and gave one to Sabre. "Goldie obviously wants to keep the trust going. Will you take her place as CEO?"

"That will be my brother, Ron. Goldie specifically put him in charge. I'd like to say he'll be good at it, but I have no idea what his responsibilities are."

Rose Marie smiled. "Does he have a good heart?"

"The best."

"Is he a people person?"

"The only thing he likes better than people are animals," Sabre said. "He gets along with everyone and is quite the charmer."

"Does he have the time to put into it?"

"Definitely."

"How is he at making decisions?"

"Good. He weighs the information he has, seeks more if he doesn't feel he has enough, and then decides. He doesn't second-guess himself, like I tend to do sometimes."

"He sounds like Goldie. He'll be great at it."

"You have certainly piqued my curiosity. What exactly does the trust do?"

"The main purpose is to find people who need a boost and provide it for them. That could range from a free movie ticket to a college education."

"And that's what Ron will be doing?"

"Yes. He'll have to investigate and file reports with the board for the big gifts."

"He has some investigative experience, so that should help."

"There are a lot of conditions set up, which have evolved over the years from Goldie's experiences and what she called mistakes." Rose Marie brought up a document on her computer and printed it. She handed the three pages to Sabre. "Here's the list."

"That's a lot of rules," Sabre said as she glanced through.

"The biggest concern is to not give money that could support a drug or alcohol problem. Goldie laid it all out, with drug testing and everything. And she felt strongly about education, so a lot of gifts are for college packages and trade schools. She looks for people who are good at heart, and every day, someone in the company has to do a random act of kindness. Ron will have to do that or assign someone to."

"What kinds of things?"

"One of Goldie's favorites was paying for other people's meals at restaurants. She focused on families with kids, veterans, people with disabilities. Or she would buy a half dozen tickets at a movie she liked and give them to the next six people in line."

"That sounds like it's right up Ron's alley."

"Goldie's wish was for one of her children to run Silent Thunder, but she finally gave up on that dream. It was important to her that whoever ran the company had a college degree, because they had to understand the importance of education. Only Langston has one, but she strongly felt he didn't have the other qualities required, specifically, compassion for others. She gave up on Micki and Rocki long ago, but she held out some hope for Travis and Chase. She eventually realized that Travis would never get an education, and Chase has a serious drug problem. And if that ever changes, and I mean a major overhaul, you can always consider a place for him in the company. Until then, they must never know what the charity does."

"Even in her death, she wants to keep her secrets," Sabre said. "There's so much I never knew about Aunt Goldie."

"The most important condition—the Goldie Rule, as we called it—is that every gift has to be anonymous. The big transactions all went through me, so the money couldn't be traced to Silent Thunder, and subsequently to her. That must remain the same."

A realization hit her, and Sabre shook her head in wonderment.

"Does this sound familiar?"

"Is Goldie the Incognito Angel?"

"The acronym originally stood for *Invisible Assistant*, but Goldie liked the title the reporter gave her. So, to answer your question, yes, she was the Incognito Angel. But now *you* are— you and your brother."

Dear Reader,

Would you like a FREE copy of a short story about JP when he was young? If so, please go to www.teresaburrell.com and sign up for my mailing list. You will automatically receive a code to retrieve the story.

What did you think of THE ADVOCATE'S LABYRINTH? I would love to hear from you. Please email me and let me know at Teresa@teresaburrell.com.

Thank you,

Teresa

ABOUT THE AUTHOR

Teresa Burrell has dedicated her life to helping children and their families. Her first career was spent teaching elementary school in the San Bernardino City School District. As an attorney, Ms. Burrell has spent countless hours working pro bono in the family court system. For twelve years she practiced law in San Diego Superior Court, Juvenile Division. She continues to advocate children's issues and write novels, many of which are inspired by actual legal cases.

Teresa Burrell is available at www.teresaburrell.com.

OTHER MYSTERIES BY TERESA BURRELL

THE ADVOCATE SERIES

THE ADVOCATE (Book 1)
THE ADVOCATE'S BETRAYAL (Book 2)
THE ADVOCATE'S CONVICTION (Book 3)
THE ADVOCATE'S DILEMMA (Book 4)
THE ADVOCATE'S EX PARTE (Book 5)
THE ADVOCATE'S FELONY (Book 6)
THE ADVOCATE'S GEOCACHE (Book 7)
THE ADVOCATE'S HOMICIDES (Book 8)
THE ADVOCATE'S ILLUSION (Book 9)
THE ADVOCATE'S JUSTICE (Book 10)
THE ADVOCATE'S KILLER (Book 11)
THE ADVOCATE'S LABYRINTH (Book 12)

THE TUPER MYSTERY SERIES

THE ADVOCATE'S FELONY
(Book 6 of The Advocate Series)
MASON'S MISSING (Book 1)
FINDING FRANKIE (Book 2)

Made in the USA
Middletown, DE
20 June 2021

42836864R00194